TEQUILA DAMNATION

THE VOODOO BASTARDS MC
BOOK 5

A.J. DOWNEY

BOOK FIVE

Published 2025 by Second Circle Press

Text Copyright © 2025 A.J. Downey

All Rights Reserved

ISBN: 978-1-950222-49-0

Editing & book design by Maggie Kern @ Ms.K Edits
Cover art Dar Albert at Wicked Smart Designs

DEDICATION

To my loyal readers. This last year was a tough one. I'm grateful for every single one of you for buying my books and getting me through. Let's hope things get easier instead of harder, like I personally fear. We really do live in interesting times.

CHAPTER ONE

Velina...

I stared up at the formidable cinderblock building behind its chain-link fence with its strapping to hide the parking lot beyond. It was filled with graffiti on the outside, and it wasn't all bad. Meaning, some of it was actually artistic, featuring what had to be the Loa of the Vodoun practice... although likely colonized and bastardized for the use here. Which wasn't it ironic? I mean, these guys *did* call themselves the *Voodoo Bastards*...

I was here against my better judgment when my half-brother, Garnett Whitcomb, had suddenly ceased his communications with me.

It'd been a hard and bitter pill to swallow. He'd told me things – things he wasn't supposed to about these men, and I'd worried about him. He was younger than my siblings and me. While I wasn't the oldest, I wasn't the baby either, at least not out of the four of us who'd grown up in our house.

I had three siblings by the same mother – my older brother, one older sister, and one younger sister – and while my dad had, ah, *stepped out* on our mom all around the country, we'd sort of been his primary family.

I'd found Garnett by accident and a few other half-siblings scattered to the four winds. I'd done one of those online, spit-in-a-tube and mail-it-in tests, and all of a sudden found out about my extended, er... nuclear... family?

Dammit, I didn't know what you were supposed to call it. I really didn't.

A shit show came to mind.

Anywho, Garnett had come up as one of them, and while the rest of my half-siblings hadn't wanted anything to do with dear old dad and had shut me out, Garnett had been different. He wanted so *desperately* to have some kind of family that he and I had kept in touch.

It'd been hard telling him about our father and what he'd been like. I'd had a complicated relationship with our dad.

He was away for long lengths of time as an over-the-road trucker, but when he *was* home? Well, I'd firmly been a daddy's girl, doing everything my effeminate and *very gay* older brother had absolutely zero interest in doing.

My dad had been stubborn on that, and he and Rafe didn't always get along. While Rafe had wanted to play dolls with Ophelia and Valencia – our two other sisters – I had wanted to learn all the things that my dad had been pretty uninterested in teaching me because I lacked the right equipment between my legs. Things like how to fish, how to hunt, how to fix shit around the house, and change my own oil... you know, *boy* shit.

As I'd gotten older, though, my dad had started calling me the "son he always wanted," which was certainly a dig at Rafe and had alienated us quite a bit.

I had some regrets about that now, but damn, Rafe was such a drama queen about it.

While our dad relented and had taught me some things, it wasn't really what I'd wanted our relationship to be like.

He'd said he had regrets about that. About not embracing the fact he had a child who was so enamored with him – tomboy that I *was*, as a kid. In the end, I'd been the only one of his progeny left to hold his hand in the hospital as the pancreatic cancer had taken him.

I'd been the one to hear his deathbed confessions about all the women and both knowing and not knowing that he had other kids out there.

I'd been the one he'd asked, his dying wish, to let them all know he was gone and he was sorry.

I'd taken on the duty, ever the dutiful daughter, and boy, did it lob a grenade in with the rest of the family.

I was the black sheep, alright. Pretty much shunned and ostracized by my other siblings. I found that Garnett had been desperate for family as much as I'd been mourning the loss of mine – even if I *did* feel as though I'd never really fit in with them.

I leaned against my car parked on the opposite side of the street from the Voodoo Bastards hangout, with my arms crossed below my breasts, and sighed.

I had no idea what waited for me through the maw of the open gate, but I felt like I owed it to both my dad and Garnett to find out why the hell the texts and emails had just *stopped.*

I pushed off from the car as a trickle of sweat made its way down my spine beneath the olive-drab, ribbed tank top I wore to try and beat some of this summer heat.

Fat chance of that happening.

I was prepared for hot, but it was the muggy humidity that overwhelmed me and made me feel like I walked through soup. I was regretting the boot-cut jeans and hiking boots and wished I'd gone less tomboy and more girly – or at least that I'd done shorts instead. Honestly, I didn't know if walking into a biker's den in a skirt wouldn't be asking for trouble I wasn't prepared for.

Sure, while Garnett had nothing but high praise for these men, I didn't really understand it. Some of the shit they'd put him through to be part of their little club had been downright disgusting.

I'd learned all about their particular brand of hazing rituals, and I couldn't say I liked a bit of what I'd heard. But Garnett? He'd sounded so *proud* of his accomplishments in becoming one of them, and I guess, in some ways, it was like any other fraternity or brotherhood.

You had to do a lot of stupid shit to get into a frat, too.

Of course, there was no way Garnett would know. College was so far outside of the reach of his socioeconomic status that it wasn't even funny.

It'd been out of mine and my siblings, too – without grants, scholarships, and a shit ton of student loans.

Only two out of the five of us had opted for a college education, and both of us had gone two very different ways about it.

Ophelia had gotten a shit ton of academic scholarships and whatnot, and had almost gotten an entire free ride. Mom and the other sibs were *so* proud of her.

Meanwhile, I'd taken out a shit ton of student loans. I didn't honestly have the grades and extracurriculars on my high school transcript to get the notice that Ophelia had. Of course, while I was some type of nerd, I wasn't that hardcore of a nerd. I actually enjoyed having friends, free time, and being a kid while I'd had the chance.

Boy, did that come back to bite me.

I was in the good ol' American debt trap after graduating, and while I had a small one-bedroom house, a beat-up almost fifteen-year-old car with high miles, and a steady and semi-decent income – if I ever had a hope and a prayer of paying off my student loans before I died – *no, I didn't* make enough money. Not even close.

I'd had to tap my savings by quite a bit just to get out here to find Garnett, and I hated that I'd had to do it this way.

The drive from California hadn't been great, but it hadn't been awful. It certainly had sucked that my air conditioning had crapped out halfway across the Texas panhandle, and I was running two by seventy A/C now. Meaning, two windows down driving seventy down the highway.

With the oppressive wet and heavy atmosphere of New Orleans in the summertime pressing all around me, I kept a big stainless-steel bottle of water on hand and had been trying to keep hydrated like crazy.

I glanced back at it, sitting on my passenger seat, and wondered if I should keep it with me when I finally plucked up the courage to go inside.

I sighed and wondered what the fuck my problem was and why I lingered out here on the sun-scorched blacktop.

I stared at the black, purple, gold, and green painted building with its larger-than-life painted Baron Samedi bursting from Louisiana's signature gold fleur-de-lis, and I decided that yeah, okay, I was nervous. I mean, I was here, and I wanted answers. About the only thing I feared was that somehow, some way, Garnett wouldn't want to see me, wouldn't want to talk to me anymore... and that?

Well, there was only one way to find out if I would be abandoned for good by literally *everyone*... and that was to pluck up my courage and go inside.

CHAPTER TWO

Saint...

It was late afternoon, and I was sitting at the bar in the club, sipping on my favorite poison – Casa Noble tequila. The liquid – spicy, flavorful, and crisp – went down smooth. I also had to admire the way the liquor coated the inside of the glass I sipped from as I swirled it.

It was a weird liquor for a born and bred Italian, New Orleans native, and wholly raised Southern boy like me to pick up, let alone enjoy as thoroughly as I did. But hey, a man liked what he liked, and I certainly was no exception to that rule.

It'd been a long fuckin' day, but the day was done, and I was just chillin' at the bar on my own, sipping my drink and keeping to myself.

I wasn't really looking for company. Didn't really feel like peopling, but sometimes the chicks that liked to come around here, lookin' to ride a man who rode motorcycles, came unbidden and uninvited. They were generally all the same – looking for a thrill in all the wrong places.

I thought that's what *she* was, at first, when I heard the scuffling footstep in the doorway. I hadn't seen her coming from behind the boarded-up windows, but I heard her, and as soon as her shadow fell into the oblong, canted rectangle of light spilling in from the doorway to the outside? I turned and looked. I took my time sizing her up from her hiking boots to a pair of shapely thighs clad in boot-cut jeans. Her arms were lightly tanned, her shoulders just starting to pink with sunburn. As much as I should have been captivated by her large, heavy breasts straining the rib knit of her army green tank top, it was the sweeping curve of her shoulder, up the long and elegant line of her neck, kissed by stray tendrils of dark chestnut hair that escaped a messy bun in a claw clip at the back of her head that caught my attention more.

Her sunglasses were perched above a sweep of bangs across her forehead, long, wispy tendrils to either side, framing her face.

It was a pretty face, but for the sour look on it.

She didn't look thrilled to be here, and I half wondered what kind of Karening she brought with her. Because she was starting to look the type.

She had a strong jaw with a hard set, but it wasn't out of place. It worked with her face with its thick arched brows and long dark lashes. I wanted to say she had some type of Hispanic in her, but then her flashing light green eyes caught mine, and I was hit with an almost feeling of *déjà vu*...

"What're you lookin' for darlin'?" I grated out, and took another sip of my tequila.

"Not what, but who," she said, approaching me cautiously.

I arched a brow. "I'm looking for Garnett Whitcomb?" she said, the name lilting off her tongue with a question mark hanging on the thick, still, and muggy air between us.

We still ain't had the air conditioning fixed from where the unit out front had taken some stray bullets.

"We don't use government names around here. You're going to have to be more specific. Besides that, who's askin'?"

"I'm Velina Young, and I think you guys called him Louie. Have you seen him?" she asked.

I straightened up in my seat and took her in, searching her face.

"Why you wanna know?" I demanded.

"I just do," she said. "Have you seen him?"

7

I cleared my throat and turned around, fixing my eyes on the back wall beside the bar. At the eight-by-ten framed mugshot of Louie hanging there and the floating shelf under it, his gunmetal gray urn sitting squat on it.

I turned back to her, made eye contact, and jerked my head in Louie's direction.

"He's right there," I said. "Afraid he's not much of a conversationalist no more. *Now who the fuck are you?*"

She paled, her tan suddenly floating over the surface of her smooth skin like a sickly oil slick on the swamp waters you sometimes got around here. She seemed frozen, staring at the picture and at the urn. Finally, her steps carried her closer, almost automatically, as if they were unbidden from any real thought from her.

I straightened up further and slipped off my barstool.

"I'm serious. Who wants to know?" I demanded, but it was like she couldn't hear me, her eyes growing luminous with unshed tears that damn sure threatened to spill.

Just who the fuck was this bitch? How did she know Louie?

"Talk to me," I ordered, and her eyes flicked from the photo and urn to mine as her nose grew red and the tears spilled down her cheeks.

"Are you serious right now?" she demanded, more than a hint of outrage to her tone. "Can you just give me a fucking minute to absorb this?"

I rolled my eyes.

"Ain't never heard of you, and don't really care at this point. Either tell me who you are or *get out.*"

"Wow, fuck you!" she cried, as she went for Louie's urn. I stopped her, with a hand on her chest, and she batted at it ineffectually.

"Uh-uh, where you think you're going?"

"Closer to my brother's urn if you don't mind!" she snapped, and I barked a laugh… and I kept right on laughing. I couldn't help myself.

"Louie ain't got no siblings, so try-a-fucking-gain," I said and put a sharp edge of menace into my tone.

"That *you* know of!" She looked up at me, high spots of color in her cheeks, her chest flushing, and those green eyes of hers flashing with temper.

I blinked, long and slow, and took a second look at those eyes.

I dropped my hand from holding her back and said, "Well, I'll be damned…"

"Yeah," she muttered. She went up to the floating shelf, bracing a hand to the cinderblock beside it and leaning heavily against the wall. Her head bowed, her shoulders shook, but she didn't make a sound.

I swallowed hard, suddenly feeling really fucking awkward when Cypress came out from the back and stopped.

"The fuck?" he demanded, in his thick swampbilly accent.

"Give her a minute, man," I said. "She's Louie's sister."

Cypress barked a laugh, but it died with the sour look on my face.

He looked surprised and asked again, "The fuck?"

CHAPTER THREE

Velina...

I wanted to take him. I wanted to pluck that urn from its shelf, rip the photo from the wall, and take him with me. I didn't know what the fuck these assholes had gotten my brother into. How could he have considered them his family? *I* was his family! *Me*! And now I really *was* alone.

"Hey, come back! Don't go like that!"

The man at the bar called after me as I turned on my heel and marched back out into the oppressive heat outside. I put my hands on my hips, closed my eyes, and tipped my face to the sun. It blazed fire through my closed eyelids, and I swallowed hard.

I would not cry anymore. I could not cry in front of these motherfuckers!

I took in a deep, harsh, cleansing breath as the pressure in my nose and at the backs of my eyes receded.

You didn't cry in my family.

It wasn't the way we were raised.

You cried, and Dad would *give you* something to cry about. I'd stopped crying about shit a long fucking time ago. There wasn't any point. It didn't fucking fix anything.

"Hey."

I turned sharply at his voice, the hulking form of the long-haired bastard filling the darkened doorway behind me.

"What?" I snapped. His jaw tightened with consternation and I stood there, waiting him out while he swept me with deep, dark, brown eyes that were honestly just enough brown in the light to keep them from being black.

"You know what?" He held up his hands. "Never mind." He backed into the doorway and, dropping his hands, turned to go back in the direction of the bar.

The other one, the one with his close-shaven head a lighter brown than the other big bastard, leaned a shoulder against the doorway and crossed his arms, squinting into the bright sunlight in my direction.

He was big and built like the first guy, with one exception. His neck was almost wider than his head – like wildly disproportionate to the rest of him.

I scoffed as he threw me some chin and pecked a kiss in the air, winking at me. Frowning, I went back across the street and opened my car door. I got in, fishing my keys out of my shallow hip pocket and sticking it in the ignition, and turned her over.

Click!

Nothing.

I drew in a long, slow breath, closed my eyes, and did what any red-blooded American woman fed up with the patriarchy would do.

I screamed long and loud and beat on my steering wheel until the shock of the blows radiated up my arm and rendered my hand achy and numb at the same time.

Did it fix anything?

No.

Did it make me feel any better?

Also no.

Did it keep me from bursting into tears or making an absolute embarrassment of myself?

Yes, *that*, but come to think of it? *No*, on that last part.

"Pop the hood, Cher. Sounds like your starter."

I blinked and turned my head to the shadow that'd fallen over me. It was the thick-necked Cajun leaning his arm against the sun-scorched and peeling clearcoat of the roof of my car. He turned his head and spit brown tobacco juice on the ground, and I felt my stomach roil.

Ugh.

Wordlessly, and with honestly nothing better to do at the moment, I reached for the lever and pulled it, the hood jumping an inch or two with a not-so-satisfying deep metal thrum.

Fuck my life.

"Name's Cypress, *ma cherie*. Welcome to Louisiana."

"Thanks," I said, non-plussed. I looked across the street at the doorway where the long-haired bastard stood, arms crossed over his chest, looking impassively on.

"What's his name?" I asked as Cypress fiddled around under my hood.

"That there is Saint," he called back.

Saint and Cypress…

"Garnett talked about you two," I said, hanging wearily onto the top of my steering wheel with both hands, leaning forward some, gaze fixed on Saint, who stared impassively back at me.

"Did he now?" Cypress asked, sounding only mildly interested.

"Yeah," I said.

"An' what ol' Louie have to say? Huh?" he asked.

"That you guys were the only family he ever knew, even if you put the fun back in dysfunctional."

Cypress barked a laugh and said something in Cajun-French that I couldn't understand.

Living in California, Spanish had been a higher priority for me, and my grasp of that language had honestly eluded me from even the most basic conversation. I think I could effectively ask where the bathroom was, call something black or white… and maybe say "thank you." That was about all I'd retained out of that.

"Try it now," Cypress called out.

I turned the ignition.

Click!

Nothing.

"Aw, yeah. No connections loose. Pretty sure it's your starter. Lemme go grab some tools, yeah?"

"Why?" I asked.

"Why what?" he asked.

"Why are you helping me?"

"That all depends," he said, coming back around to lean over my window and look me in the eye. "You really ol' Louie's sister?"

I raised my chin defiantly and said, "Half-sister, older by seven months," I said. "We shared the same father."

Cypress gave a nod. "Thought so."

"Oh?" I asked.

"Louie had his daddy's eyes. His mamma's was brown. You got the same ones." He straightened up and knocked on the roof of my car.

"Come on outta there and come have a cold one. I'll see if I can't get you sorted, yeah?"

"Why?" I asked again, getting out of my car.

"You're family. We do right by a fallen brother's family. That's our way."

He walked away, ahead of me, heading into the front of the club, stopping only when Saint barred his way, asking something. His voice floated toward me on the breeze, unmistakably masculine and deep – but the words unintelligible from this distance.

Cypress answered, and Saint stepped aside – sort of – more turning in the doorway for Cypress to slide past him like a human door.

"Leave your keys," he called out to me. "Cy's gonna need 'em, and it's not like that piece of shit's going anywhere anytime soon."

The fuck?

"It's old, but it's not a piece of shit," I argued.

"The fact it won't start and it's left you stuck here to annoy the piss out of me suggests otherwise," he said.

"You're a fantastic host," I said sarcastically, passing him by and rolling my eyes.

He snorted a slight laugh and shook his head.

"We don't generally gather out here in any significant numbers anymore," he said when I moved to clamber up onto one of the bar stools. "Grab yourself something cold to drink and follow me."

I turned and looked at the plywood over the windows and let my gaze meander over the dimly lit interior of the bar space.

The smell of fresh paint and the dry tang of fresh drywall hung in the air with a faint underpinning of fresh mud.

"Don't touch the walls back there," he said over the fans circulating the air here.

"Everything's still wet," I said, and he nodded like I'd put a question mark on the end of that – which I hadn't.

"What happened here?" I asked, reaching into the cooler and coming up with an icy can of Coke.

"Some rivals of ours shot up the place one night, only a couple three weeks back. We're still working on fixing things up."

I cracked open the soda can and looked back to my brother's urn and mugshot behind it.

"Is that how my brother died?" I asked, putting two and two together.

"Right where you're standing, actually," the man said coolly as I took a drink of soda, which I promptly choked on, the searingly carbonated liquid coming out of my nose as I coughed uncontrollably.

Saint was suddenly just kind of there, smacking me on the back hard enough I swore my spine was going to shoot out the front of my body, and my ribs rattled together like ghoulish windchimes.

"Here, here you go," he said, thrusting some of those blue shop paper towels into my free hand. I stuffed them against my face to sop up the worst of the cola and snot mixture evacuating from my nose and squeezed my watering eyes shut.

"You really need to work on your bedside manner for breaking bad news to a bitch," I squeezed out of my aching, spastic lungs through my equally traumatized voicebox.

He threw back his head and laughed at that, but I was dead serious.

"What the fuck?" I demanded.

"If it's any consolation to you, I believe you, now."

"Again, and with all due disrespect, I say, *what the fuck?*"

"Come have a seat," he said and tried to draw me by my elbow out from behind the bar.

I obliged him, setting down my can of Coke on top of the cooler or whatever back here and dropping onto my ass right there on the dusty concrete floor. I put my hand to the warm concrete, a coating of drywall dust chalky against my fingertips and palm as I rubbed along the polish of it.

"Right here?" I asked. "Are you serious?"

He put his hand against the bar and leaned against it.

"Ah, yeah. Right there."

I pressed my hand flat against the floor and closed my eyes, trying desperately to reach back in time, to feel even the smallest echo… which was silly and stupid, I knew, but I didn't have anything else. I never would. Nothing but the sight of my brother's cold, impersonal, gunmetal gray urn sitting on that floating shelf. The eight-by-ten of him holding that plaque and the scrunched-up, disrespectful face he was making at the camera behind it.

That was it. That was all I'd driven all those many miles to find.

What the fuck?

"What happened?" I asked through numb lips.

"I told you—" he said.

"Don't spare me the gory details now," I said spitefully.

He shook his head.

"You don't need 'em."

"And what if I say I do?" I asked.

"I say that's too damn bad. Now c'mon. There are more people out back that knew Louie to meet."

"Just gimme a minute," I said. "Alone, if you don't mind."

"Suit yourself," he said with a shrug, and pushing off from the bar, he disappeared around the corner and down the hall somewhere deeper into the cinderblock building.

All this way, and he was already gone.

That knot of dread I'd been carrying in the pit of my stomach all the way from California unfurled into a twisted flower of nausea and regret.

I should have come sooner.

CHAPTER FOUR

S aint...

"Where she at?" Cypress asked, looking up from the club's shop bench and dumping a socket wrench into a random tool bag he'd scrounged up from somewhere.

"Takin' a minute at the bar," I grated.

Hex looked up from his phone, head still bowed, givin' me a Kubrick stare. I rolled my eyes at him.

"Ain't nothin' compromising on the property. Relax."

"Not what I'm worried about," he said, and he glanced back down at the face of his phone.

"Looks like LaCroix's got the part her car needs. Should be at the ol' boat scrapyard within the hour. I reckon you ought to give the lady a ride on out that way."

I arched an eyebrow. "Doesn't sound like a suggestion," I said.

"It ain't," Hex declared, pushing off the pillar back here in the wide-open garage, looking up as he slid his phone into his back pocket.

"Well," Hex said. "I don't know about you two fools, but I can see Louie all over her from here. Those two certainly were written in the same font, as my girl likes to say."

"And what turn of phrase would you use?" she called from the doorway leading back here into the garage from the front of the clubhouse.

"Where I come from, we'd say you was both picked right out your daddy's ass."

She barked a laugh and it sounded bitter.

"From what I understand, Garnett wasn't anything like our father – gonna have to trust me on that one. I actually knew the man."

"Gone then?" Hex asked, holding out his hand.

"Pancreatic cancer, a year or so ago," she said, taking it to shake.

"Shame," Hex said. "I'm Hex, you've met Cypress an' Saint."

She nodded. "Mixed feelings on that," she said.

"On what?" Cypress asked, hefting his tool bag.

"Whether it's a shame my daddy's gone. Some days it's a relief. Other days it's a curse." She shrugged.

Hex laughed. "Yeah, that was ol' Louie, too."

"He said you called him that because he saw a Loup Garu... although he also said you guys corrected him mercilessly."

"Roux Garu." Cypress gave a nod.

"Yeah, that was it," she said, capturing her bottom lip between her teeth.

"Cypress is gonna take that problem starter out of your car, and Saint here is gonna run you out to a place to pick up a replacement."

She smiled faintly. "And just how much is this going to run me?" she asked.

"Nothin'," Hex declared. He gave me a hard look, which told me all I needed to know. I was the hook for the part and possibly to grease Cy's palm for taking it out and putting it back on.

"If only it was so easy to fix my AC," she said with a wry grin.

"What's wrong with it?" Hex asked.

"Dunno. Just quit on me halfway across the Texas panhandle on my way here."

"Where you come from?" he asked.

"California," she answered.

"Hollywood?" he asked with a grin.

She laughed. "'Fraid not. Riverside."

"Riverside..." Hex sounded thoughtful.

"Suburb of LA," she said with a shrug. "So I guess close enough to Hollywood."

"I reckon," he said.

Cypress had left our presence already to see to yanking her starter.

"Have Cy look at her AC. See if it needs recharging or a new compressor."

I gave a reluctant nod.

"Nice meeting you..." he trailed off.

"Velina," she said, and she was eyeing Hex curiously.

"Velina." He repeated her name.

"Pretty name."

"Thanks," she said. "Mom wanted Valencia like the orange, but Dad talked her out of it. No such luck for my little sister, though."

"Ouch," Hex said with a good-natured laugh.

Velina shrugged.

"Come on, I'll take you out to the junkyard," I muttered. "Can I borrow your truck?" I asked Hex.

He gave me a shit-eating grin and said, "No can do, my friend. You're just gonna have to take your bike."

Shit, I thought to myself and turned to look at Valina, her eyes wide and showing a little too much white. I got the impression she was thinking the same thing.

"C'mon," I muttered and went back out the way we'd come to get the busted part off Cy and to relay the message about the compressor.

Velina fell into step beside me and muttered under her breath, "Shit's totally bizarre, little brother."

"What is?" I asked, curious.

"How the fuck we went from you being a total cock goblin to giving me a ride to pick up a part to fix my broken car for free in the span of," she checked her watch, "less than an hour."

"Welcome to the life," I said sarcastically.

"Garnett's life," she said. "Mine's back in California, I guess."

"You guess?" I asked as we crossed out the gate and headed for Cy, who was balls-deep under the hood of her car and already cursing.

She didn't respond.

"Surprised you made it all the way here in that piece of shit without anything breaking before now."

"I take good care of her for the most part," she said defensively.

I eyed the peeling clear coat off her paint critically and said, "Uh-huh."

"From the look of things under the hood down here, I'd say she ain't lyin' bro," Cypress declared and came up with a crusty dusty part in a greasy shop rag.

"Hex said to check her A/C. See if it needs a new compressor or just a recharge," I said.

"Hard to do that when I can't start the damn thing," Cy said, spitting tobacco juice off to the side.

I heard a faint "ugh" from just off to the right and behind me, where Velina stood.

I felt my lips twitch with a smirk that I barely suppressed. Cy didn't seem to hear her, which was no surprise. With how much time he spent on the airboats, even with ear protection during gator season, he was damn near as deaf as a post.

Judgy little thing, I thought to myself. I guess I shouldn't fault her for it. She grew up citizen, clearly, and didn't know the life. Still, I did fault her. We were out here bailing her ass out for nothing, other than for the fact that she seemed to be who she said she was – Louie's older half-sister.

My phone vibrated in my pocket, Hex's pattern and a snippet of Tennessee Whiskey blaring out of the speaker.

I pulled it out and checked the text.

Part is officially on its way to LaCroix – find out how much she knows.

Just how the fuck was I supposed to do that from the back of my bike? Fucker. He just loved making shit complicated.

"We gotta go," I said. "Figure it out and text me," I told Cy absently.

"Yeah," he muttered. "I got you." It was more work and a pain in the fucking ass, but there were some basic things you could do to diagnose the compressor was fucked without the car running. They weren't super reliable, but a couple of 'em were pretty tried and true. For instance, if it was seized? It wouldn't turn, and *that* was an official "the compressor is fucked."

I was betting she just needed more refrigerant, but the only way to test *that* out for sure was with the motor running and a set of gauges. Couldn't get that going without the starter, so *off we fucked to see the wizard...* and by wizard, I meant the big cheese, the president, and head honcho. When it came to Miss Velina, it could go either fuckin' way.

She had an attitude and a mouth on her – was brazen in a way that Louie hadn't even begun to reach until he'd been with us a while.

Seemed he'd been talking pretty freely about us. Hex and LaCroix were right – I mean, Hex was just about *always* right. We needed to know just how much Louie'd been flapping his gums. He was a loyal one, but he had a lot of moments where he wasn't particularly bright. Kid had been knocked around so fuckin' much, there was a real possibility there was some permanent brain damage or some shit like that to it.

Right now, the car trouble she was having was a whole *by-the-grace-of-God* thing. Time to exploit it.

Exercise a little goodwill, fix her car, answer some questions about her brother, and while I was at it, covertly do a little fishing to see if Louie had spoken out of turn any. See whether or not that could or would be a detriment to us.

"Ever ride?" I asked Velina, stuffing my phone into my pocket.

"No," she said.

"No time like the present to learn, I guess."

"You don't have a car?" she asked.

I made a face like it was offensive she'd even suggest such a thing because, well, it was.

"I got a work truck, but it ain't anywhere near here. Here's what you need to know…"

I ran her through just about everything a first-timer should know. Granted, I probably forgot some shit, but that was easy enough to instruct on the fly at a stoplight or whatever.

"You sure I can't just wait here?" she asked, her eyebrow arched and dismay written all over her face.

"No," I answered curtly. "LaCroix wants to see you."

She looked like she paled a bit under her California tan, and I didn't know if I liked that.

"Guess you've heard of him," I said.

She swallowed and put on a face like she was tougher than she felt and said, "Garnett mentioned him a time or two. He's the president of…" she stopped and chose her words carefully. So, she wasn't as dumb as Louie could be. "Your club," she finished tamely.

"Guess you're getting sort of a crash course," I said.

"I mean, my guide into all of this is sitting in an urn in your bar… so uh, sorry if I'm not as up to date as I could be."

"I'm sure he left a lot of things out," I said casually.

"Not really," she said.

Shit.

"At least, I don't think so."

"Stick a pin in that. We'll come back to it later." I clambered aboard my bike and dropped into the seat.

"You ain't got a jacket or nothing in your car, do you?" I called out over the bass rumble.

"In this heat? No!" she called back.

"Should always dress for the slide and not for the ride, but you can't be more than ninety-eight pounds soaking wet. We shouldn't have any problems, but next time you ever get on a bike, you make sure you got on leather. At the very least, a denim jacket."

She blinked at me in surprise and blurted out, "Why do you care?"

"Good point," I said bluntly. "I don't."

She rolled her eyes and got on behind me, settling onto the back seat. I checked to make sure her feet were on the proper pegs and that she hadn't rested the soles of her hiking boots on the rapidly heating pipes.

Had a bitch melt the soles of her sneakers to my shit once. Dumb cunt did it and had the intestinal fortitude to get mad at *me* for it. I'd left her ass at the bar in the Quarter and hadn't thought twice about her until now.

She'd been blonde with big fake titties… not like Velina, though.

When she wrapped her arms around me and scooted forward against my back, what pressed into it was all natural.

I tried not to think too hard about it, dismissing it as I pulled us out onto the street. The borrowed helmet was a little loose on her head, and her fucked-up starter was stowed safely in one of my saddlebags.

Low-key, I was surprised Hex hadn't sent one of the other guys with us. We weren't riding alone anywhere these days, especially into the swamps and shit.

The Voodoo Bastards and the Bayou Brethren were slowly circling one another like fighting dogs, looking for a good drop in the other's defense to lunge and sink teeth.

The heat was pretty high right now, and as soon as the pigs stopped looking? It would be back on like Donkey Kong, but for right now, we were in a bit of a stalemate ceasefire while the authorities were circling and sniffing.

Not that they were doing much when it came to running down who'd been out there and shot Louie.

They didn't care *that* much. Just enough to keep us minding our p's and q's so some precious citizen didn't get caught up in our crossfire. Fuck us biker pieces of shit – they just didn't want us accidentally dropping a kid or somebody's grandma.

Anyway, Velina held on, and she was pretty strong for such a little thing. When we took our first turn, she was a natural, leaning with it, with a strong core. She was as stiff as a board behind me, both trying to hold on and not press too tight at the same time. Made me chuckle. As soon as we were off the surface city streets and making for the highway, I caned it. Twisting down on the throttle, the engine's power kicked like a mule underneath us as we lurched forward at breakneck speed.

I could swear that she squeaked behind me, this cute little sudden noise of fear that was quickly swallowed and drowned by the kiss of the Harley's low growl of satisfaction at the beast being turned loose.

Her arms crushed around my ribs with a near-brutal cracking force, and her thighs pinched around my hips as she pressed to my back, molding up against me like she was almost meant to be there.

She shouted over the deafening rush of the hot wind around us and

I was pretty sure it was to call me a name. I laughed at that, and she squeezed around me tighter, a quick jerk of her arms almost like she was trying to give me the Heimlich. The message of her scolding was as clear and as loud as the brap of the pipes as we rocketed past the people in cages all around us.

It was a good ride, and I was glad I hadn't been but part way into my first glass of tequila and was good to make it.

I would always take a good ride over a drink, but I just didn't have someplace to go and wasn't quite in the frame of mind to want to ride without a destination.

This was honestly just what the doctor ordered.

We rode the hour and some change outside the city into bayou country and right past Jessie-Lou's place, where Collier fell in beside me.

Leave it to Hex. I wasn't riding alone – not out here.

I threw Collier a salute, and he threw one back. Where Velina had just started to relax behind me, I felt her muscles tighten up again as she went very still at my back.

I checked my side view and took in her face. It was unreadable between her aviator sunglasses and the hard line of her mouth, the stubborn set to her chin.

She wanted to seem tough, but she honestly just reminded me of one of those fucking little adorable terrier purse dogs that looked more like a fluffy rat than a dog.

We pulled up at the old boatyard on the edge of the swamp and its gray-weathered front end with its rusty-ass old tin-roof awning over the plain six-by-six posts holding it up.

Around the door to the place, old license plates and taxidermy gator snouts were the main décor, along with old posters faded by the sun advertising different types of motor oils and fluids for maritime use.

On the posts, old pistons and random gears, rusting and sun-scorched, practically floated on the silvery wood that was so dry it held that wind-worn satin finish.

I pulled up carefully across the wash of gravel that comprised the lot and killed my engine. She jumped off almost as soon as we'd rolled to a stop. I turned on her quick to make sure she'd done it carefully enough to avoid touching even her denim-clad leg to the pipe.

"Watch how you do that," I said. "Always get off from this side." I indicated the side opposite where she'd gotten off.

"Got it," she said, unhooking the trident clasp under her chin by pressing the two prongs together.

It popped, and she took it off, her hair windblown but still stylish. She kept it in a layered cut just above her shoulders, and it looked good on her.

She held the helmet out to me and I took it, putting it upside down in my lap.

"Collier," Collier said by way of greeting, sticking out his hand to her. She shook it.

"Velina," she said, eyeing him carefully.

"Louie's sister, huh?" Col asked.

"Yeah," she said, and her voice dropped an octave, a heaviness dripping from it, thick like honey and unmistakable for what it was – sorrow.

Her shoulders drooped with disappointment, and Collier said, "Sorry for your loss."

"Not sure if it counts when you never got to meet in person and you'd only been talking less than a year," she said.

"Aw," he said. "It counts. I reckon that makes it even worse in some ways."

She eyed him and nodded, and he smiled.

I took my own helmet off and hung both hers and mine from my handlebar before getting off the bike myself to get into the saddlebag for her busted-ass starter.

"Have a smoke," I told him. He gave a nod, leaned against one of the pillars under the shade of the awning, and lit up the cigarette he was going to have anyway.

I held open the door for Velina with one hand and had her fucked-up starter in the other.

"Thanks," she muttered and went into the junkyard's front office.

I followed her in, letting my eyes adjust to the dimly lit interior, putting my sunglasses on top of my head, mimicking Velina just in front of me, who did the same.

"Saint," ol' Frank behind the counter muttered as he clicked his mouse on its filthy mousepad beside his old computer screen, likely playing solitaire. That's all his fat ass did all day on the junkyard's antiquated computer system. Just answered phones, played solitaire, and two-finger pecked out invoices to print up on the old dot-matrix printers he had set up behind him.

He'd tack the yellow copies to the board for the boys out back to pull the parts and stuffed the white ones in a file folder for the yard's records. The pink went to the customer when they picked up their shit and paid for it, and the yellows went on to fuck knows where. I wasn't all that intimate with their simplistic system. Shit, more than half of those invoices were fake, anyhow.

The yard here was just one of many ways the club laundered their cash.

"LaCroix out back?" I asked, setting the dead starter on the counter.

Frank looked over and raised his eyebrow.

"Yeah."

I thrust my chin at the open doorway behind Frank and told Velina, "Go on through there. You can't miss him," I said.

"Just look for the big, bald, tattooed fucker," Frank agreed.

She looked from Frank to me dubiously and floated around the counter in such a way that said she didn't really want to find out what was on the other side of the door but was forcing her feet to take her there anyway.

I smirked at her back, and once she was out of sight, asked Frank, "You got one of these in yet? LaCroix said he was having one delivered."

He eyed the starter and nodded, thrusting his double chin at the shelf off to one side and behind me.

"On there somewhere," he said.

"Thanks," I said flatly.

Frank didn't answer, just kept clicking away, his beady eyes darting back and forth behind his glasses, which were outdated and looked like Dahmer's.

Seriously, that's all I could ever think when looking at glasses like that anymore. I knew they were aviators without the dark lenses of sunglasses, but when the lenses were clear like that, or just barely tinted – all I could see was that evil, sick fucker's face behind them splashed all over the headlines.

My momma liked true crime, and I was an impressionable kid when she'd deep-dove everything about him like she was his greatest fuckin' fangirl – wasn't the only thing she'd done accidentally to fuck me up. Lord knew she'd done plenty.

I probably needed therapy. Granted, unlike Louie's mom, mine hadn't *meant* to fuck me up. She, for the most part, had tried her best, but there had definitely been a few things that, looking back on 'em, made me realize my mother wasn't as smart as I'd given her credit for when I was a kid.

That was the thing, though. When we were kids, we always seemed to think our parents were some kind of a paragon of virtue, the best, the brightest, the ones we aspired to be when we grew up.

Looking back on a lot of shit as adults, it didn't take a rocket scientist to figure out that they were basically just fucked-up kids themselves, barely outta their own parents' house and trying to make the best of a bad situation, which was having us kids when they probably really shouldn't have.

Louie's mom had *definitely* been one of those. Knocked up at something like sixteen by a dude way too fucking old for her, by the sounds of it. Her parents pitched her out on her ass like the good, upstanding Christians they were – for a while anyway.

Just long enough for Louie's mom to get hooked. It was a lot of downhill for them after that.

Louie'd felt pretty alone when it came to some of the things his mom let happen to him when he was a kid. It'd fucked him up. He wasn't alone, though.

I'd been an altar boy when it'd happened to me.

That's where things went off the rails with me and my mom. I'd told her. She slapped the shit out of me – lost her damn mind on me, calling me a liar.

That's when I first figured out that I was on my own. I'd stayed that way until the club. Kept my secret until I was old enough, big enough, and strong enough to get myself out of that kind of trouble by just *not going back.*

I was such a disappointment to my mother, but I didn't care about that much anymore. I'd found my freedom, and I held onto that shit.

The club had just given me direction. Power. The power to never be a victim again.

It'd given Louie that same power, and he'd used it. That'd made the kid stronger than me in some ways.

I didn't know how many times I sat outside my old childhood church with a gun up in the back of my waistband, too chickenshit to do what Louie had done to his primary abuser.

The kid had balls. Still managed to be kinder, softer, than the rest of us. I didn't know how, but he did.

I couldn't say the same about myself.

Made me think about some things.

"Need one?" Collier asked me when I got out front.

"Yeah," I muttered, and he held out his pack. I pulled out a cigarette and leaned over as he flicked his Bic to life to light it for me.

I took a long, thoughtful drag.

"Got the wheels turning in there," he said.

I nodded.

"You think she's who she says she is?" he asked.

I nodded at that, too.

"I'll be a monkey's uncle," he muttered, and I huffed a laugh.

"The fuck you say?" I asked.

"You heard me," he said, grinning.

"Just shut up and smoke your cigarette," I grated, but he had me laughing. Sometimes the shit that flew out Col's mouth was just so fuckin' weird.

It made me miss Louie even more. He used to be the club's comedic relief.

Damn.

CHAPTER FIVE

Velina…

I stepped through the doorway that the fat man behind the counter in his stained, light blue, vertically striped, dirty coveralls had indicated and found myself in a sort of little antechamber with filthy, wet, concrete floors populated by several engine stands with a mix of boat and regular-looking motors strewn all over.

The workbenches around the perimeter of the small room were piled with rusty and greasy leavings of mechanical parts that I couldn't even begin to tell you what they did.

I knew a thing or two about car engines, which some of these motors looked exceedingly similar to – but it was like looking at an AI-generated image of what a car engine was supposed to look like. Yeah, it looked *almost* right, but then you would see hoses that didn't make sense or vacuum lines that didn't go anywhere recognizable. Then you realized the smiling mechanic in the photo had little stubby nubbins for fingers and that he had eight on one hand and only three on the other – because Artificial Intelligence was too dumb to get the hands right on most of what it spits out.

I steeled myself, unsure what to expect on the other side of the bright portal of a doorway leading to the outside in front of me. I took a deep breath and, letting it out slowly, squared my shoulders and went through the door and back out into the muggy and oppressive heat.

The sun beat down through a canopy of trees that ringed the property's fence line, and inside that fence line was a myriad jumble of both defunct cars and boats… mostly boats, though.

I swallowed hard, eyes darting over the mayhem and wreckage in front of me, looking for any movement or sign of a single living soul among it.

I mean, their president was out here somewhere, wasn't he?

A tall, lanky, older man with a big, long, white-and-gray beard slid out from between two piles of cars and boats and looked my way. He had on the same blue coveralls the fat man behind the counter wore, and when he spotted me, he gave me the creepiest grin. It was only with almost every other tooth in his mouth, all stained brown and rotting away. For reals, with his hunched back, leathery skin from too much time in the sun, and those teeth behind thin lips spread into what could only be described as a rictus grin – I could almost hear the banjos in the distance.

I know I was being a judgy cunt, but it was hard not to. The sight of him making lanky long strides toward me made me physically want to cringe. I thought I was holding my ground but then I bumped back into a person standing behind me who I hadn't heard so much as a whisper from.

I jumped and let out a startled little shout, whirling in place to set eyes on a man who wasn't that much taller than me, but was infinitely scarier than backwoods, swampbilly Bob out there in the ruins.

I bit off a startled shout, the strangled cry dying in my throat at the sight of this bald, built, and tattooed man's deep, dark eyes.

And I do mean dark. As in wall-to-wall darkness, the whites of his eyes turned black with, if I had to guess, ink injected into them somehow.

I swallowed hard, and he loomed silently, dragging those eyes over my face and back and forth between my eyes, which I already knew were too-wide with a combination of shock and fright.

I watched his mouth turn down with what looked like certainty, and he grunted and nodded once before relinquishing my personal space by taking a step back away from me.

"You're Louie's kin, alright," he said, his voice somewhat low and surprisingly pleasant to the ear.

"Why do you say it like that?" I asked.

"It's in the eyes," he answered quietly. "You've got Louie's eyes – or rather, he has yours. He was the youngest out of the two of you, right?"

"Right," I said. "He was born after me – and we both get them from our dad."

The man grunted and gave a nod, whipping out a stained and faded, red mechanic's rag from somewhere behind him, working at the worst of the grease on his hands.

"Boy's 'll handle whatever you need," he said. "You can git on back to Saint."

"Thanks?" I said with a lilt to my voice, the sarcasm apparently lost on him as he grunted, gave a nod, and moved out into the yard with all its sad and dejected wreckage.

The skinny man melted into the heaps of junk boats and cars, and I watched the man who'd startled me retreat in a straight line to the back of the junkyard, his broad shoulders narrowing in an almost perfect triangle to narrower hips made bulkier where he had the coveralls he wore tied at his waist. He wore a thin, white wife beater, his skin around it glistening with sweat, and as he moved, the hard cut of his muscular frame deepened in shadow where hard muscle bulged and flexed over the other parts of him.

He looked like he could snap me like a twig, which scared me.

I retreated from the odd exchange, back into the gloom inside the building, pausing in the little engine-filled antechamber to allow my eyes a moment to adjust.

When I returned to the main front register area, only the fat man on the stool behind the cash wrap remained, playing his game of solitaire on the outdated computer monitors.

"Boys are out front waiting on you," he said without looking up from the screen.

"Thanks…" I said, and I knew it sounded lackluster. This whole thing was bizarre and confusing.

Like playing a game of chess where none of the rules had been spoken aloud. Like I make a move, and the piece moves back to where I moved it from in a silent, *you can't do that,* but no one is bothered to explain *why.*

I hated it, but so far, whatever the rules of engagement, I seemed to be doing okay.

It was nerve-racking, for sure, like I was walking a tightrope, but I wanted to learn everything I could about my late little brother, and these guys seemed to hold the keys to that kingdom…

…and then some with the state my car was in.

Blast it.

Saint and Collier looked up from their bikes as I turned in the direction where they'd parked them. While Collier lifted his chin in a sort of greeting with an easy smile, Saint was obnoxiously inscrutable. His deep brown eyes roved my face as though reading me like an open book, while the rest of his features might as well be carved from stone.

"Got the part, just waiting on you, princess!" Collier called with a grin.

"How'd it go?" Saint asked, his veneer of uncaring cracking over his burgeoning curiosity.

I frowned. "I honestly have no idea," I said.

"Sounds like LaCroix," Collier said, voice cracking over the laughter he was trying to suppress.

"Went fine," Saint said, glancing at his phone.

I rolled my eyes and said, "Peachy."

"C'mon, let's go find some lunch," he said, more to Collier than me.

"I'm fine," I said. "I'd like to get back to my car."

"You will," Saint declared. "After lunch."

I frowned at him and opened my mouth to argue. He just stared at me, stoic as a tree, and fired up his bike to drown out whatever protest I was going to conjure up. My frown crushed down into a glare and he finally cracked a smile at *that.*

What the fuck? What an asshole, I thought to myself, but still, be that as it may, that asshole still had me at his mercy with the part to my busted car spirited away somewhere on his bike or person.

Lunch, huh?

I could eat.

The question really was, *could I afford it on my extremely limited budget?* It depended on the place and the prices on the menu.

I climbed aboard the bike behind Saint and was doing the math in my head, crunching the numbers on the limited funds I had left and trying to factor in how much I might be charged for the parts and labor on my car. While I would have been cooked at a regular garage – I might be okay with Garnett's… *friends…* doing the work.

Still, I was an anxiety-riddled mess by the time we rode into the gravel lot at this swampy dive bar kind of a place right off the highway.

I must have looked as dubious as I felt because Collier laughed at the look on my face when he turned around after getting off his bike.

He held out a hand to assist me with my dismount, but I waved him off verbally with a testy "I've got it," before I got up.

He gave a nod, and I realized he was legit just trying to be polite, but still, looking back to Saint, who was rising from his seat like a leviathan from the deep and looking back on our interactions so far… I didn't trust it.

The inside of the bar was… rustic. The walls had the same boards as the exterior walls, yet, somehow it managed to remain cooler in here. Maybe that was from the dim crisscross of Edison bulbs strung back and forth along the ceiling, the strands draping artfully over each other over the scuffed square of linoleum flooring in front of the low stage, serving as a dance floor.

The windows set high in the back wall along the ceiling were so dirty that barely any sunlight came through them.

It was bare rafters above us and the metal sheeting of the bar's roof over that. All I could really think as we stepped across the worn path of silvery warped boarding under our feet that comprised the rest of the bar's floor was the cooling costs of this place must be astronomical.

There was no ceiling, no insulation, no drywall, no nothing – but as absolutely bare bones and rustic as the place was? It was charming.

Cozy even, with its shot-up street signs on its walls and stuffed alligator heads on plaques lining between them.

The booths were clean and cozy too, where they ringed the dance-floor on two sides – the vinyl of the benches green and relatively new. No cracks or tears. A single light fixture illuminated the table from the half wall that separated our booth from the booths on the other side.

"Best fried alligator and gumbo in Louisiana served here," Collier said.

I made a bit of a face. "I've never eaten alligator. Doesn't even sound appealing," I told them, sliding into one side of the booth. The two men slid into the side across from me, and I was secretly relieved one of them hadn't boxed me in.

"Can't knock it 'til you've tried it," Saint said as he took his seat after Collier. He leaned back against the backrest of the booth and stuck one of his long legs out into the walkway. I eyed him and tried to get a read on him, but it was impossible. He was as inscrutable as they came.

"Fair," I conceded.

"Tastes like a gamier, stronger version of frog legs," Collier said.

"Now that *really* doesn't sound appealing," I told him. Of course, that might just be leftover trauma from having to dissect the fuckers in science class. Blech. Whenever I thought of frogs, the smell of formaldehyde stuffed my nose, and I wasn't a fan.

"Tastes like fishy chicken," Collier said with a one-shouldered shrug.

"Can't knock it 'til you've tried it," Saint said with that same impassive look.

"If it's all the same to you, I think I'll pass," I said, looking out into the bar and rocking in my seat a little bit. "Is anyone even here?" I asked.

"Thought you weren't hungry," Saint said.

"I didn't say that," I said. "I just said I'd rather not stop and would like to get back to my car. Besides, how much does this place cost, anyway?"

"Doesn't matter," Collier said.

"To you, maybe," I said.

Saint shook his head.

"He means lunch is on us. We said we were stopping, and you said you didn't wanna. That means it's our responsibility to at least feed you." He sniffed, and it was almost dismissive. Like he wanted to add, *so quit being dumb* onto the end of it, but he didn't.

I blinked and let my eyes flit back and forth between them.

"You're buying?" I asked, surprised.

Collier grinned. "He is," he said, jerking his head in Saint's direction. "I got a growing teenage boy at home. I'm fucking broke."

Saint's lips twitched, almost like he was going to smile, but that was all we got from him. He was staring at his thick fingertip, tracing the whorl of a knot in the plank on his side of the table – the gears in his head turning slowly. I wondered what he was thinking about, but before I could ask, a woman appeared from in the back somewhere.

Her uniform was jeans and a tee shirt, with a thin strip of apron with just enough pockets to hold rolls of napkin-wrapped silverware on one side, paper-wrapped straws in the other, and her notepad and pens in the center, which she plucked from their pocket as she approached us.

"Sorry y'all, I didn't hear you come in. Hope you wasn't waiting long."

I looked up at her. She was a middle-aged woman, strong-featured with her curly brown hair in a high ponytail in a purple-and-gold LSU scrunchie. She wore the bar's tee shirt, in gray, the logo small and on the right, like so many businesslike tees and polos. I still couldn't quite make out the name of the place in the dim lighting, but it had a fleur-de-lis in an outline behind it, sort of like the club's logo, only not with the purple-hatted zombie.

"Can I have a menu?" I asked.

She blinked at me and said with a laugh, "Ain't had that question in a while here. Guess I'm so used to locals. Let me go on an' see what I can scare up, now."

"No need," Saint interjected.

"Thank you," I said pointedly, giving Saint a withering look.

I would order my own food. Thank you very much, and goodnight.

"Cuppa gumbo and a salad," he said. "For the lady."

I raised my eyebrows.

"That alright with you, cher?" the woman asked, waiting on me.

"I'd like to look at the menu," I said.

"I'll get one for you." She walked away and came back a moment later with a laminated page that had listings front and back.

The guys ordered while I perused the menu, and fuck if he wasn't right... the gumbo and a salad *did* sound good. I half contemplated choking down something I didn't want just to stand on principle but opted against it.

"A *bowl* of gumbo and a side salad," I said. "Cup doesn't sound like it would be big enough. Is it very spicy?" I asked.

"Aw, yeah." The waitress laughed. "You in the swamp now, sweetheart."

"Damn," I muttered.

"You want it from the pot we keep goin' for the tourists?" she asked.

"Please?" I asked.

"I gotcha," she said.

Both men stared at me like I'd done something weird, and when I looked up and asked, "What?" They broke out into snickers and laughter.

"Never seen someone handle being insulted so hard so well," Collier said.

I shrugged. "I like what I like, and I *don't* like to taste my endorphins."

"How do you like them?" Saint asked, and his gaze had lost its curiosity and had switched out for an uncomfortable intensity.

I felt my mouth go dry and answered him starkly with, "That's private and likely something you'll never find out. So change the subject."

Collier busted up laughing while Saint's eyebrow went up as a slow grin spread across his lips. He leaned back in his seat and nodded slowly at me like I'd got him, and that was okay. But it held an edge of *"it's on, now"* that I didn't know if I quite liked.

I wasn't here to spar or to flirt. I was here to find my little brother and keep a tenuous hold on "family" only to find that I'd been too late.

35

Now I only had one thing left – learning about who he *was,* but I didn't know if I would be so lucky that any of these fools would tell me.

"That was good," Collier said, wiping a tear from his eye.

I felt a smile of my own start to crack my lips just as our waitress returned with some glasses of water and asked what else we wanted to drink, flustered at the fact she'd forgotten all about the beverages since we'd been so quick with our food order.

It was a welcome change of subject with the way Saint let his gaze drift over me as though I'd finally said something interesting.

CHAPTER SIX

S aint...
She'd finally said something interesting.
She was into kink, and I found myself wondering what end of the spectrum she found herself on – dominant, submissive, or somewhere in the middle where she switched between the two. It finally made me curious.

I liked her fire. It was hot. In that regard, she was kind of a diametric opposite of ol' Louie. He was as beta as they came but had his moments. I missed the kid. He'd been a good dude – made the best out of the shit sandwich life had handed him. Hadn't let it change him for the worse. It'd been something watching him grow and come into his own, and he'd had so much further to go. It was a fuckin' shame he would never have the fuckin' chance to fully find himself.

I let my eyes rove the woman in front of me as Collier chatted her up. It wasn't long before the conversation turned to Louie, and Collier tapped my foot under the table twice with his. I clued into the conversation as she called Louie by his government name and said, "Garnett said why you all called him Louie. What's with that, anyway?"

"You asked him?" I asked.

"Well, yeah," she said. "Is that supposed to be off-limits or something?" she asked.

"Actually, yeah," I interjected before Collier could say something. He gave me some side-eye and clarified my point.

"Road names, while given to you, are deeply personal things," he explained. "It's considered rude to ask."

"All Garnett would tell me is that it was stupid. That I wouldn't believe him if he told me."

I chuckled at that. He'd been right, but that wasn't Louie. Louie never hesitated to tell his story about his run-in with a Roux Garou. Although that's not *why* we made fun of him for it. It was that he called the thing a *Loup* Garou – which wasn't *wrong*, per se. That was the French word for "werewolf," but Roux Garou was the correct nomenclature around these parts.

Made me think, though, the way she said it, her voice softening and somber as it was, that maybe Louie didn't tell her because the kid had finally been growing up – learning about what he should and shouldn't be talking about.

That was my mission, though, wasn't it? To see how much Louie may or may not have been talking out of turn. To learn if big sister here was trustworthy, or if she was going to be a problem.

"Guess I'll never know unless you tell me," she said. "I get that it's a deeply personal thing, or whatever, but does it go beyond death for you guys, or...?" her expression was a study in neutrality, and I let my eyes catch hers. She tipped her chin, barely, raising it, a subtle act of daring or defiance, and I felt a little thrill.

"Not much transcends death, as far as I'm concerned," I said. "When you leave the mortal coil, you leave everything's between you an' God at that point."

Her eyebrows went up, and her interest seemed piqued.

"Does that mean you'll tell me about my brother?"

"Quid pro quo," I said, seizing the opportunity. "You ask, I'll answer, but I get a question of my own for every one you ask."

Her green eyes flashed, and she leaned back into the backrest of the booth, which was pretty unforgiving. The food in this place made up for it, though. For real.

"Why do I feel like I'm about to make a deal with the devil?" she asked, a hard set to her jaw as the wheels turned behind those brilliant green eyes.

"I'm a perfect Saint," I said, raising my eyebrows, doing my best to look innocent – which I knew was a joke. "It's even my name."

She snorted and laughed, and I felt Collier shake with silent laughter beside me, his arm and shoulder next to mine, hitching with it.

"Bet," Velina said. "Why was Garnett's name Louie, then? Seems as good a place as any to start."

"Around these parts, there's an old legend." Collier, the natural-born storyteller, took over. "The Acadians and Cajun around here call it the *Roux Garou*. You know it as a werewolf – but it's also known by another name in French – the Loup Garou."

"Okay." She drew out the word and gave a look like *is this getting somewhere?*

"Louie swore he saw one, one night," I told her, cutting to the chase. I liked that about her.

"Except he kept calling it a Loup Garou rather than a Roux Garou," Collier said.

"The boys never let him live it down," I said. "Neither that he said he saw one nor the fact he kept calling it the wrong thing for around these parts."

She cocked her head and asked, "Do you know the story?"

Collier snickered. "Only heard it about a thousand times," he said.

"Every time he got drunk, an' every time he was sober and encountered someone who ain't heard it from him before. It was his favorite story to tell," I said.

She swallowed hard and looked like she wanted to ask but didn't.

"Your question," she said.

I smiled, and I knew it was a feral thing. I wasn't quite capable of smiling any other way. I took it easy on her and lobbed a softball one at her, or so I thought.

"What you do for a living?" I asked.

She hitched a laugh and looked to the ceiling, blowing out her cheeks as she contemplated how to answer that one.

"I'm a cleaner," she said, finally. "Specializing in biohazardous materials."

I frowned at that, reading in her face there was something more to it than that. I was almost ashamed to admit Collier caught on quicker than I did.

"What, like one of those crime scene cleanup outfits?" he asked.

"BINGO," she answered.

"You work with the cops?" I demanded, and I knew my expression darkened.

She shook her head. "Only in that they refer us out to families and businesses that need our services, but I'm just a grunt, a pleb. I don't dispatch. I'm the one who shows up to clean up the human soup when someone's been left to rot in their apartment for weeks."

"Eww," Collier said, sniffing like he could almost smell it. "How the hell did you get into that line of work?"

She shrugged one shoulder and said, "I was going for a degree in Criminal Justice and Forensic Sciences. I got my Associates, but I couldn't make it to a Bachelors. I got most of the way there, but it just got to be too cost-prohibitive. Turns out, you can't do much with an Associates these days. Couldn't even apply to a lab to try and gain experience. About all I was good for was security work – which just wasn't my thing. I did have an aptitude for all the really gross shit and enough of a cast-iron stomach that I could deal with it just fine. Turns out there's some pretty good money to be made cleaning up a scene and I already had most of the education and certifications to be able to do it. I switched tracks, and I've been doing it ever since."

"No shit?" Collier asked, and he sounded impressed.

"No shit," she said, nodding slowly.

Ain't that a hell of a thing, I thought to myself, but it made me wary. Doing a thing like that meant she was closer to law enforcement and the law enforcement side of things than what made me comfortable. I couldn't do much about it other than follow LaCroix's orders, so I filed it away to report to him or Hex on it later.

She had a strange sort of smile on her lips, one full of something that I couldn't pin down until she said to me in a sarcastic, almost self-deprecating tone, "Does that lose me cool points with your little club?"

I smirked back and told her honestly, "No, but the disrespect certainly does."

Her eyebrow went up. "Disrespect?" she echoed.

"Don't even try to pretend," I said. "Can't say we aren't used to it. We don't expect a citizen like you to understand."

She looked non-plussed at the disrespect I flung right back at her. I was thinking that she could dish it, but she couldn't take it, when her smile turned genuine, and she laughed a little and said, "Touché, to-fucking-ché."

I sat back, eyeing her, and before I could say it was her question, she spoke up and said, "I think the key difference here is that I *want* to understand, though. I'm just really bad at processing emotions, and I've got a lot of them right now. Big ones. Probably some of the biggest I've ever felt, so I'm sorry if I'm coming off like a bitch. It's a defense mechanism."

I glanced at Collier, who glanced at me, and I raised a questioning eyebrow. A sort of, *do you believe her?* He picked up what I was putting down and nodded. I simply said in her direction, "Your question."

She looked thoughtful, her green eyes searching my face keenly, and finally sat back on her side of the booth and looked out over the empty bar dance floor.

"Now I feel like anything I'm going to ask is going to be considered rude or whatever."

I shook my head. "We cleared that up."

"Just like that?" she asked.

"Just like that," I said evenly.

She took a deep breath, huffed it out, and said, "Tell me my broth-er's story – the one how he got his name. That seems safe enough right now."

I nodded, and Collier and I exchanged a look, mostly to gauge who was gonna start talking.

He deferred to me, and I started…

"It all started when…"

I told her the story as Louie had related it to us damn near a thou-sand times or more. About how he'd only been a teen back then, out late at night with some buddies, playing hoop and cuttin' up – when it hit that appointed time and the park lights went out.

How they decided to walk along the old train tracks down a ways to the corner store, lookin' to score some beer or malt liquor from some good Samaritan who was alright with contributing to the delinquency of some minors. About how they was smokin' a joint, passing it between 'em as they walked.

"The way Louie told it, things got real quiet," I said. "No birds, no bugs, no nothin' – and a real eerie calm came over him an' his friends."

"Yeah?" she asked, leaning forward, rapt.

"Yeah," Collier said. "Happens sometimes when a predator is nearby."

"It got one of Louie's pal's attention, and he got 'em all to shut the hell up and listen," I said.

I told her the rest, as detailed as Louie had ever told the story. Funny thing was, he never wavered in the retelling. Didn't deviate from his story one bit. It was the same every time. Sure, a lot of the guys gave him shit, claiming there was more in that joint they was passing back and forth than just weed – but as much as some of the guys gave him shit about it, we'd all, at one time or another, talked among ourselves and came to the conclusion that Louie wasn't just tellin' stories. That he definitely saw something that night.

I was in the camp that firmly believed he saw what he saw and, truthfully, it made me uncomfortable. That was some kind of evil I didn't want no part of. I fought the urge to cross myself just recounting the story.

"He said they were all standing there, in the quiet, in the dark. Said it was so dark that you had to stand within five feet of each other, or you'd lose track of your homie next to you, right?"

She nodded, rapt.

"Then he said they all heard it, out there in the trees along the side of the tracks, this low growling – foul and evil – enough to scare the fucking piss out of every last one of them."

"A werewolf?" she asked. She didn't look or sound too incredulous, which surprised me some, given she'd stated she had an interest in forensics and shit – a science-based field.

"Said that's what it was," Collier said, leaning back in his seat, playing with the edge of his napkin under his flatware absently.

"Did he see it?" she asked. "Like, actually see it, or just hear it and decided that's what it was?"

I chuckled and said, "Now just hold your horses. I'm getting to that part. He said he heard it first, a growling out there in the dark, in among the trees, and all he and his homies could do was look at each other for a moment, crapping their pants. Then whatever it was *moved*, and they heard it a rustlin' out there. That was enough for them. They booked it. Started runnin' up the tracks like hell itself opened up a portal behind 'em."

"Jesus," she said. "Then what happened?"

"Whatever it was back there *howled*, just like a wolf – scared the piss out of 'em even more," Collier said.

"Okay," she said, and I could tell we had her hooked. She was hangin' on every word, and I hoped for just a second there, I was doing ol' Louie proud in the retelling.

"So, they're all running like a bat out of hell, and Louie always said he heard one of his home boys – Tony or some shit – well, he heard him eat shit behind him."

"I'm not familiar with the term," she said, shaking her head.

"He fell," Collier said.

"Garnett?" she asked for clarification.

"No, not Louie – his friend," I said.

"Okay, I follow." She nodded.

"So ol' boy falls, and Louie, being the guy he is, he stops and turns around—"

"No shit?" she asked, smiling, and I could see the pride in her eyes.

"Ah-huh." I nodded. "So, Louie, he turns around, and that's when he saw it, for real – said his homeboy is lying there on the ground trying like hell to crabwalk back from the thing. Louie says he saw it. Said it looked like a half-man, half-dog thing, rearin' up on its hind legs over his homeboy."

"What?" she asked incredulously. "How'd they get away?"

"His buddy J-Dawg pulled his piece, an old .38 special, and started plugging away at the thing. It took off running," Collier filled in.

Velina sat silent for a long moment, looking troubled.

"I can't believe he never told me this," she said as our waitress returned and started setting dishes in front of us.

"Why's that?" I asked, seizing on the opportunity.

"I mean, he's told me literally *so much else*," she said.

"Yeah, like what?" Collier asked casually. He took the words right outta my mouth. We glanced at each other, both trying to remain looking lax and casual, but both of us simultaneously were on high alert – hanging on every word Velina dared to utter next.

The tension fizzled into a disappointing payoff when she said, "Private things. Things I doubted he would want you to know," she said pointedly and stared fixedly into my eyes as if daring me to contradict her point.

I didn't take the bait she laid out to start an argument, nor did I try to piss her off any further by simply blowing her off.

I simply dropped back a step and said, "I can respect that."

Collier looked like he swallowed a whole-ass bait hook sideways and opened his mouth, but I kicked him under the table. He shut his gob and nodded, trusting in me that I had a plan – but fuck me. I didn't have so much as a *concept* of a plan. I was just falling back to regroup and the food had arrived at the perfect time to do it.

We were digging in, and the conversation had its natural but not entirely uncomfortable lull.

I sniffed as the dash of hot sauce I'd slapped on my first bite of gator tickled my sinuses and made my nose start to run. That was some good shit.

She picked at her salad, stabbing at it a few times to build up a forkful and paused, her eyes rising to catch mine looking at her. She froze and didn't say a word, just put her bite in her mouth while holding full eye contact and chewing thoughtfully as she stared me down.

It was hot. Hot and cute.

Made me want to bend her over the table and fuck that attitude right out of her, which took me by surprise.

My thoughts changed track just then, and it was a runaway train, and it didn't head nowhere good.

CHAPTER SEVEN

Velina...

The gumbo and the salad paired with it were both pretty good. We were silent for the majority of the meal when Saint cleared his throat and asked me, "Ever tried gator?"

"Can't say that I have," I answered him honestly. My thoughts had been on my little brother, lost again after having been barely found. I wondered why he had been willing to tell me so much about himself and yet hadn't told me his tale of his brush with the supernatural, which, to be honest, I didn't ordinarily believe in those kinds of things. But something about the repeated tale of his encounter had sent a shiver down my spine. Enough that I believed him, even if I hadn't heard it directly from his lips to my ears.

"Here." He held out his fork with what looked like a fried chicken nugget dashed with hot sauce.

I made a face. "I don't like to taste my endorphins," I reminded him.

"Fair," he said, pulling the chunk of tender meat off his fork with his teeth and chewing, spearing another smaller piece without any of the spicy taint on it. He held it out, and I eyed it warily.

"What's it taste like?" I asked.

45

"Try it and find out," he challenged.

I plucked it off the end of his fork, tossed it into my mouth, and chewed. The breading itself was some type of spicy with the seasoning mix they used, but it was the kind of spicy that was just this side of tolerable. The taste of the tender white meat was akin to chicken... but not. Earthier, somehow... fishier... it wasn't bad. It wasn't bad at all.

I made a face like I was impressed, because I was, and nodded. "I would eat that," I said, and he gave me a crooked grin.

"Ain't good like this just any place. This place is the best around," Collier said.

"Noted," I said dryly, and still, I struggled internally with all I had learned and all I had yet to learn about my little brother.

I didn't want to alienate these guys. They were my only tenuous link to Garnett. Likewise, I was still pretty damn unsure about them all. It was a cognitive dissonance that left a bitter tang in my brain and the discomfort of it was real.

We finished up eating, the banter and further discussion kept to a minimum as the food sank into our systems and we all calmed down just shy of a food coma. The place had been good, like, really good. When I went to pay my share, Saint waved me off.

"You're a cheap date," he grated non-committedly, and I frowned.

"Thanks," I said curtly, and he nodded tersely. I didn't like not paying my own way, but I also had to admit to myself, my budget was fucking *tight*, and I needed to take it where I could get it.

As for the cheap date comment? He wasn't wrong. I tended to eat like a bird. Partial holdover from when I had an eating disorder, thanks to the kids at school and my own family constantly calling me fat.

Had, at one point, half-starved myself to death while everyone complimented how good I looked. I hadn't had a period for like three months and ended up collapsing at school.

Mom and Dad had been furious with me, and I hadn't been allowed to get up from the table until my plate had been clean. Although, thankfully, Mom hadn't overloaded it.

For their part in it, my siblings hadn't been allowed up, either, which had been both a blessing and a curse.

I shoved the uncomfortableness of my broken childhood back in its battered toybox at the back of my brain.

I hadn't had it half so bad as Louie, so who was I to bitch?

We went back out into the muggy, oppressive heat of the late afternoon, and I made the comment, "Whew, I can't wait until the sun sets around here and it cools off."

Saint and Collier barked a laugh, and both looked my way, amusement sparkling in their eyes. "Never been to Louisiana before, have you?" Collier asked.

I made a face. "It doesn't cool off after dark?" I asked, and they both shook their heads.

"Not really," Collier said.

"Peachy," I shot back flatly, the word laden with every ounce of sarcasm intended.

"You'll feel better on the bike. Get some wind moving," Saint said, and I sighed.

Something was better than nothing, I guessed.

We rode back to the club, and like before, I wasn't sure why he thought that riding would somehow make things cooler. The airflow *did* help make things a little drier, the wind moving past and over us, drying the sweat against my skin. But it honestly felt like the girl at the salon had her blow drier set to high and was blasting me in the face with it, letting it carry all the humidity of my wet hair into my face.

There was just no escaping the uncomfortable mugginess of it all.

When we rode up back outside their club, my poor car still sat where I'd parked her, hood up and lonesome on the side of the empty road. The sun was making its way for the horizon, and the light would only be good for a little while longer, which bummed me out. I liked taking still-life photography in my spare time. Had myself a nice digital camera. Had found I'd had an aptitude for good, clean, and focused shots when we'd been in the photography phase of learning for forensics.

I even managed to sell some shots on the side in some coffee shops around my city that I'd framed up nice.

My thoughts wandered from good light to photography, to the thrifting I did for a lot of my frames and the time I'd spent stripping, sanding, polishing, re-painting, and gilding to get them just right for a particular photo I had in mind for them. I wished I could take some time for myself and go wandering. Maybe do some thrifting. Who knows what treasures I could find in a place so rich with history.

From there, my thoughts drifted back to my brother and all of the promises he made, of the places we would go and where he would take me. He would always talk so big about the adventures we would have and of the hidden beauty in this city and her surrounding swamps and I just… I guess I would never know now.

Shit.

"Come on inside," Saint said as I worked the chin strap of the borrowed helmet and stared across at my forlorn car. "Cool off a minute before you pass out."

I scoffed at that and shook my head. "I've only ever passed out once in my life, and it wasn't from overheating," I declared.

"Must be nice," Collier said, eyeing me, and I felt like a privileged ass all of a sudden for saying it.

I shrugged. "I know, it's a flex," I said casually, attempting to deflect like I always did with sarcasm and humor.

I got a bona fide chuckle out of Saint and had to work harder than you'd expect to *not* smile.

Looks like you finally scored a point, Velina, I thought to myself. Saint was a stoic motherfucker and a tough nut to crack. That lone little chuckle was, for sure, the ice starting to crack and the iceman starting to thaw. I felt it in my bones.

I passed him as he held open the door to the clubhouse for me and slipping past him, I murmured a "Thank you."

Inside was cooler, for sure, the air conditioner working overtime to combat the oppressive heat, and likely drowning in the humidity it was pulling out of the air and dumping… well, somewhere.

Collier and Saint led the way, and I followed, going past the barroom and down the long hallway, past a room with what looked like a long table and chairs all around it – an altar of some kind at the end all aglow with those church candles in glass cylinders. The door to that room hadn't been open the first time I'd passed by it earlier in the day. As much as I wanted to, I didn't linger to look more fully, as the guys were walking with some purpose. After they passed the room, Saint looked back at me specifically to make sure I was keeping up.

At the end of the hall was a metal door that had been spraypainted in the club's colors to resemble a purple and green flag with a golden fleur-de-lis, the artwork really well done, the flag rippling in an imaginary wind. There was a tall, narrow window with the diamond pattern of chicken wire in the glass set to one side, and without breaking stride or hesitation, Collier hit the crash bar in the middle of the door and stepped through, holding it for both Saint and myself.

"Thanks," I said, slipping through, my view obstructed by Saint's broad back. What lay beyond was still just as unexpected as the first time I'd been back here just a couple hours or so ago. But with how fast life was coming at me at the moment? Felt like eons had passed already.

I knew the club was two stories from the outside, but in here, there was no second floor. The room just opened up huge to chains hanging from big thick steel girders high up above. It was... creepy, eerie, and made all the more eerie by the dim natural lighting coming through the high, high, dirty windows up near the ceiling and a couple of opaque off-white skylights set in the metal roofing.

"Creepy," I muttered, looking at the still, hanging chains and their hooks.

Saint chuckled again, a low, dark, and oily sound that sent shivers down my spine in such a way that I couldn't decide if I liked it.

"Hurricane proofing for the bikes," he said. "We pull 'em in back there." He indicated an open roll-up garage door, with a view across a short lot backed up against the next building over – some kind of a warehouse, maybe with a jazz mural painted on its uniform cinderblocks to liven it up.

"Hoist 'em up, and it don't matter how much it might flood. They're good to go until the water recedes," he said.

"And the power comes back on," I said dryly. I mean, how else would you get them back down?

He pointed along a wall in shadow at a metal staircase and catwalk against it, a generator of some kind sitting squat and waiting at the end of the walk like a toad.

"Gassed up and ready to go at the first reports there might be trouble," he said.

I raised my eyebrows. "You all are real Boy Scouts," I said, impressed. "Prepared for anything."

"I guess that would make me Scout Master Hex," a voice called from nearby.

I turned, and Hex stepped out from the same pillar he'd been leaning against the first time I'd seen him.

"How was the ride, sugar?" he asked.

"Hot," I said.

"Well, hopefully, we'll get you squared away here and back in your cage in no time."

"Excuse me?" I asked, unsure what he meant.

"Your car," Collier said. "We call 'em cages."

"Ah, gotcha," I said, and my eyes flicked back up, unbidden to the hanging chains up above.

"Cypress!" Hex hollered, and I jumped at the unexpected boom of his voice. It reverberated off the ceiling and sort of echoed back at us as a shadow fell into the doorway of the open garage door at the back of the big space.

Cypress came trotting up and threw some chin at Hex. Hex looked to Saint.

"Where's it at?" he asked.

"Left saddlebag," Saint called to Cypress, who nodded and walked out toward the front.

On this side, the door into the club was just a flat black, as though waiting for an artist to shake a can and depress the nozzle in its direction.

"Can I ask who's your artist?" I asked, dragging my eyes away from the door and back toward Hex.

He huffed a bit of a laugh and said, "Saint, why don't you give her the ten-cent tour of the place while she waits for Cy and Col to get done with her car, yeah?" Hex winked at me. "You know the art and the stories behind it better 'n anyone around here."

Hex held up his phone and said, "I'm fixin' to make some calls before the day is done. If y'all will excuse me..."

He wandered away a few paces and, after touching the screen a few times, raised the phone to his ear.

Saint grunted and said, "This way. We'll start outside first."

"Uh, okay…" I said, and fell into step beside him, heading into the back lot, shading my eyes against the setting sun to have a look at the big mural of the jazz artist on the wall up over the fence on the neighboring building first.

CHAPTER EIGHT

S aint...

I gritted my teeth and glared daggers at Hex who had entirely too much of a bemused sparkle in his eyes for my taste.

Fuck yeah I knew the artist for a lot of the rattle-can art around here. I did most of it. It'd been a hobby of mine since I was a fuckin' kid. Started out in dank abandoned places post-Katrina. Places where it'd be a while before they'd get to it, giving me the time to perfect my skills. The type of graffiti I was into wasn't that low-brow tagging shit. I worked on *art*. Drawing on a lot of local color and flavor to do it.

Velina stopped next to me outside and shaded her eyes, looking up at the largest mural I'd done to date on the side of the warehouse we'd purchased next door. We rented it out, but we were looking at turning the space into the distillery, Hex was trying like hell to get the proper permits and shit for us to build.

"Who is that?" she asked, as her green eyes roved the face of Buddy "King" Bolden. "A young Louis Armstrong?"

I barked a laugh. "That ain't even a trumpet," I said.

"Looks like one," she said.

"It's a cornet," I corrected. "Pretty fuckin' similar, but not the same."

"What's the difference?" she asked.

"You'd have to ask Axeman," he said. "He's the jazz lover. I like it and all, but I don't know a trumpet from a cornet until he corrected my ass when I was already partway through this beast."

She froze and turned slowly. "You're the artist?" she asked, her voice dripping with disbelief.

I sniffed. "Sometimes," I said. "It's really just a hobby, not like I do it for a living."

"Why not?" she asked. "This is incredible!"

"Yeah?" I asked, genuinely surprised.

"Yeah!" she said. "Your stock just went up in my book. You went from Neanderthal to Cro Magnon."

Her response caught me off guard and I laughed, like genuinely laughed.

"Yeah?" I nodded. "Alright. Okay."

She smiled at me and wrinkled her nose in this impish way that was entirely too cute.

"As I was going to say," I said. "That's King Bolden, one of the grandfathers of jazz. He was popular in the early nineteen-hundreds when the genre was still in its infancy and was still called 'jass'. Armstrong murals are a dime a dozen in this city, and I wanted to do something different, so I asked Axeman who he would like to see and this is the guy he picked. I had no idea who the fucker was before then. He's a cool cat, though. Played a cornet, which is visually similar to a trumpet only with a mellower tone. Axe sat out here just a jabbering on about the guy while I sprayed, playin' his music. It was some good shit."

I held back the part about how Louie had hung back here with us, soaking up what Axe had to say about the guy like a sponge, getting me regular drinks and shit to keep me hydrated as I worked in the heat and under the sun.

Velina's eyes wandered the image of Bolden, his sharp part in his slicked-down hair, and his even sharper and smarter suit. He dressed for success and was a born performer who lived up to his last name – bold and adventurous in his music. I tried to capture that in his eyes, the fire and the passion for his trade. I felt like I fell short, but hey – you are your own worst critic. You know how that shit goes.

"Did he watch you paint it?" she asked softly, and I nodded silently, unsure of what to say in the face of the utter defeat in her tone. I'd never heard someone so crestfallen.

"He was a genuinely good dude," I said awkwardly, unsure what else *to* say.

"Look, I get it," she said with a sigh finally. "I'm a civilian, or whatever, with a background in law enforcement in education if not in actual *practice*... but..." She struggled with the point she was trying to make and finally just closed her eyes and shook her head.

"You know what? Never mind."

Her stock went up with me in that moment. Maybe from a... fuck, I don't know. A fuckin Malibu Barbie to something more down to earth... like whatever the hell Barbie's younger cousin or sister's name was. Chipper or whatever. Not quite as bad or obnoxious as a Barbie, but still not great.

"Come on," I said after a long, uncomfortable silence. I was done stewing out here, and she fell into step with me without protest or complaint when I started walking.

We went out the back lot and turned along the fence. I'd spray-painted all kinds of shit along the strapping out here. Decorated the fence all along the block on this side with a scene from a Mardi Gras parade, the float a representation of the Baron throwing out party favors to the crowd, beads mostly, some candy.

She slowed her walk, falling behind me, and let her eyes rove the street art slowly as if she was taking in some kind of masterpiece in a museum. I studied her face as she looked, fully absorbed in picking out the details in front of her. Her green eyes jumped from one thing to the next, filing things I couldn't see or think of away as she looked.

"Louie looked at my pieces like that, too," I said suddenly.

She jolted slightly and turned her attention back to me.

"Yeah?" she asked.

I nodded, slowly. "Yeah," I said, but I didn't elaborate more.

There were echoes of him written all over her, and it was strange.

Knowing that they had never met and that it was likely all genetics…
well, maybe not *all* genetics.

Louie had grown up *rough*, and I do mean rougher than most.
Pimped out by his mamma in order for her to score, the sexual abuse
he suffered was just the tip of the fuckin' iceberg when it came down
to it.

It was low-key a miracle he hadn't been *more* fucked up.

All of us sort of had that going for us in some regard. I certainly
wasn't immune to a rough past. My mother never acknowledged what
happened to me, though. I was pretty certain it would destroy her now
if we got back into it.

She'd been a single mother, too – after a fashion. My daddy was a
drunk and away more often than he was home, out on the oil rigs out
in the Gulf. Still, she'd done everything right according to the Southern
Italian mamma traditions.

Church every Sunday, and sometimes mass on Wednesdays, too.

I still went, despite having been an altar boy and despite Father
Daniels and his… perversions.

I was bigger, tougher, now, and was pretty good pals with Father
Castelucci, who *would never*. How did I know? We'd grown up
together and had suffered side by side in some ways. It was a bond
forged in a different sort of fire but stronger than iron all the same.

"Tell me?" she asked, and her voice was beseeching. I wanted
nothing more in that moment to spill my guts and tell her *everything*
about Louie – but it just couldn't work that way.

"I believe when we last left off in our tit-for-tat, it was my question," I said, but truthfully, I couldn't honestly remember if it'd been
my turn or hers.

"Fair," she said, but she looked unhappy about it.

"What'd Louie tell you about *us*?" I asked, deciding to cut right to
the point, but trying to do it in such a way she didn't know I was
fishing for some really specific information out of her on the subject.

Her light green eyes searched mine, and she swallowed hard.

"Not a lot," she admitted nervously, and I could taste the lie as
soon as it was off her lips. "Said that Bennie was a war hero, and
LaCroix gave everybody the heebs. But that LaCroix, while scary, was

evenhanded and fair. Said that you had to watch out with Hex. That he's smart, and always six steps ahead of you whether you knew it or not."

I nodded slowly, feeling like now we were getting somewhere.

"All true," I said.

"Said that Axeman loved jazz and was a wealth of knowledge and that he got his name from some infamous New Orleans serial killer who loved jazz, too, and who was never caught. We went down that rabbit hole for a few days," she said, slowly walking forward. We just sort of naturally fell into a slow stroll along the fence as she spoke.

"A few days, huh?" I asked.

"He ended up sending me a book," she said.

"Yeah?" I asked.

"Yeah, he started writing letters. Old-fashioned, you know? Through the mail, even though we still primarily kept up through text and email."

You smart motherfucker, I thought to myself. Emails and texts you could track. Old-fashioned snail mail, not so much.

"What was in his letters?" I tried to slide in casually, but she was stubborn and shook her head.

"My question, if we're heading there," she said.

"My bad, my bad," I said and gave a low chuckle.

"Hey, you made the rules. I'm just following them," she said with a smirk that'd like to have me pin her to the fence if we were on closer terms, but we were definitely not that. Also, *no.* That was Louie's *sister* and I hadn't felt even so much as a pang about *anyone* in that direction in a minute. It was a *"what the fuck?"* kind of moment, even if it was just a fleeting one.

"You were saying…" I said.

"Give me a minute. You guys are like some kind of demented *Snow White and the Seven Dwarves.*"

I barked a laugh outright.

"How's that?" I asked.

"Can *you* name all those little bastards?" she demanded.

"Dopey, Happy, Grumpy, Doc, uh… Bashful, Sleepy, and… *fuck.* You got me "

She bit her bottom lip to keep from laughing, but her wide grin gave her away.

"What?" I demanded.

"Sneezy," she finished for me. "But I'm impressed!"

"I have a goddaughter," I said defensively. "She's seven."

She stopped walking and genuinely looked surprised.

"Seriously?" she asked.

"Her name is Hazel," I said. "And she's so happy and plucky I call her 'Yayzel.'"

She blinked, and I could almost see in real-time her opinion of me somehow unmaking and remaking itself behind her eyes.

"Careful," she intoned. "Your image of badass biker is cracking."

I chuckled and it was a mirthless thing. "I don't honestly give a fuck what anyone thinks about me, princess. I just want to live my life, make some art, and be left the fuck alone for the most part."

"Garnett said that about you," she said.

My eyebrows went up in silent question.

"That you were the most extroverted loaner in need to be around people that he'd ever met, which is why the club life suited you so well."

I turned that over in my head and nodded slowly.

"Perceptive little bastard, after all, wasn't he?" I said almost to myself.

She snorted. "Definitely my question now. What do you mean by that?"

I shrugged a little lamely and said, "Louie was young, yet. He made a bunch of dumbass mistakes and didn't always think shit all the way through." I sniffed. "We all knew he'd grow out of it, eventually, but he sure took his sweet time doing it."

Velina smiled faintly and nodded. "He said you all thought he was some kind of a dumbass."

"Sometimes," I agreed carefully. "But he was also a lot of other things. Funny, loyal, and kind, I guess. Always there, willing to lend a hand. A real *give you the shirt off of his own back* type. He had his dumb-assed moments, sure, but he more than made up for it in other areas."

"A good soldier," she said quietly to herself.

I frowned. "What was that?"

She stared at me for several moments and finally came to some kind of a decision because she said clearly, "He said you all described him as a good soldier behind his back. He heard you, you know. When you were discussing whether or not to patch him in, or whatever you call it. He heard everything you all said about him. The good, the bad, and the indifferent."

"Guess we can add 'crafty' to that list," I said, and I was duly impressed. I guess I hadn't thought Louie had it in him to listen in, because I remembered Bennie saying that about him during our deliberations. Ol' Louie must have been listening at the proverbial keyhole or some shit.

I filed the information away to let Hex know later. Louie shouldn't have known a thing about what we discussed inside the chapel while he'd been a prospect.

If he'd talked out of turn about *that*, what other information had he inadvertently or purposely passed along?

It was enough to make me worry, and I could tell by the bold look in Velina's eyes that dead or not – she would protect her brother and his secrets to *her* dying breath, which was a good thing. It gave her a chance. Still, all of it bore further exploration, so the tit-for-tat continued.

"What else did he have to say about us?" I asked, bringing us full circle and back around to Louie and his mouth.

She smiled and said, "Whatever he said, he said in confidence, and I wouldn't tell another soul. You know that, right?"

Guess we could tick the *crafty* box on big sister, Velina, too. She wasn't stupid – that was for sure, which was surprising given she was a California girl. Guess the stereotypes weren't all true.

Low-key, she reminded me of Cutter's Hope out there in Florida. She was originally a California girl, too.

"Doesn't matter if it wasn't something he was supposed to say in the first place," I said, and I tried to be gentle about it. "If he wasn't supposed to be talking, he wasn't supposed to be talking, *period*."

"What are you going to do?" she asked, eyebrows raised. "Spank him?"

I snorted a laugh at that one as she drew up and stopped at the corner before we had to turn right to walk along the front of the club.

"Touché," I said.

She sighed and said, "You don't have anything to worry about. He loved you, all of you. You were the closest thing to family he had right up until I showed up, and nothing was going to alter that for him."

The look on her face changed, the lines of her expression deepening with something that looked like it weighed her down. It was a bone-deep weary in her eyes and the set of her mouth that I recognized. One of those deep tireds that wouldn't or couldn't be remedied by sleep. It made me less curious about Louie and what he may have told her out of turn and piqued my interest in *just* her."

What'd put that tired on her soul?

That wasn't a level of exhaustion you found from work or the daily grind. That was a grind that was put on you by other people. Louie had that look, too, sometimes. When he didn't think we noticed. When his memories of his life *before* club life hooked their demon's claws through his ribcage and drew him down, down, down, and down, into the depths of his own personal hell.

We all had that haunted look for one reason or another, and I wondered, what was Velina's reason?

It was food for thought. Serious food for thought.

Citizen or not – maybe we were a lot more alike than either of us gave each other credit for.

"Appreciate you saying so," I said gruffly as I made the turn around the corner of the fence. She moved with me, and we turned it just in time for Collier to crank her car and for it to start up.

"Guess that's my cue to go, right?" she asked.

I shook my head.

"Not if you're not done talking," I said.

She looked at me. "You're not?" she asked.

Again, I shook my head.

"No."

"Interesting…" she said in a pondering tone.

"Yeah?" I asked.

"Yeah," she said. "Right up until a few minutes ago, it felt like you couldn't wait to get rid of me, and now?"

I laughed a little. "Now, I think you're interesting," I said. "Besides, they just got it started. Now they got to properly diagnose your AC issue and see if they can get that fixed."

"You know I can't afford that, right?"

"Part of this life is your family gets taken care of long after you're gone," I said.

"Just like that?" she asked.

"Just like that," I answered. "It's just how it works."

"I don't understand that," she said.

"Spoken like a true citizen," I said back.

"What was the art piece in the room with the long table?" she asked, and it threw me for a second.

"Come on," I said. "I'll show you, but put your hands in your pockets and keep 'em there."

She raised her eyebrows but stuffed her hands into what passed for pockets on women's jeans and threw me some chin to indicate I should lead the way.

I maybe liked that she could follow orders so cleanly, just a little too much.

CHAPTER NINE

V elina...

They fixed my car – both the starter and the air conditioning. I guess the only thing that was wrong with the air conditioning was a need for some kind of recharge of the refrigerant. It took
them a little while to scare some up, but they wouldn't hear of me
leaving until they did it, and after? The vents blew blessedly cool and
then cold air.

I was grateful for that.

Saint had shown me every piece of art he'd spray painted inside the
club and out – and each piece was more impressive than the one
before. We'd wound up back at the bar in the front room next to
Louie's urn and photo.

He'd told me the story about how Louie had ended up in the
mugshot behind his urn. A drunk and disorderly in the French Quarter. Dumbass shit... you know?

I let slip that I'd never been arrested, and Saint had poked fun at
me for being some kind of a virgin. Never arrested, only ever passed
out the one time, next thing you'd know, I'd tell him I'd never broken a
bone.

That one I had done. More than once.

I'd told him about it, opening up a little about my dad and what he was like on a bender.

He'd said his dad was a drinker, too.

All I'd been able to say was, "Guess we aren't so different after all."

I'd come back to the hotel in Metairie after all was said and done. Hex had told me to come back in a day or two and they'd have pictures and stories. They'd hold another sort of impromptu wake for my brother, just for me.

I'd asked why, and I'd been met with the same sort of lackadaisical shrug and the explanation, "You're family."

I sat up in bed, trying to ignore the roach-infested motel surroundings as I scrolled through old text messages with Louie. The last ones were all about a girl named True and how she wasn't a girl – at least not all the way, not yet – and I had to smile.

She was trans, and I was surprised that Louie was so enamored with her, but the way he was gushing about her in his texts, he was absolutely mad for her.

I guess it was later that very night that he'd died, and the texts had just… stopped.

It was an interesting maelstrom of emotions keeping me awake, not just about Garnett but also about Saint. He was inscrutable. I mean, *hard to read* is the understatement of the year here. Just when I thought he hated my guts, he would crack a smile and banter with me or laugh at one of my sarcastic remarks, leaving me all sorts of confused all over again.

Color me shocked when he'd handed me a card at the end of the night – blank but for the phone number in black block numbers on its face in the center of the card.

He'd told me to call him if I needed to. I didn't honestly know if I *needed* to, but I couldn't help but find myself *wanting* to.

I picked it up from the side table under the golden pool of lamplight, frowned, and tried not to shudder at the thought of the tiny brown roach I'd seen crawling on it a few minutes ago. I'd seen another in the bathroom, when I'd flipped on the light, making a break for it off the top of the toilet seat under the lip of it.

I wished like hell I could afford better than the La Chiquita on

Veteran's Boulevard, but I wasn't here on vacation. I was here to find my missing brother, and now, I was here to learn what I could about him, now that I'd found he was dead.

I sighed, set the card aside and switched out the light, sinking into the uncomfortable, but thankfully bedbug-free bed. Making sure my phone was plugged in, I closed my eyes.

Saint had resisted telling me the details of my brother's death beyond that of he'd been shot in some kind of a drive-by shooting.

Tomorrow, I would go another route on that and hopefully find justice for Garnett before my time in New Orleans was through.

I WAITED the better part of an hour for the detective or, hell, for *anyone* involved in my brother's case to come fucking *talk to me*. It was almost one hundred percent apparent from the time I hit the front desk of the station to the time I waited in the cubical and watched who I was pretty sure was the detective I was waiting for shoot the shit with another bad suit at the water cooler and coffee maker for at least twenty more minutes while I sat there, staring, waiting, and yes, *seething*.

I mean, tell me you don't give a good goddamn without telling me you don't give a good goddamn.

When he finally decided to look up and down the line of cubicles in my direction, the laughter on his face turned dour, like it was somehow *my* fault he'd been standing there fucking off, leaving me waiting while he talked Saints football for twenty minutes with his dude-bro coworker.

I was pissed, but I did my level best to hold back my father's famous temper. *Our* father's temper, because screaming at this cop about what an inept fucking troll he was wasn't going to get me anywhere. Would it make me feel better? Probably. Would it get Garnett anything close to resembling justice?

No.

Of course, it didn't look like Detective Troy Malcom was working too hard at it anyway – a notion that was only about to receive further reinforcement when he slid past me and went around his desk to take a seat.

He dropped heavily into the desk chair that sank several inches under his considerable bulk, and I wondered vaguely when this guy had last passed a fitness test.

"How you doin', Miss…"

"Velina," I said. "Just call me Velina."

"Miss Velina," he said finally.

"Velina is my first name," I told him. He gave me a smile that, if he had been eighteen and strapping, *might* have done something for fifteen-year-old Crystal Methalina down at the trailer park but didn't do anything for me except make me like him even less.

Was I biased?

Maybe just a little.

I had more than one occasion to show up to a scene and have to wait around for forensics or detectives to finish up, and man, these assholes thought they were God's gift to a crime scene and looked down on me like I was just the janitor.

Which was annoying, considering I probably had more education than both detectives partnering combined, if a lot less experience. Still, it was always a satisfying feeling for me when I found missed evidence and had to call the detectives or forensics team back in to pull a walk of shame to collect what they'd missed.

That part of my job never got old, and yeah – I called *every time.* I wasn't so petty as to deny anyone justice because I was pissed at the cops for treating me like I was some fresh-off-the-boat, didn't-t-speak-a-lick-of-English, hotel maid… who, truth be told, put in more work in a week than these overstuffed egotistical motherfuckers probably put in all year.

All it'd really taken for me to hate the cops and forensics teams I had so much wanted to *be* when I grew up was a few months working in a position that they felt was beneath them.

That was the truth.

"Well, this is the South, Miss Velina, so anytime you're properly addressed by a good ol' Southern boy or gentlemen, 'miss' is going to be a part of the mix," he said and chuckled.

Which... *ew.* The correction dripped with condescension and more than a little misogyny. Looked like I had two things working against me, I wasn't Southern and I had a vagina.

Fucking peachy.

"What can I help you with, *Miss* Velina?" he asked, and I heaved an inward sigh that I hoped I managed to keep any outward appearance of under wraps.

Unfortunately, I could be one of those people who it didn't matter what my mouth was saying, my face told the truth anyway, which in this particular setting could be a detriment to getting what I wanted.

"I'm here about the Garnett Whitcomb case," I said in my most professionally bland tone I could muster. Mustn't seem too eager.

"Whitcomb, Whitcomb, Whitcomb," he muttered to himself under his breath, spinning in his chair to the low filing cabinets behind his desk and a stack of file folders on the top of one of them. He pulled a disappointingly thin and barely battered folder out from under three much fatter ones, and I felt my heart sink.

Did they even fucking try?

"Here it is," he said absently. Tipping it up so I couldn't see its contents, he flipped it open.

He let his watery blue eyes travel down the page and spread a few pages to skim over their contents.

"Not much here," he said with a gusty sigh. "Why are you interested in a Voodoo Bastard? You know they're bad news, don't cha?" he asked me, flipping the folder shut and tossing it on his desk. The corners of a few photographs slipped out, but just enough to let me know they were photos with no actual discernible content.

I made eye contact and said, "Most motorcycle gangs are, aren't they?"

He huffed a bit of a laugh. "Hell, just them one-percenters, as they call themselves," he said, leaning back in his chair. "Most of the rest of 'em are law-abiding citizens and responsible riding clubs – but the Voodoo Bastards?" He made a face and shook his head. "Why you wanna know anything about that?" he asked.

"Because he's my brother," I said point blank and let the period at the end hang between us.

He grunted and leaned forward in his chair, a frown furrowing his brow below his receding hairline as he picked up the folder and flipped through the pages.

"Says here, he didn't have no family. His mamma died in a drug deal gone bad – never solved… no siblings to speak of…"

"We shared the same father," I said. "I have a commercial DNA test that says we are, most definitely, related."

"Is that what brings you down to New Orleans?" he asked.

"Yes," I said. "We were in constant contact for almost the last nine months or so, and then everything just… stopped. I got worried, and so I came down to find him."

"Ah." He nodded. "I can see how communication would, ah… cease under these circumstances."

"Yeah," I said unhappily.

"Well, I hate to be the bearer of bad news, but there ain't a whole lot here to work with," he said with a big sigh that, to his credit, sounded genuinely frustrated. "What do you know about it so I can fill in the blanks?" he asked.

"Nothing, really," I said. "Drive-by shooting – some kind of club turf war thing."

"Mm-hm, I know that's right now," he said. "Some new group outta the bayou causin' a mess of trouble tryin' to move into the city onto the Voodoo Bastard's territory – like either one of 'em have a claim."

I nodded.

"I wish I could say this would be solved," he said, looking sorry, but I could tell it was a painted-on emotion that he didn't genuinely feel. "But no witnesses on the outside and no real cooperation from the boys on the inside. I'm afraid this is one of those cases that's destined to just… sit until someone gets to talkin' out of turn around the right set of ears, if you know what I mean."

"You're stalled," I said. "I'm also getting the impression that you're not even going to try."

He sighed and gave me a disappointed look. The way he leaned back in his seat said I was about to get a stern talking to and that I wasn't going to like it.

Bring it on, I thought, as he flipped through a couple of the top pages and unfolded a long, old-fashioned, dot-matrix printout that was at least three pages long.

"Assault, drunk and disorderly, drunk and disorderly, drunk and disorderly, possession of a controlled substance, looks like marijuana for some personal use – not sure anyone cares about that these days." His eyebrows went up. "Battery – with a domestic enhancement – looks like he shoved his mama into a table—"

I snorted.

"Something funny about that?" he asked.

"If you knew his mother and how he was raised, you'd have pinned him with a medal for that one," I told him.

He made a sort of *eh* face and went on, "Assault, assault with a deadly, drunk and disorderly, *another* possession, this time with an intent to distribute... are you getting a clear picture here?" he asked me.

"That my little brother was no saint? You should have met our father," I said. "That doesn't mean someone gets to drive or ride by, shoot and kill him, and that there's no justice to be had."

"No, that's true," he said gently. "But do you know how many homicides come through here on any given day?" he asked.

"I know that once upon a time, New Orleans was the murder capital of the United States before it lost its crown to DC."

"That's right, and that makes for *a lot* of homicides... and this one? Dead end after dead end, and no family to speak of—"

"I'm his family," I cut him off. "Me."

"I do apologize, but if you'd let me finish, I was about to say 'until you walked in the door.'"

I nodded and let my posture, which had tensed, ease back down.

"Now I'll see if I can't find the time to give this another look, but darlin', I'm not sure that even with another stab at it, I can get somewhere with it."

Tell me you don't want to try without telling me you don't want to try, I thought to myself. I let my eyes flicker up and down his face and said finally...

"I clean up crime scenes for a living. Sometimes, I find things that were missed. Can I?" I half-heartedly reached for the file, but he drew it away from me.

"All due respect, Miss Velina, I think that might be a bad idea. You don't want to remember your brother like that."

My shoulders sunk in defeat.

I knew he had a point, but *damn.*

"What if I spot something?" I tried, and I think I failed at keeping the pleading out of my tone.

"It's a big 'if,' and I promise to go over these again, thoroughly, and with another pair of eyes – but again, the likelihood of a case like this ever being solved really does come down to dumb luck and the wrong people talkin' around the right ones. I'm sorry. I wish I had better things to tell you, but that's just how it is."

"It is what it is," I said bitterly.

"Exactly," he said, but at least he genuinely didn't sound happy about it.

He stood up and held out a hand, and that was my cue. I reluctantly stood up, too, and sighed heavily.

"Thank you for your time," I said as professionally as I could.

"Don't mention it," he said. "Thanks for stopping in. Again, I wish I had better news to tell you."

I nodded, turned, and said, "I'll see myself out."

He gave a nod, and I left the floor, stopping at the elevator and stabbing the button to go down with my finger.

I wanted to scream with the unfairness of it all, and I felt like I was being sucked into a whirlpool and thrashed about on the inside.

I hated it, but by the same token, I wasn't giving up.

It sounded like anyone and everyone in Garnett's life had – our dad, his mom, the cops, society as a whole… but you know who hadn't?

The Voodoo Bastards.

They hadn't, and maybe it was time for another talk with Saint.

CHAPTER TEN

S aint...

"We need to talk. No bullshit, no games."

My eyebrows went up as Velina's no-nonsense voice came over the airwaves.

"Oh, yeah?" I asked and tried to keep my tone easy and uninterested.

"What part of *no games* did you not just understand?" she asked, sounding both tempestuous and impatient.

"Slow your roll, there, Turbo, What's got your underwear wedged up your butt?"

"First of all," she said. "I wear thongs. I figure if my underwear is going to get wedged up my ass crack anyway, I might as well buy some that's meant to be there."

I lost it and started cracking up. That had been unexpected, but shit, she was a quick study. She kept talking, never missing a beat.

"Second of all, I talked to the detective handling my brother's case," she said and she didn't sound happy about that at all.

It figured.

"Yeah, and what'd he have to say?" I asked nonchalantly.

"Basically told me without telling me that Garnett's case was a low priority and that no humans were involved."

I recognized the term – *no humans involved*, and yeah – that about summed it up. There were a lot of us out here that fell under that category. Outlaw bikers, druggies, hookers, homeless, headcases – pretty much anyone who was considered the dregs of society. Those of us who fell through the cracks, or like us, wedged ourselves right on through deciding it was better to reign in Hell than it was to serve in their idea of heaven.

A gilded cage was still a fucking cage, man.

I grunted.

"Sounds about right," I said and sighed. The truth was ugly, and the truth was that to the majority of the citizenry – our lives didn't matter. It was just more cost-effective for us to kill each other rather than suck up taxpayer money and resources by sending us to prison.

"Yeah, well, it's bullshit," she said fervently.

"You noticed," I said with no little sarcasm.

"Meet me at the Café du Monde on Veterans," she said. "I'm already here."

I snorted. "You think I'm at your beck and call?"

"Knock it off," she said moodily. "We're on the same team on this, and I think we can help each other."

"Oh, yeah? You think you can help me?" I couldn't keep the amusement out of my tone or the grin off my face. She had a brass set of ovaries, alright.

"That douchebag detective had more sympathy for Garnett's piece of shit druggie abusive mom rather than Garnett," she said and then lowered her voice. "I'm glad he shot her in the face."

I froze.

Fuck me. She knew. Louie had told her… *fuck, fuck, fuck, fuck, fuck!* What else had he told her?

My tone was cold as ice when I said, "I'm on my way."

"Thought so," she said, sounding dangerous.

I ended the call and immediately phoned Hex.

"We got a problem," I said as soon as the line connected, but before he even had a chance to speak.

"What kind of problem?" he asked, cutting through the bullshit.

"Louie talked to his sister."

"How bad?" Hex asked.

"She knows it was Louie who did his mom," I said.

"Shit," Hex swore softly. "What does she want?"

"Me to meet her at the Café du Monde on Veterans in Metairie," I said. "Said she talked to the detective on Louie's case this morning. Seems all fired up about it – wants to help me, she says."

Hex voiced my exact thoughts on that when he scoffed.

"Her, help us? How the fuck she plan on doing that?" he demanded.

"Beats me. What do you want me to do?" I asked.

"Meet her," he said. "Gather more intel and bring it straight to the chapel. I'll make some calls, see if we can't put tabs on her."

"Sounds good," I said. "Let you know what I find out."

"Uh-huh, you do that," he said, ending the call.

I sighed and set the phone down by my hip, lying there, watching the ceiling fan of my bedroom spin lazily above me. I'd tied one on pretty hard the night before, trying to drown out those haunting green eyes of Velina's framed in the silky fringe of bangs and longer pieces of her dark brown hair. She did a thing with it, where she'd dyed it red, which didn't look like much on her dark natural hair until the sunlight hit it and sparked it like she'd spun rubies into fire and woven it through the strands.

I whipped back the covers and sat up, wincing at the aches and pains and how my stomach roiled with the sudden motion.

I lived in Metairie – right down the street from the big park with the lake, just a few blocks over from Veterans. I knew which Café du Monde she was talking about. I wasn't but three minutes from it, but she could cool her heels for a bit while I put myself through a shower and at least whipped some mouthwash through my mouth to get rid of last night's bender.

Swear to God, my mouth tasted like dog shit smelled at the moment. The shower helped the throbbing in my head. I brushed my teeth while I was in there, swished some mouthwash when I got out, and found last night's jeans on my bedroom floor. I pulled on a fresh tee with the sleeves cut out of one of my drawers and pulled down my cut from the hook on the back of the bedroom door. I left my jacket at home. I wasn't feeling like a safety Nazi. I was feeling like a rebel – only I had a big damn cause set up in front of me, and that cause was protecting my fucking club.

I didn't think it was more than fifteen minutes from the time I hauled my big ass up out of bed to the time I pulled in the lot at the Café du Monde. It was mid-afternoon and pretty empty. Not even so much as a car in the drive-thru.

I could see her through the windows at a front corner table, her phone lying flat and a cup next to it. She had her chin in one hand, elbow propped on the table, and the other rested on the table. She stared off into space, her index finger on the hand resting on the table, tapping out her nervous and impatient energy with the even measure of a metronome – albeit one on crack.

It didn't miss a beat, but the pace was pretty frantic.

I went in and held up a finger at her when she straightened, going for the counter myself.

"Coffee, black," I said.

"What size?" the older woman behind the register asked me.

"Fuck, better make it large," I said.

"Coming right up, your total—"

I held out a five. "Keep the change."

"Thank you, sir. I'll have that right out."

I stood and waited while she poured and took the paper cup with its cuppy condom cardboard sleeve thing from her with a muttered "thanks."

Velina was turned sideways in her seat, watching me over the back of her chair as I threaded my way through the empty tables to her. I hooked a boot in the leg of the chair opposite her and pulled it out from the table with a clattering screech.

"Thought you'd never get here," she said.

"Yeah, well, I was at home," I said, perfectly content to let her assume it was a ways a way.

She harrumphed and said, "So I got your attention."

"Seems ol' Louie's been talking out of turn," I agreed carefully.

"Don't be pissed at him," she said, immediately coming to her brother's defense. "While he told me, he didn't tell me who else was there or involved, if anybody. Just said he'd been the one to handle it and talked out some of his feelings about it."

"Yeah, and what were those?" I asked, mildly interested but pretty sure I already knew.

"Never mind that," she said. "Anything Louie told me, he told me in confidence, and I'll take his secrets to my grave."

The look in her sparking green eyes was dead-ass serious, and I nodded slowly.

"Let's say that I believe you," I said. "You got me here, now what?"

"The cops aren't doing shit about my brother's case," she said. "What are *you* doing?"

I scoffed a laugh and shook my head. "That's club business," I said automatically and expounded on it by telling her, "Even if we were doing anything, it's not something to be talked about. Especially with a citizen like you."

"So, you're not doing anything," she said stubbornly, seemingly ignoring the insult about her being a citizen.

"I didn't say that," I shot back and she gave me a look like *don't be stupid*. "Better question is *what do you think you can do that we can't?*" I demanded.

She leaned back in her seat and looked contemplative before saying, "First of all, I'm not a citizen. I'm his sister. Second of all, I can get in."

I frowned.

"Get in? Get in *where*?" I demanded.

She looked at me, blinking several times, and finally said, "You can't seriously be that thick."

I shot my eyebrows up and leaned forward.

"You want to infiltrate the Bayou Brethren and do exactly *what*?" I demanded.

"Well, I can either broker what I learn to you or the cops. Take your pick," she said, leaning back in her seat.

"Why am I your first pick?" I asked.

"I thought you said you were Louie's family," she said.

"We are." The two words were resolute, and I glared at her, daring her to argue the point.

"Well, *so am I,* and I know the likelihood of getting any kind of *real* justice for my brother is higher with you lot than with the cops and the system."

I shook my head. "You don't want justice. Otherwise, you wouldn't be sitting across from me right now."

"Not so thick after all," she quipped, and I scowled. "You're right," she said. "I want revenge."

We sat across from each other, the silence dragging out as I thought furiously about it.

"Look," I said. "Despite my better judgment, I actually *like you,* and what you're proposing is fucking *crazy.* You know that, right?"

She lifted a shoulder in a blasé shrug and looked almost bored, like she saw the whole me trying to talk her out of this shit coming a mile away, and she had no designs on entertaining me or my bullshit.

"You really are related to Loup Garou," I said finally. "He did some crazy shit, too."

"Like what?" she asked.

"Walked straight up to a cop in the Quarter and headbutted him once – got charged with an ag-assault, pled down to a drunk and disorderly. Spent ninety days in jail for it. Was some funny shit, though."

"He had a laundry list of charges. The detective read some out for me, like he was trying to convince me somehow that Louie's case wasn't *worth* solving because my brother was some kind of a piece of shit. That pissed me off," she said. "He wasn't a piece of shit. He was an abused kid who got turned into a fucked-up adult who was just trying to find his way in a world that showed him and told him at every turn that it just didn't give two shits about him."

I stared at her and was pretty sure I was getting a chub. The passion in her voice, the fire in her eyes, and the cold, hard look on her face… all of it was leading to one conclusion – she was a warrior queen and she was out for blood – sure, that part, but the part that was important to me?

She got it.

She was, at the very minimum, starting to understand that for kids like Louie, he didn't choose the life. The life chose *him*.

It was like that for a lot of us.

"You're right," I said, nodding slowly and evenly. "The world didn't give a fuck about Louie. Doesn't give a fuck about me, or you either – and in *this* world? *My world?* You're even less than that. This life will chew you the fuck up and spit you the fuck out, little girl." I shook my head. "Whatever you're thinking, I'd stop if I were you before you get yourself into some deep shit."

She snorted. "Too late for that," she said and stared at me pointedly.

Damn. She had me there.

"Touché," I said. "You got our attention, and not in a good way. But what you're proposing is *nucking futs.*"

She smirked and said, "I know it sounds ass backward, but look. They don't know me from fucking Adam," she argued. "So gimme the crash course, tart me up, and turn me loose – it's either that, or I do it myself. At least with some pointers from you and yours, I have an icicle's chance in hell."

"Shit, Hell would have to freeze the fuck over in order for me to get on board with your crazy, woman."

She laughed then and shook her head.

"Of all the crazy shit I've thought or done, believe me, this seems like the one time I feel completely and comfortably *sane.*"

"Then you've really lost the plot," I said.

"Look, if you're worried about me being slapped around, raped, or getting hooked on something or whatever – you can stop. I'm a big girl. I've been through some things already. There's nothing they could do that hasn't been done before."

She maintained eye contact, and I said, "They could kill you."

"Yeah, done that too," she said, and I raised an eyebrow.

"I drowned when I was eight. Was clinically dead for nine minutes. The medics and the ER docs got me back, and I got lucky. No permanent effects."

"I don't know about that last bit," I argued, and she cracked a smile.

"Everything has risks," she said. "Louie's never had blood show up for him in his entire damn life. I know something about that. I know he's gone, and thus this won't really change his track record, but I'd still like to try."

"We gotta run this by Hex and LaCroix – the rest of the club," I said, coming to the decision that she was going to do it, come hell or high water.

She was either brave or stupid – likely a stiff combination of the two.

"Why?" she asked.

"Because, like any family, Daddy and Mommy have the final say on what the kids get up to," I said, my voice laden with sarcasm.

"Okay, fine," she said.

I sipped my coffee, the bold and rich flavor flooding my mouth, that bitter zing of chicory just hitting mighty fine in that instant.

"Ugh, is that black?" she asked.

"Yeah, why?" I asked.

"Nothing," she said, shaking her head. "I just use cream and sugar because I like myself."

"Yeah, well, I'm a psychopath, and I like things simple."

She snorted. "Not so much a psychopath," she said. "You seem worried about me and what I'm doing too much to be a psycho."

Tou-fucking-ché.

Damn, she was good at that.

"I DON'T LIKE IT," Chainsaw said almost as soon as I'd got done talking.

"Well, now, hold on a minute here," Hex said, looking thoughtful. "Let's have a look at the whole big picture."

The table was quiet for a moment, and LaCroix was as unreadable as ever.

"This could present a real opportunity," Axeman declared, and I nodded.

As much as I hated to admit it, I'd come to the same conclusion.

"I'm with Chainsaw," Bennie said. "I feel like we've already let Louie down a metric fuckton, and letting his sister do this?"

"We didn't even *know* he had a sister until she showed up," Cypress said. "She's fine and all, but in the real of it, who is she to us other than just another fuckin' citizen?"

"Harsh," I said, and he gave me a look like *so?* I couldn't help but chuckle. I'd had the thought myself. Shit, all of this was moving faster than greased lightning for my tastes.

"Sounds like she's got Louie's tenacity," Collier said, and I nodded.

"Stubborn and crazier than a shithouse mouse," I said.

"She got Louie's dumb, too?" LaCroix asked simply. I looked at him.

"No," I said, cutting right to the point. Was she inexperienced? Yes. Dumb? No, not at all.

"Set this up right, the inexperience could help weigh in her favor. Gonna have to take the long road goin' in that way," Hex said.

"Get outta my fucking head," I said, and he nodded. We did that sometimes – thought along the same lines at the same time without meaning to. We'd taken to telling each other to get out of our respective heads when it happened. No more needed to be said.

There was a lapse in talk at the table as we each retreated inside our heads to think through all the implications.

"Pros and cons, boys. Pros and cons," Hex said.

"Pro – she finds out what the fuck pissed in these asshole's Wheaties for us," Axeman declared.

"Con – she gives us up, gets raped, tortured, and killed all for nothing," Chainsaw argued.

"She knows the risks," I said. "Either she does it with us and our backing, or she goes it alone."

"Jesus." Bennie blew out his cheeks and tipped his head all the way back to stare at the ceiling as though it was some kind of Oracle that could pull the will of the divine out of thin air.

"We take her to the swamp witch," LaCroix said evenly. "Get her blessed and send her with all the right juju."

"I'll just stick to prayin' if you don't mind," I said.

"Shit, sounds like we gonna need all the help we can get if we go through with this, non?" Cypress said, and he was staring off into space, the wheels and gears turning inside his skull.

"For?" LaCroix asked.

He noted the hands that went up around the table.

"Against?" he asked.

"It passes by simple majority," Hex declared.

It was far from unanimous, though.

"She seems to have taken a shine to you," Hex said, grinning and I scowled at him.

"Fuck you," I declared.

"So, it's decided, then," LaCroix muttered. "You're her handler."

"Yeah," I agreed, but I didn't have to be happy about it.

"This is one hell of a Hail Mary pass," Chainsaw said.

"If anyone might be able to pull it off, I think she could, though," I said.

Bennie frowned at me. "You voted against it," he said, and I nodded.

"I guess I like her," I said, which took a lot for me to admit, but there it was.

"This is fuckin' crazy," Bennie muttered.

"Yeah, yeah, it is," I agreed.

CHAPTER ELEVEN

Velina...

I hadn't expected Garnett's club to accept my offer, but they did. Honestly, my meeting with the detective on my brother's case left me feeling like even if I *did* get any information, up to and including a recording of a confession straight from the horse's mouth, that he wouldn't do anything with it.

In the absence of justice for my brother, revenge would suit me just fine.

Saint came and got me out of the back, where I waited, protected by the thick cinder block walls of the garage. I wondered if they would ever use the front of their clubhouse again after what happened to my brother.

I didn't want to ask.

If you had told me when I'd started out from California that I would abandon literally everything – my job, my home, - all of it – to pursue revenge for a half-sibling I hadn't even gotten to meet yet before he was murdered, I would have said you were crazy. But this wasn't going to be an overnight kind of a thing here.

As the boys of my brother's club had laid out, this was going to be one of those things that took *time* and potentially a lot of it.

They suggested I start looking for work out here, and they weren't necessarily wrong.

I had some serious choices to make and little time to make them.

Of course, I was also the kind of girl who figured you might as well go big or go home, and going home wasn't an option for me.

Not once had anyone in Garnett's life showed up for him, and I maybe knew a thing or two about that. I would be damned if I was going to be yet another in a long line to let him down, too.

Wild? Sure, but also true.

"So, fill me in," I said, sitting down with Saint in the back. It was just him and me right now. The rest of the men were still in the chapel.

"Where you want me to start?" he asked.

"Let's start with motive," I said, automatically falling back on what I knew.

"You're thinking like a cop," he said sourly.

"Sorry, not sorry. I was raised on the right side of the law, but that's where we're at," I said. "So, let's start with *why*. I'll try to keep the big words like 'motive' to a minimum since they seem to chap your ass."

"*Watch it,*" he warned me.

I sucked in a deep breath and let it out slow and measured.

"Sorry, I'm on edge and I'm angry. I guess I'm used to fighting for literally *everything* – so it's my default setting."

"We'll get into that later," he said, and my eyebrows went up at that. "Right now, let's get into it. You want to know why – *why what?"* he asked.

"Why are the Bayou Brethren so hard up to bone you boys?" I asked, and he barked a laugh.

"You're picking up biker life quick," he said. I shrugged.

"Not so far from trucker life," she said. "Lewd, crude, tattooed, with a heaping side of chauvinism and misogyny – about right?" she asked.

"You forgot loyalty," he said.

"Territorial?" I countered. Oh no, I got that.

He laughed and said, "They don't even sound the same." He shook his head finally and made to get up.

"This'll never work," he muttered. I reached out and caught his index finger with my hand, wrapping it around it like a child.

"Wait," I beseeched him, staring fixedly at my hand wrapped around the thick digit of his finger, the Harley Davidson logo of his bulky silver ring, looking suddenly vicious over stylish. "I'm sorry," I said. "I know this is a lot, and I'm scared. I deal with being scared with sass." I swallowed hard. "I'm not very good at peopling."

"That's not going to work for this kind of a thing," he said gently, sinking back down into the folding metal chair across from mine, extracting his hand from mine.

"No, I know," I said, lacing my fingers and wrapping them around my knee that was up over my other one. I let the sweat collecting in my palms be wicked away by the denim of my jeans.

"Having second thoughts?" he asked.

I shook my head, stopped, nodded once, and then resumed shaking my head.

"You're right to be scared, but you can't show it," he said. "I need you to deal with them with the same confidence you have around me." I looked up at him, a little surprised. He thought I was confident around him? "But take the sass down *several* notches. These mother-fuckers don't play, and to answer your question? We don't *know* why."

I frowned. "You don't?" I asked.

He shook his head.

"No," he said. "They just started muscling in on our turf, acting like the baddest motherfuckers on the block, and like we had beef when we don't have a clue *why*. But that's not what we need to worry about right now. Right now, we have to worry about you going in there, not knowing how this all works."

"How *does* it work?" I asked softly.

He sighed and said, "That's gonna take some time, so settle in. We've got a lot of ground to cover before we can even consider turning you loose into the beast's lair."

"Okay," I said warily.

It wasn't a no, and he was right. I needed to learn how to operate within their organizations – even though, by the sounds of it, biker life was more like barely organized chaos rather than a criminal mastermind organization.

"So how's this work?" I asked.

He smirked and said, "You're gonna hate it, but you're gonna need to leave all this feminist bullshit at the fuckin' door. You start that up, they're liable to bend you over the nearest pool table and fuck that attitude right out of you."

I shuddered, the thought coming unbidden of Saint doing that very thing, which I was more than a little confused at the tingle in my vag and the way my nipples hardened at the thought.

His deep brown eyes met mine, and his grin turned something akin to feral. I realized that the tank I wore and the bra I had on underneath didn't do much to hide my sudden arousal at the thought.

"You're something else," he said with a bit of a chuckle.

"Shut up," I said, flustered and growing redder by the minute with embarrassment.

He laughed then, a real laugh, long, genuine, and loud. All I could do was sit there in the flaming wreckage of my embarrassment of having been caught out and wait for him to finish.

"You done?" I asked when his laughter died down, and he wiped tears from his eyes.

"Not even close," he wheezed, trying to get a grip. I rolled my eyes and threw up my hands, which just made him laugh harder, but I had to admit, I was having a hard time keeping from smiling and laughing with him.

Maybe I *was* nuts.

CHAPTER TWELVE

S aint...
"You think she can do this?" Hex asked. I kicked back in my chair and looked at him and LaCroix in turn. LaCroix leaned in, looking at me intently.

"I think she can, but by the same token, I still don't like it."

"I get that," Hex said. "The pragmatist in me wants to say, 'who gives a fuck? who is she to us anyway' but..." he sighed.

"That wouldn't be doing right by Louie," LaCroix said.

"Easy, yes, right?" I snorted.

"Who would have thought going straight would be so fuckin' hard?" Hex mused aloud.

"We didn't take the fight to these assholes," I said.

"Something about it damn sure feels personal, don't it?" LaCroix asked, speaking up at last.

"Too fuckin' personal," I agreed.

"Where she stayin'?" Hex asked, and I could see he was already working logistics.

"La Chiquita on Veterans," I answered. "She's looking for work – maid or cleaning stuff. Says it's her niche, and any gig she lands out here will be easier than the crime scene shit she did back home."

"How much does she know about our business?" LaCroix asked.

I heaved a sigh. "Louie told her he's the one that did his mom… but from the sounds of it, he made it out to be like he was the sole actor on that whole shit show."

"Still, if he told her that, what else did he talk about out of turn with her?" Hex was staring off into space, his expression unreadable but for whatever social or club political equations he was working on up in that head of his.

"Enough that she didn't hesitate about this hare-brained idea of hers, fuckin' hell-bent on revenge."

"She's not stupid," LaCroix said, leaning back and bringing his glass of bourbon to his lips.

"If Louie could do that, she knows what kind of men we are and by extension, has an idea of what the Bayou Brethren are about. The practical thing to do is let her go in, let her feed us any information she can – she dies…" he shrugged. "Either way, it's a problem solved for us. We only stand to net gain in all of this."

"And if she doesn't die but rats to the cops on everyone?" Hex asked.

"That's where you come in," LaCroix said, looking at me. "You have the most rapport with her. If she's anything like Louie, you gain her loyalty, you gain her trust, you gain everything." I nodded slowly.

"You ain't wrong," I said, but what did it say, that as practical as it all was? I didn't want to see any harm come to Velina. Did I think she was tough? Yeah. Did I think she could take it? Yeah.

'Cept the only one I want her taking it from is me, I thought, and the thought made me scowl.

Hex chuckled. "She's a pain in the ass, I reckon," he said, sipping his whiskey. I nodded, but I kept it to myself the real reason it probably looked like I'd just sucked on a lemon.

"How you gon' go about this?" LaCroix asked.

"How do you mean?" I asked.

"She moving here, or what?" Hex demanded.

I shook my head. "Don't think we got that far yet," I said.

"Well, I reckon we better figure it out before long." Hex heaved a sigh.

"Appreciate all the brain power on this because this is kind of huge," I said.

"Louie's big sister," LaCroix muttered and harumphed. "Didn't see that one coming," he said, downing the rest of what was in his glass.

"Makes three of us," Hex said, and I snickered and finished off my tequila.

It made for a long night – plotting, planning, and conniving.

CHAPTER THIRTEEN

Velina...

I lay in the dark, waiting for what had woken me to sound again. I was just starting to relax, when it happened – *whump, whump, whump, whump, whump!* I sat up, heart pounding, and realized that there was someone at the motel's door.

I threw back the blankets and tip-toed across the grimy linoleum floor to the curtains, peering out the window carefully and letting out an explosive breath when I spotted Saint's hulking shadowy form at my door. He was leaning on his arm in that way that said *drunk*, and I rolled my eyes as he called out through the door, "Velina, come on! I ain't got all night."

I went to the door and, against my better judgment, turned back the safety latch with one hand and the deadbolt with the other. I opened the door, and he dropped his arm.

"About fuckin' time," he grated as he brushed past me, narrowly missing my toes with his big, booted feet.

I shut the door behind him and tipped around to the bedside, clicking on the lamp.

He winced and put up his hand, and I startled back from a pair of roaches running from the light.

"Oh, hell no. They got roaches in here?" he complained.

"Yeah, one of the other rooms, I think. They're filthy, and the bugs are migrating through the walls. It's gross, but it's what I can afford."

"Not anymore," he said. "You're moving."

"Saint, it's the middle of the fucking night. Why are you here?" I asked.

He came up to me, and he was most assuredly drunk. He put an arm around my waist and hauled me up against him, thrusting one of his powerful thighs between my legs. I sucked in a sharp breath and pressed both hands to his chest over the soft, broken-in tee he wore.

"What the hell?" I demanded.

"Shut up," he ordered, and automatically, my teeth clacked as I closed my mouth on what I had been going to say next.

"I like that," he muttered, and he dipped his head, running his nose up the side of my neck and nuzzling just behind my ear. His breath was hot and fetid with the tequila he'd been drinking as it rushed over my skin, and he made this deep growl next to my ear.

My body loosened, and I practically melted at the sound.

"That's what I thought," he said, and he captured my mouth with his.

I stiffened but didn't try to push him away. Instead, I parted my lips and darted my tongue out to meet his.

We stood there in the golden lamplight, exploring each other's mouths, both of us standing stiff but not in an awkward sort of way. More like his body silently challenging mine, and mine answering the challenge, stiff against his, the heat building between us, a game of defiance between a predator and prey that wasn't known for backing down.

A larger apex predator stalking a smaller, yet equally dangerous apex predator, but in the end, like most things, size, speed, and presence mattered, and Saint had more of each of them in spades.

Fuck, it was hot. He was hot, clad in his faded denim and leather, his hands big, strong, and so very warm through the thin cotton and Lycra blend of my cami and matching panty set, which I tended to like to sleep in.

"What the hell?" I demanded breathily against his bearded mouth as he drew back from me.

"My big dumb ass just needed to see if it was my imagination or not," he said.

"If what was your imagination?" I asked.

He thrust his leg up tighter to my sex between my own, and a slight moan escaped my lips, and I caught myself rubbing against him.

"That," he growled, and his mouth captured mine once more.

Shit-fire, motherfucker! I thought to myself.

It'd been so long for me, at least a couple of years. Part of that was because the California boys didn't know the difference between being dominant in the bedroom and just plain being a douchebag.

Oh, trust, I thought Saint could be a real asshole sometimes, but legitimately – you could *feel* the difference. I was, most certainly, feeling *something* about Saint that had nothing to do with anger, ire, or irritation. More like passion, desire, and a very real want to crawl out of my skin and into his. But *holy shit*, that would be so wrong! Wouldn't it?

Talk about complicating things!

I pushed against him, tore my mouth from his, and gasped out, "Hold on a minute!"

To his credit, as strong as he'd come on to me, he was equally strong in a different sort of way in letting me go.

He lowered his upthrust knee, his hands, which had migrated from my waist to my ass to haul me up against him, lowering me gently so my feet could rest flat to the floor.

"You're all good," he said between heaving breaths, and I shook my head.

"Far fucking from it, but I'm okay," I gasped back.

He chuckled then.

"Seriously, Saint. What the fuck is this all about?" I demanded.

"I'm drunk as fuck and thinking with my dick," he answered honestly and dropped onto the edge of the rumpled bed with a big sigh.

"I appreciate your honesty," I said and dropped onto the bed beside him, a considerable wanting ache developing between my legs that was almost too persistent to ignore.

"Hell of a way to let a girl know you're interested," I said, and he chuckled and flopped onto his back across the bed sideways. I turned over onto my stomach and stretched out beside him.

He opened one eye and said, "Probably best not to complicate things any further than they already are."

I snorted and said, "Took the thought right out of my head, but hey – in for a penny in for a pound."

"What does that even mean?" he asked.

"Fucked if I know, it's some sort of British turn of phrase I heard on some show or whatever."

"Fair," he said, turning on his side to prop his head on his hand and look at me.

He slid his free hand up under my cami, along my back, smoothing it over my skin.

I closed my eyes and relished the roughness of his palm against my smooth flesh and tried not to shudder.

"You react nice to my touch," he whispered, and I sucked in a sharp breath at the small praise.

"Tormenting me isn't the only reason you came by in the middle of the night like this, is it?" I asked. He chuckled and smacked my ass, the sharp report echoing back at me from the walls and ceiling of the small room.

"Ow! Hey!" I cried, frowning.

"I haven't even begun to torment or torture you yet," he said. "But I bet you suffer beautifully."

Fuck, fuck, fuck, fuck, fuuuuuuck! That was hot.

"You having second thoughts about backing my play?" I asked him.

"No," he said. "But full honesty – I don't like it, and I voted against it."

"Why tell me that?" I demanded.

"Because you need to understand, the guys who said yes? They see whatever happens as a net gain for the club. You need to understand that until you prove yourself, going into this – about the only friend you've got is *me*."

"Hell of a pep talk you're giving me, Saint," I said with all sarcasm intended.

"It's not meant to *be* a pep talk, baby," he said. "This is my half-drunk and half-assed last-ditch effort at getting you to understand what a bad fuckin' idea this is. How fuckin' dangerous this is—"

"I'm good," I said. "I understand."

"I don't think you do," he said.

"I'm not some insipid California Malibu Barbie cunt," I snapped. "Louie was my brother, my blood, and Goddammit – I'm going to do this. I'm going to show up for him!" *The way no one has ever shown up for me,* I thought, but didn't want to admit out loud.

"You got a death wish," he said.

"So, give me what I need to know to stay alive," I said evenly.

"There are fates worse than death," he tried, and I scoffed.

"I know," I said. "I've lived some of them. Louie's mom wasn't sunshine and roses, but neither was his dad. *Our* dad."

"You get diddled like we did?" he asked, and I paused.

"No, the whole rape thing came later in high school for me, and it wasn't family that sold me up the river. It was a date rape turned gang rape sort of a thing, but that is neither here nor there," I said. "I know you're drunk, but did you mean to say 'we' in that sentence?"

"Yeah," he said. "It's how I got my road name. I was an altar boy growing up, and I still go to church every Sunday, Wednesday mass, too, if I can manage."

"You're a biker who goes to church?" I asked.

"Yeah," he said simply.

"And I assume you being an altar boy is somehow centric to your abuse?" I asked softly, trying to get a clear picture as gently and diplomatically as possible.

"Yep to that, too," he said.

"Yet you still go to church?" I asked.

"I don't always get it either, but the priest is one of my good buddies who I grew up with. Not the fuckin' pedo we *both* had to up with while growing up ourselves."

"That's a strange and sordid CliffsNotes version of your child-hood," I said.

"We all come from fucked-up places," he muttered, and it sounded as though sleep was starting to suck at his edges, blurring his words along with his consciousness.

I scooted closer as he rolled back onto his back and stretched, and tucked myself into his side, laying my head on his chest.

"We all come from fucked-up places," I murmured in agreement. His arms sort of went around me, and he sighed out.

He fell asleep first.

I was still awake when the light started to press at the edges of the blackout curtains.

I had a lot of thoughts, most of them with an eye on the prize – the prize being standing on business when it came to my little brother.

Someone had to.

Someone needed to.

I had a feeling if he could have, he would have for me. He couldn't stand up for himself, dammit, so I would stand up for us both. Because fuck the world, that's why.

CHAPTER FOURTEEN

S aint...
   I woke up sideways in an unfamiliar bed with a warm, shapely body tucked into my side and half draped over mine. Which was strange, given that as my hand glided down the back of the woman against me, it was to discover she had clothes on. I looked down my body, and yep, I was fully clothed too.

What the fuck? I thought.

She sucked in a sharp breath at the movement of my head and shot up, pressing a hand flat against my cut. Brilliant green eyes framed in dark bangs and longer tendrils at the sides met my own, and I almost felt my breath stolen from my lungs at how beautiful she looked, even sleep-mussed and fucked-up first thing in the morning.

I coughed and damned if my mouth didn't taste like dog shit smelled. I sat up quickly, coughing some more, and tried to spare her a blast of my rancid morning breath right in her pretty face.

"You, okay?" she asked dubiously.

"Yeah," I grated out, clearing my throat. "How the fuck did I end up here?" I asked.

"Your guess is as good as mine. I was sound asleep when you cop knocked at my door at like three a.m., trying to talk me out of doing this."

I turned, looked at her, and said, "Yeah, well, it's stupid on your part."

She grinned and wrinkled her nose in that cute, impish way of hers, a sparkle of mischief in her eyes. "Guess I'm more like my brother than y'all want to admit," she said.

"You got a damn toothbrush?" I demanded.

"By the bathroom sink," she said, and I got up and staggered that way.

I loaded the brush with paste, stuck it in my mouth, and heard her scoff incredulously behind me.

My hands on the counter to keep my big ass up, I twisted enough to stare blearily back at her, mumbling around the brush in my mouth, "Weren't complaining when I had my mouth all up in yours last night. If it bothers you that much, I'll buy you a new one." Shit was coming back to me, just slow.

Her response was to roll her eyes and flop back down on the bed.

I turned back to the mirror and finished up with a good brushing to get the taste of hungover ass out of my mouth.

When I finished, I straightened up and turned back around to find she was right where I'd left her, her back against the bed, her green eyes staring without seeing the water-stained ceiling of this shithole motel. I felt my cock stir in my jeans and wondered, briefly, how far she would let me take it.

I let my eyes wander her body encased in its tight-fitting sleep set, her breasts heavy and all-natural under the straining tank, her legs slightly parted, and that thin strip of cotton of the crotch of her boy short panties, the only thing between me and what I so desired.

I took steps over the disgusting floor, my boots sticking, as I undid my belt and thought to myself, *if this doesn't work to deter her, nothing will.*

"What are you doing?" she asked, her head coming up at the rattle and snick of the leather sliding through the buckle.

"Fucking you," I answered succinctly. I gripped her panties at the hips, and she rose her ass up off the bed for me to shuck the garment out of my way, and, well, *that* hadn't gone according to plan.

"Can't rape the willing," she argued with a wicked smile, and my cock just got all the harder for her sass.

I gripped her by the throat and slammed her back down onto the bed with one hand. She let out a throaty moan and writhed beneath me as I worked to find purchase with my cock in my other hand against her body. She was slick, hot, wet, and wanting – and *shit*, that really hadn't been according to plan. This woman was my kind of freak.

I thrust into her. She let out a cry that I choked off by tightening my hold on her throat, just to the point it would start to hinder her blood flow and breathing, but definitely *not* to the point that it would choke her off or cause any damage.

I was just playing here. Granted, it was a dangerous game, but I was just playing, nonetheless.

"What you gonna do?" I demanded, thrusting up in her savagely until I bottomed out. She definitely writhed at that one, but it was a lot less wanting and a little more trying to take what I was dishing. "When they throw you down on a table, and they each take their fuckin' turns with you?" I finished my thought and tried not to lose my hard-on at the mental image of the Brethren pulling a train on her. But it was precisely what could happen if she smarted off to the wrong guy at the wrong time, going in there as anybody's meat.

"Mm, take it like a fuckin' good girl," she answered as I drove into her. *Fucking son of a bitch* – not the answer that I wanted, but precisely the answer I fuckin' *needed*.

"Yeah, and when you got one of 'em in that sweet cunt of yours, another at your back door, and one shoving into your mouth, and it ain't nothing but hands and cocks using your holes until they bleed, what then?" I demanded.

"I'll survive," she answered breathily. "I'll survive and come back to you."

Something wrenched and twisted in my chest, or maybe it was my gut, at the look in her eyes as she looked up at me, inside her, legs parted, hand on her throat, and perfect... perfect iron will and trust mixing in those eyes of hers as she looked at me.

"I'm prepared to fuck one of them or all of them, if I have to Saint, but - *mmm*," she moaned and writhed on my dick. "I'll pretend it's you and that it's this if that's what you want to hear. I'll take every inch of their small dicks if it gets me closer to fucking them all up for what they did to my brother. I'll take every inch of yours like this a thousand times over, though – just because, *Goddamn*, you feel fucking *good*."

I took my hand off her throat and put it on the bed by her head, bending over her and kissing her just as fiercely as I vaguely remember having done the night before with a shit ton of liquid courage on board.

She wrapped her hands in my ponytail and kissed me back with a delectable edge of violence. Before long, she pulled my head back, tore her mouth from mine, and breathily demanded, "Harder! You gonna fuck me, or make love to me?"

I slapped her on her outer thigh. The smack was loud in the small space, made better by the peal of wild laughter that came from her, her wild giggles music to my ears. I couldn't help myself. I smirked.

"Haven't decided yet, little one," I declared. "Just let me find my rhythm," I said. I rotated my hips, giving it a bit of a back-and-forth on my next thrust up inside her, and she gasped and then moaned.

Most dudes failed to realize there was an art in loving a woman, even an art to fucking one properly. A nice guy will *always* finish last – hopefully after he's satisfied his woman *multiple* times. I aimed to fuck Velina Young until she felt it with every step later on. I wanted her to remember this every time she went to do *anything* in the next day or two.

Mostly, I just wanted her coming back for more at this point, and I couldn't help but think to myself, *fuck if I've really lost the fuckin' plot here.*

This was Louie's *sister*. Granted, we hadn't known a damn thing about her, let alone that she'd even *existed* until she'd shown up at the club, but the more she talked, the more she walked the walk, the hotter I'd found her, and the more I thought about her, the more that she'd turned into a fucking *obsession*. Then my drunk fucking ass had shown up here and pounded on doors until I'd found her.

Now she was writhing under me, around me, her nails biting into my exposed ass cheek, pulling me deeper inside her, and I wondered who had ensnared who?

Who really had the fuckin' power here? Because one night with her in my arms, without even so much as anything beyond a few kisses, and I was losing my motherfucking mind over her.

"Oh, God! Yes! *Please!*" she begged, and I could tell she was getting close. I grunted, picking her up by her hips, my fingers curving under her ass, and I pulled her down onto me as much as I thrust forward, giving a wiggle back and forth every time I had myself buried to my root inside her, brushing over that spot with intention, and it paid off.

With a sharp, piercing wail, she came apart underneath me, her body at once going limp before seizing up as her tight pussy squeezed and pulled at my cock in silent begging for me to fill her demanding little cunt with my cum.

Shit, I didn't know if she was on any type of birth control, and I wasn't quite ready to be a daddy yet.

I pulled out, probably not even close to the nick of time, but it was better than filling her up with my baby gravy on the first fuck without that discussion.

Instead, I shoved her tank top up over those big bouncing tits of hers, letting them spill out from the bottom hem of her shirt, and shot gleaming jets of pearly cum onto her stomach and between them. She arched, taking every bit of it on her milky skin, and I felt a deep satisfaction at the sight.

"Good girl." The words of praise fell unbidden from my lips, and I watched hers curve into an almost shy smile.

Hmm…

She turned her head, blushing furiously, and put the backs of her fingers against her lips to hide that smile from me. I didn't like that.

"Drop your hand," I ordered, and she did, but the smile disappeared, replaced with wide-eyed surprise.

I got out from between her legs and flopped down beside her, propping my head in my hands. She lay on her back, my spunk cooling on her body, and those green eyes of hers held wonder but also question-ing. I traced patterns on her skin through the beautiful mess I'd made of her.

"I hope you're on some kind of birth control," I said a minute later.

"I am," she said. "I hope *you're* clean." I snorted.

"Fuck you," I said, laughing. "I am, but fuck you."

"Fuck you, too!" she said, grinning, and we sort of collapsed into some giggles.

"That was nice," she said a moment later, and the shyness was back in her tone.

I glanced up to her face, which was guarded, and nodded against my hand.

"Yeah, it was," I agreed. I put my hand flat in the mess on her skin, slid it down to her ribs, and gave her a little shove.

"Go take a piss, get cleaned up. We've got shit to do today. Places to go, people to see."

"Like where?" she asked. "Like *who?*"

"Get cleaned up, and I'll tell you," I told her.

She rolled her eyes and got up, turning into the smaller room that just housed the toilet and a bathtub and shower combo common to these cheap motel setups.

"You can talk to me while I do this," she said as I listened to her pee.

I tucked myself back into my pants and zipped and buttoned up, working my belt back into place.

"Just hurry it up. Find some sturdy clothes – jeans and boots prefer-ably. You're gonna need 'em."

"We going for a ride?" she asked.

"And into the swamp, later tonight," I answered.

"The swamp? What for?"

"LaCroix wants you to see the Bayou Baroness," which is what we called her – but she was much more than that.

Rumor had it, she was some kind of many-time adjacent descen-dant somehow related to the Voodoo Queen of New Orleans herself, Marie Laveau. I didn't know if I put any stock into that bullshit. I didn't even know if Laveau had any kids who survived the times to have any kids of their own – but that wasn't what was said.

It was said she was descended from some brother's kid, a nephew or niece or something of Laveau.

You know, I'd lived in New Orleans my whole life, saw, and heard a lot of weird shit in that time – but Voodoo? The actual closed practice religion? I and anyone with any goddamned sense in these parts avoided that shit like it was the plague. All but LaCroix, but no one ever accused him of having any sense.

He didn't practice, but he believed in all that occult bullshit, and me? I had to admit, there was some veracity to it, but anytime I was around it, I crossed my damn self and took my ass on into confession shortly thereafter.

The Bayou Baroness creeped me the fuck out. Said she could commune with the dead – had some kind of a pact with the death deities – and not just the Baron Samedi, but other ones, too, from other faiths.

It didn't make much sense to me, to be honest. Said she was some kind of a solo practitioner, but of what, I wasn't certain. Whatever it was, though? It worked for her, and any time we'd had an encounter with her and received her blessing, shit had gone pretty okay. Anytime she warned us, we heeded that warning.

The one time the one who hadn't? Well, let's just say, she'd been right on that, too.

"I'm going out for a smoke," I said sometime after the toilet flushed and the shower had started up.

"Those things will kill you," she called out from under the shower spray, and I huffed a laugh.

"Not fast enough some days," I muttered.

I went out the room's door and stepped up to the railing. She was on the second floor of three or four. I fished out my smokes from my jacket pocket and lit one, sucking in a drag and holding it for a moment, blowing a smoke ring into the shadow of the building, the sun coming up behind it as it was.

It wasn't early, but it wasn't late, either. At least not by my reckoning.

She was going to do this, she needed to do it right. She wanted to be tarted up, that was on her, but I was definitely going to make sure that if she got onto one of those chuckleheads' bikes, she was going to do it as safely as possible without going too far out of pocket.

I didn't want to put her in full-on chaps and leather. She didn't know enough about the life to walk into that den of vipers looking the part. She couldn't talk the talk and would stick out like a sore thumb, looking the part without the smarts or wisdom to back it up. We're talking a plethora of red flags that would just get her killed, probably after a whole lot of hurt.

To that end, I had a mind toward denim. A jacket at least, some sturdy jeans, and those boots of hers did just fine.

When she opened the door, and I turned, she looked like liquid fire, bold in her boots, jeans, and a rust-colored tank top, ribbed like the first one she'd shown up at the club in.

"So, what's the plan?" she asked. She stepped up beside me, leaning against the railing and running a towel over her hair. I'd suspected right about the red dye over her brunette – the white motel-issue towel coming away pink where the water from her locks saturated it.

"Hit a couple thrift stores and find you a sturdy denim jacket."

"Yeah?" she asked, eyebrows going up.

"Yeah, to start with," I said, taking another drag.

"Sounds... fun," she came back with, and I barked a laugh.

"Yeah, not my idea of a good time either," I shot back, flicking my butt out over the parking lot down below.

"Oh, I wasn't being sarcastic," she told me. "I love thrifting."

"Yeah?" I raised an eyebrow at that.

"I take pictures," she said. "I thrift old fancy frames and refinish them for the photos."

"No shit?" I asked.

"No shit," she said.

"Fuckin' A." I jerked my head out over the lot and said, "Just waitin' on you, princess."

It was her turn to bark a laugh, and she followed it with a giggling, "Fuck you."

I couldn't help but smile.

CHAPTER FIFTEEN

Velina...

The day was actually pretty nice. Almost, dare I say, *normal*. I wasn't sure if letting Saint fuck me had been the brightest idea I'd ever had, but for as much as a sarcastic asshole as he could be, he did give a damn fine dicking – so there was that.

We went to a thrift store looking for a denim jacket and some jeans that were on the sturdier side. The jacket, unfortunately, remained elusive at the first thrift store, but I did find a nice pair of steel-toed boots – which was better than hiking boots – that looked fairly grunge/industrial. Which, if I had to go for a look, I would much prefer that to anything else.

I wasn't a metal chick. Goth was too flowery for my tastes, but I damn sure didn't want to look like hippy hiker California girl going into a biker bar around here.

Let's face it, in the South? Nobody liked Californians – and I got it, believe me. Most of them had more money than sense, hadn't really *worked* a day in their life, and no, it wasn't lost on me that I'd done it too – but they were judgy as fuck.

We had lunch at an Italian place in Metairie – that I swore was run by the mob, but good *God*, the food was fantastic – before we carried on in our adventures looking to re-fashion me.

The second thrift store had a better selection of denim jackets, but the ones that I liked were lined and would be way too hot in the humid New Orleans' summer heat.

I couldn't resist, though. I took a wander down the aisle with the art and looked through the photo frames. I was *not* disappointed.

"What?" Saint had asked me when I found a particularly nice eight-by-ten frame, and I whimpered at how much I wanted it.

"I refurbish frames for the pictures I take and sell them as a whole art piece. The things I would do to this frame… it's perfect."

"It's… gold," he said, and he sounded non-plussed.

"It's gold *right now*, but I would strip it, sand it, and paint it flat black."

He cocked his head and asked, "What'd you put in it, though?"

"That I don't know yet," I said.

"Get it," he told me.

"I'm on a tight budget," I said.

"Get. It." His tone brooked no argument and was as final as anything I'd ever heard. I couldn't help but smile.

"Sir, yes, sir," I said flippantly.

"Was that disrespect?" he asked with a bemused smile. "Thought I'd already fucked some of that out of you, but if you're begging for a round two – that maybe can be arranged."

I laughed and turned to follow him up to the registers with my treasure.

The third time was the charm. We'd found a pair of jeans or two that made my ass look good at the second thrift in addition to my treasure find of the frame, but it was at the *third* and final thrift of the day that we found a suitable jacket.

Actually, we found *two* suitable jackets.

One a light denim, and the other a clearly vintage, but still in wonderful shape, brown leather coat from the 1970s.

It wasn't heavy, but it was nice, if a little thrift store musty – and we got that, too.

We'd taken my car – erm, *cage*, which I had been grateful for, but when we pulled up at the hotel, he said to me, "I'll help you take this shit upstairs, switch into those other boots and put on a jacket. *Now, we're going for a ride.*"

When he said we were going for a ride, I thought it was to the club, which it sort of was. We headed in that direction, pulled up just long enough for Cypress and LaCroix to get on their bikes, and then we turned right around and fell in with them, heading to God knows where.

Turned out, it was the swamp… again… although I couldn't tell you if it was the same swamp we went and got my car part or if it was totally in the opposite direction.

All the swampland down around here looked the same to me.

It was dark by the time we pulled up outside the dilapidated house under the big old oak tree in the yard.

"Where are we?" I asked.

Cypress answered, "Oh, we ain't there yet, Cher. We're just gettin' started."

Wonderful, I thought to myself.

At least it was still light out, which wasn't terribly much comfort because the light was starting to fail.

The three men walked me to a dock and a dingy of some kind moored to it.

"Cy, stay at the house," LaCroix ordered. "Saint, with me."

Saint got into the boat first and held out a hand to help me down into it. It rocked perilously, and I bit off a yelp as it shifted. Saint laughed and said, "Sit before you tip us." I did, dropping to the middle bench and sitting, gripping the edge of the seat with a white-knuckled grip as we rocked while Saint took a seat at the bow of the little flat-bottomed boat. I didn't honestly know what you called it.

LaCroix boarded next and dropped onto the seat back by the motor while Cypress unwound lines and helped us cast off, putting a booted foot against the side and giving us a shove away from the dock.

"See y' after a while, y'all," he called and waved as LaCroix thumbed a switch, and the boat's motor tripped over itself to kick to life.

I swallowed hard as LaCroix steered us out into the wide, flat, shallow, dark waters. "Aren't there alligators in here?" I asked.

"And water moccasins, and spiders, and all manner of creepy crawlies," Saint affirmed behind me. "Just stay in the boat, and you'll be fine."

"I'm not used to being in places where the flora and fauna would like to eat you. I've got no problem staying my ass in the boat," I replied. LaCroix, with his creepy blacked-out eyes, cracked a smile, which only made him *more* terrifying to look at, not less.

I carefully turned around on my seat to face forward and Saint instead.

The sun was getting low in the afternoon sky as things tipped on toward evening. I found myself catching my breath at the beauty of things as the light filtered through the cypress tree canopy and touched on the drapery of Spanish moss.

I pulled out my phone and asked, "It be alright with you, fellas, if I took some pictures of this?"

Saint looked over his shoulder past me, at LaCroix, and I swiveled my head on my neck to look too. LaCroix gave a single nod, and I smiled and turned back.

"Still photos only, no video," he called from the back of the boat, and I nodded.

"Of course," I called back.

I wished I had my good camera, but my phone would have to do.

I played with settings and took a few snaps, messing with filters and the like that I could. There was no signal to speak of out here, and I would be a liar if I said I wasn't worried for myself.

I didn't know how much I could or should trust these men, but I was willing to go out on a limb. What did I honestly have to lose?

My mother and siblings didn't talk to me anymore, and Louie was gone already.

I turned forward and looked at Saint, curled in the bow of the boat, one hand braced on the lip of the side, staring out ahead of us. The patch on his back was on full display even though he was turned slightly to the side. It was such a striking image, I couldn't help myself.

I took it for myself and spirited it away to upload to my cloud storage as soon as I got someplace with a signal.

I didn't know where we were going or how far it would be. I tell you, I hadn't expected our destination to be a house on a barge in the middle of the swamp, nothing around it for what was probably miles.

It looked cozy, the outside done in wood shake tiles, or whatever you called them, solar panels, and what looked like some raised garden beds off to one side.

Golden light spilled from the windows in the deepening gloom, and as we made our approach, the door to the place opened, and a woman slipped out from behind the screen door.

She was in jeans, her long red hair pulled high in a ponytail. She crossed her arms over her chest, and her flowy green peasant blouse strained across her shoulders.

"Hey, baby," she called out, and I stiffened at first before I realized it wasn't Saint she was talking to but LaCroix.

"That's my little Alina," he said when I looked back at him. Something about his hard face had changed, smoothing just a bit, becoming softer somehow just at the sight of her.

"Alina and Velina," I said with a dry smile. "This should be fun."

"How d' y' mean?" LaCroix asked.

I shrugged. "They sound so close I'm sure we're both going to look up no matter who you're actually talking to."

"Ah," was all he said.

He was a man of few words. I honestly liked that about him. Made him seem careful, I guess, and with what I was about to do, careful was going to be exceptionally warranted.

We pulled up to the barge and Saint used a handle like you would see at a set of pool steps to hoist himself up. He caught a line tossed by LaCroix and tied the skiff dinghy boat thing we rode in off at one of those horned boat moor things you saw on docks.

Hell, I didn't know what any of it was called. Riverside was a way away from the ocean, and I was too poor to come into contact with boats regularly.

Closest I'd come was for a suicide cleanup on some McRich

bastard's yacht after he'd suck-started a .45. I'd had to scrub his brains off the expensive veneer wood paneling and priceless painting that'd been hanging behind him after he'd done what he did.

I never did find out the *why* of it.

Sometimes I did, sometimes I didn't.

Saint reached down and helped me up onto the barge, and LaCroix followed us, sliding right on past us to pull the redhead into his arms and kiss her fiercely. A kiss she enthusiastically matched in fervor.

"I thought you'd never come home," she murmured, and he smiled.

"Got enough supper cookin' for four?" he asked her.

"You're in luck," she said. "I do."

"That's my girl," he said. "Want you to meet somebody." He turned so that she could take me in.

"Louie's sister?" she asked, eyebrows going up.

"Shit." Saint laughed. "Can't keep anything from you girls, can we?" he asked.

"I guess that's why my getting in among them is the perfect play," I commented dryly.

"Didn't say it was a *bad* idea, just stupid for so many reasons," he said.

"You're a braver woman than I am," Alina followed him up, stepping half away from LaCroix to extend her hand.

I shook it.

I felt like I knew her already. Louie had talked about her a ton. About how she was kind, but tough. How LaCroix was literally obsessed with her, and how if there was anyone to respect attached to the club, it was her, but not like it was hard. He said Alina was just easy to like and/or love.

I smiled, and I knew it was cool. I just couldn't instantly like *anybody* anymore. It just wasn't how I was built. Trust issues, mommy issues, daddy issues *for sure*. Hell, I had a C-17 cargo jet *full* of fucking issues that were too many to list, and it kept me really guarded for the most part. It also kept me *safe* for the most part, too.

"Velina," I said by way of greeting. "Nice to meet you."

"Nice to meet you too," she said with appraising cool blue eyes.

I forced a smile, and she forced one, too. I guess it was all about getting to know one another after that.

"Come on inside, I'm starving," LaCroix said, and Alina led the way. LaCroix opened the door for her and smacked her ass, making her jump and yip on her way through. I grinned, I couldn't help it as I passed through, but LaCroix kept his hands to himself. So did Saint, and at this point in whatever it was we had going on, I was low-key glad for that.

The inside of the little house was as cozy as you'd imagine – the kitchen tucked back with a host of delicious smells emanating from a crock pot on the small counter space by the sink or the stove. The table was set for four, and there was a candle lit at its center. A salad bowl filled with leafy greens and a basket with a checkered napkin with some rolls waiting nearby.

"Sit," Alina urged. "Beers?" she asked.

"Yeah, I'll take one," Saint said. LaCroix just nodded.

"Sure," I said.

"I have wine if beer doesn't do it for you," she said.

"Wine would be great," I said.

I took a seat at the table, and Alina came around with two plates loaded with some kind of pasta dish.

"Guest first," LaCroix said when she went to serve him first. She served me, setting a plate in front of me, and then set the other before LaCroix.

"You're not a guest," she said to Saint with a wink. "You've been here before. You might as well be furniture."

Saint laughed and nodded as she told us she'd be right back. She set two more plates down, one at Saint's place and one at her own, and then returned with the boy's beers after popping the tops.

Her last trip brought two glasses of white wine and then she sat.

"Help yourself to salad and garlic knots," she said. "I've been dying for some company out here for the last day or two."

"You stay out here all alone?" I asked.

"Sometimes," she said. "Sometimes Cor, Jessie-Lou, or Sandy will stay out here with me. It's just been a quiet week this week to myself, though."

I recognized the other names. Garnett had talked about them. Sandy or Sandrine was how he'd met True. I guess True was her best friend or something. Corliss was a teacher and Hex had been a janitor at her school, while Jessie-Lou was Cypress's sister and had somehow wound up with Collier.

"I have to ask, and please, don't think I'm being rude, because I'm not. But did you guys really start out as LaCroix *stalking you*?"

I looked from LaCroix to Alina and back. LaCroix was unreadable, shoving a forkful of the cream pasta into his mouth and chewing carefully. Alina's smile was somewhere between impish and chagrined.

"Uh, yeah," Alina said with a little laugh. "Louie told you about that, huh?" she asked.

"Among other things," I said with a smile, swallowing the cool, crisp sip of wine.

"Not sure I'm too keen on Louie running his mouth about our business." LaCroix's voice was deep but steady, and I sighed inwardly and nodded.

"It was all good things," I promised him. "He loved you all like the family he never had until I showed up. And even then, we were still new to each other and just trying to learn. You guys were his whole world. What else was he going to talk about?" I asked.

LaCroix grunted and said nothing. Saint said, "Touché."

"Don't mind them," Alina said, rolling her eyes for my benefit. "They're an intensely private lot."

"I can understand," I said, putting some salad onto my plate. Looked like Ceasar. I wasn't sad about that. It was my favorite if I had to eat a garden.

"What about you?" LaCroix asked. "How about you volunteer some information about yourself?"

"Babe!" Alina said sharply.

LaCroix's eyes found hers, and something passed between them, but hey – had to hand it to the girl to be brave enough to stand up for me, even if I didn't need her to.

She certainly earned some points with me for that.

"It's a fair question," I said, partially coming to LaCroix's defense but more coming to Alina's by taking the heat off her so-to-speak.

Saint sat by and said nothing, just speared food onto his fork and chewed silently. His eyes found mine, and there was a silent intensity there, as though daring me to share more.

"I was born and raised in Riverside. My dad was a drunk, a trucker, and a carousing piece of shit who was gone more often than he was home. But hey, that just probably spared us more of his ire and discipline, so it wasn't really a total net loss in that respect."

I cleared my throat.

"Apparently, when he wasn't home, he was fucking anyone and everyone under the sun with a vagina. I've found six other half-siblings, *not* including Louie, and none of them wanted to have fuck all to do with me or him, which I can't say that I blame them.

"My own family that I grew up with are pissed at me and not talking to me because I went looking after my dad died. It was sort of his dying wish that all his kids knew he was sorry. Too little, too late, if you ask me, but it's not like anyone else was stepping up. I've got enough daddy issues that I'd give my non-existent left nut to have even one iota of his approval even though I disappointed him so by being a girl and not the son he wanted.

"I've got three other siblings by him and my mom. Rafe is the oldest and gay as the day is long, followed by Ophelia, me, and finally, Valencia. Mom's still alive and in the same house. None of the sibs give a shit. She doesn't give a shit, and I dunno, maybe that's why Garnett and I clicked."

I glanced at the three other faces around the table and said, "If you want to know anything else, all you really have to do is ask. I'm not always the best at volunteering information if I don't have to, but I'm an encyclopedia as long as you crack the book."

There was a gleam of something in Saint's eyes as he stared at me. I glanced at LaCroix, and the same was there, just harder to discern with the way the sclera of his eyes was blacked out with ink.

"I guess we'll see," LaCroix intoned cryptically, and I nodded.

"Garnett didn't let you down, and neither will I," I said. "Especially considering that letting you down would let *him* down, and I'm not about to be another in a long line of rejects to do that. His mom, my dad, the system… you guys were there for him when no one else was. I want to be there too, even if it is too little too late."

The rest of the meal sort of fell into silence after that, each of us under our own heavy mantle of thinking. All thoughts none of us really wanted to share, apparently.

CHAPTER SIXTEEN

S aint...
The Bayou Baroness wasn't a new thing as far as the Voodoo Bastards went. She'd been in the shadows of the club since its inception, long before even Ruthless had become P.

While the guys in charge before Baby Ruth had put stock in the Bayou Baroness, he hadn't, while LaCroix had remained true to her. It was what had supposedly decided him when Hex had brought up how shit just wasn't right the way the Bastards were headed under Ruth's leadership.

Hell, we all saw what was happening. Ruth was out of his mind on drugs and greedy as fuck. He kept taking, and taking, and *taking* – the club growing, growing, and growing – too fast for the likes of a lot of us. Still, he wanted *more*. We all saw it. Ruth living high on the hog while the rest of us rooted in the muck from his table for scraps. The money went to the top under him, but it damn sure wasn't trickling down.

That's part of what started it.

We did what we did to get what we wanted, but we weren't *getting anywhere*.

It was a story as old as fuckin' time, and a bunch of us were getting disgruntled. By the time we all started whispering our mutual dissatisfaction to each other, and found the majority of us didn't like what was going on one bit? Well, as far as LaCroix was concerned, there was only one thing left to do – consult the Oracle of the swamp, the Bayou Baroness.

Trouble was, it was hard getting a meet with her... eminence? Grace? Not sure what you called royalty of her stature. Not out here.

Still, somehow, LaCroix had managed to get an audience tonight, and he wanted to bring Velina.

I knew the shit that was about to go down, but she didn't. Still, if I didn't think it was safe enough for her, I would have said something.

I'd seen the Bayou Baroness do her thing a time or two, and while it left me wantin' to run back to the church, I couldn't argue with the results. You couldn't get a thing past her.

We finished dinner, boarded back into the boat, and headed out deeper into the swamp.

There was a place in the deepest part of Manchac Swamp that was cursed back in 1915 by a Creole voodoo priestess named Julie Brown. The place we headed now? It was a similar place, just closer to the coastal waters of the Gulf.

I'd been to ol' Manchac in the middle of the night before, and while it was deathly still and creepy as all get out, it still ain't hold a candle to the little ol' settlement we made for now.

The place we went was along an old bayou that had no name, and it ain't have a town left to it, either. It was an old spot with even older graves that were barely left standing themselves and, more often than not, were under the black water of the swamp, only the tallest vault tipping precariously above the waterline.

Tonight, the water was low. As we slipped between the knees of two cypress trees like a cock sliding lovingly home, we could see that Lavinia was already here and waiting, small fires and torches dotting around the old cemetery to light the space she'd drawn out whatever sigils and ciphers that meant something to her and her loa or gods.

I didn't begin to understand any of it, but I didn't need to. Some things you just didn't understand, but you had to respect them.

"Where are we?" Velina breathed, and I looked past her to LaCroix.

He had a grim set to his mouth but didn't say anything, and I followed my president's lead.

"Saint?" she asked as we bumped the bottom and slid halfway up on shore.

"It's all good," I reassured her. "Promise."

I got out of the boat and held down a hand to help Velina out. The ground was spongy with moss, and the mud beneath sucked at our boots as we made for the slightly higher ground.

LaCroix stepped past us and went to greet Lavinia.

"You bring a guest," she said, and her old crone's voice was that of a fifty-year chain smoker. She held out her hand, and LaCroix placed a large wad of cash in it.

"Bah!" She dropped the cash. "You wait, boy! Gimme the sack of dimes first!"

"Apologies," LaCroix intoned, and he pulled an old Crown Royal bag out of his back pocket, heavy with the weight of coins that jangled in the dark.

Lavinia took it and shook it, laughing her old, wizened crone laugh that wheezed on its end.

"Pick dat up, and save it for now," she ordered him, and LaCroix complied, stashing the fold of bills in his back pocket where the Crown Royal bag had come from.

"You! Girl! Come forward!" Velina looked up at me and I nodded, thrusting a chin at Lavinia.

Velina gave me a dubious look and went to the older woman. Lavinia was a skinny thing and had a lighter, almost golden cast to her skin. Her long silver hair was in braids that went past her waist, and she was draped in what could only be called colorful robes. Her wrists clattered with beads, her neck heavy with necklaces that jangled with bones and chicken or hawk's feet.

She reached out a hand, heavy with silver rings and decorated with henna, to Velina, and Velina took it.

"Ol' Louie in them eyes," the old woman said, her brown eyes watery and turning a milky blue at the edges with her age. There was no telling how old Lavinia was – somewhere between sixty and ancient. Old enough to have grown grandchildren who had made her great-grandchildren who were approaching adulthood in their own right. Wasn't saying much around these parts where a lot of girls found themselves pregnant young, and their kids found themselves having babies when they were still but kids themselves.

A lot of late thirty, early forty-year-old grandmothers out here. A thing that was common among a certain socioeconomic caste but certainly transcended race.

"He was my brother," Velina said to the old woman, and the woman frowned.

"Psht! Ain't gotta tell me! Ol' Louie already did. Come sit down."

Lavinia led Velina over by the fire she had going and pointed to a folded old woven blanket. "Sit," she ordered. Velina sank to the blanket, and Lavinia gathered her robes and told us, "You boys, stay out there, outside the light."

LaCroix and I exchanged a look and stepped back away into the shadows to wait.

"What's your name, girl?" Lavinia asked before she started muttering and making hand gestures at the fire.

"Velina," Velina answered politely.

"Mm." The old woman didn't sound impressed, and Velina made a face in my direction like *what the hell?*

I thrust my chin at the old woman, and she turned her attention back to her.

Watching Lavinia work her old magic was always a harrowing experience, but she was the mistress of her craft. I didn't know anything about it or how it was *supposed* to work – just that it did, and when it did? *Woo boy.*

This was no exception.

She sipped her whiskey, spit some into the flames, and handed the bottle to Velina.

"Drink," she ordered.

"Whiskey isn't really my thi—"

"Drink!" Lavinia shouted and hastily. Velina put the bottle to her lips and sipped, and that was it.

She was halfway to handing the bottle back when her eyes rolled up into the back of her head, just the whites showing. She tensed as though seizing and just sort of froze in place.

"Ask your questions," Lavinia told LaCroix, and he moved into the firelight at her invitation.

He crouched in front of Velina and asked, "How much did Louie tell you?"

"Everything."

Velina's voice was a strangled whisper.

"Why'd you come to New Orleans?"

"To find him."

"Why?"

"He stopped texting."

I hated these questions and answers. I *especially* hated it for *her*, but LaCroix was right in bringing her here. We had to know, and there were worse ways to find out if she was telling the truth than a little of that voodoo that the Bayou Baroness do. Still, she sounded like a hand was at her throat and that she could barely breathe to speak. Her breath strained and rattled in her chest like she had one foot in the grave.

"He tell you that he killed his ma?" LaCroix demanded.

"Yes."

"He say that anyone else was there?"

"No."

"What else did he tell you?" he demanded and she told him. It took a while, but she told him everything that he wanted to know.

When LaCroix was satisfied, LaCroix stood up from his crouch and nodded to Lavinia.

"Bring her back," he ordered, and Lavinia emptied some sort of powder from one of the many pouches at her belt into her palm. She blew it over the fire and into Velina's face. Velina fell back, coughing and choking, rolling onto all fours, gasping for air.

The Bayou Baroness stood as straight as her wizened old frame would let her, and she snapped her fingers three times. Velina collapsed, unconscious.

"You can pay me now, boy," the old woman said, and held out her hand to LaCroix.

"Saint," LaCroix ordered, and I looked to Lavinia for permission before I went to Velina. The Bayou Baroness nodded at me, and I gave a nod back and went to the prone woman on the ground.

Getting her turned over was the easy part, bringing her into my arms and up off the ground was a little trickier, but I managed.

"She's a strong one and loyal," Lavinia said as I went to pass her, and she gave me a wide, toothless grin. With a wink, she said, "Just like her brother. It's a good match, you and her."

I frowned at the last, and she laughed, that creaking, wheezing thing that made her lungs sound like they were made out of old leather.

"It's not like that," I said, non-plussed, and that only made the old woman laugh harder at my departing back.

"Go on back to the city with you!" she called. "Ol' Louie rides in spirit and protects her from beyond the grave. He craves revenge as much as she does. He's out for blood – and you boys'll have it. The bayou'll run red, and your haunting will be over."

"What the fuck is *that* supposed to mean?" I asked LaCroix as he climbed aboard the boat and I settled Velina in the bottom.

"Fuck if I know," he said. "But I suspect we'll find out."

I shoved us off and jumped in, settling on the bench at the bow and pulling Velina against me.

She slept and slept deep. No telling how long she would be out.

We wound our way up bayous and through swamps, passing a glimmer out there in the dark that had to be LaCroix's place. It took a while to get back to shore at LaCroix's daddy's old place, where Cypress now lived to get out from under his sister's roof.

LaCroix had no interest, that was for sure. He was either in his houseboat out there on the swamp or in Alina's apartment. Seemed to be his home was wherever she was apt to be and that suited him just fine.

I looked down at Velina in my arms, her face pale in the moonlight.

A good match?

I snorted and shook my head, but there were very few things the Bayou Baroness was wrong about.

CHAPTER SEVENTEEN

Velina...

"You came. I didn't expect you to come all the way here."

I looked up from where I was kneeling on the folded blanket before the fire. The clearing in the little old and decrepit cemetery was empty now. No Bayou Baroness priestess lady, no LaCroix, no Saint, and no boat. The colors were almost more vivid than life, and lit across the fire from me was Garnett, my little brother, his keen green eyes made luminous by the under-lighting of the flames.

"Where are we?" I asked, my heart stilling in my chest, squeezing down almost painfully tight.

Garnett sniffed. "A place between worlds," he said. "A crossroads. I've been here a while, it feels like. Even before I died." He took a hit off the joint he was holding, inhaling deep and holding his breath as he said, "Got some good shit here on the other side. All the good and none of the bad."

I blinked and looked him over. He looked... fine. His cut sharp, and the patches still nearly new, having not been road-worn to the extent of the other guys. There was a 1% diamond patch, and over his right breast was the name patch that proudly proclaimed Loup Garou. His tee shirt underneath was white and almost gleamed in the firelight, his jeans baggy and a light wash but likewise clean. His boots worn but serviceable as he shifted his feet and planted them more firmly in the leaf litter of the ground. He rocked on the fallen log he sat on and blew out a big plume of smoke that drifted my way.

I expected to be hit with the dank green smoke of some quality fucking weed, but there was no smell... nothing smelled, actually. I didn't smell the deep green and brown of rich earth and green growing things. I didn't smell the underpinning of rot or decay that was pervasive along the bayous and in the swamps.

I didn't smell the smoke from the crackling campfire in between us, and I felt my heart drop as I realized... this was just a dream.

"Aw, no, don't be sad," Louie said and sniffed. "It's not a dream. It's more like a vision – and you just got here, so don't go yet. I mean, we don't have a lot of time, but I want to talk. You came. I didn't expect you to come. It's really cool that you came."

"Of course, I came! You big idiot. You couldn't keep me away!" I said, and I swallowed back down the thick feeling in my throat and willed the red in my nose to back down and the watering in my eyes to stop its bullshit.

"Hey, don't cry! For reals, sis. It was my time. While I'm bummed that I didn't get to get further with True, and I miss her and the guys, it's not going to be so very long for me. It's going to be a while for you guys, but I'm here, and I'll wait forever."

"You don't have to do that," I said. "You don't have to wait for us. You've been through enough, little brother. It's totally okay for you to rest."

He shook his head, smiling, and it was a rueful thing.

"Nah, I have to watch over you and the rest of the boys," he said. "Make sure you all get through what you got coming unscathed." He flicked the butt of his joint into the fire.

"What's coming?" I asked.

He grinned, and it held a reckless and savage quality to it.

"Revenge."

"God, I hope so," I said bitterly.

"You should know!" he crowed. "You're leading the charge."

"You're damn right I am!" I cried. "Why wouldn't I?"

He smiled and said, "Our time's up – but I see you, Vel. I see you and what you're doing for me, and I'm right there. You may not be able to see me or feel it, but I am."

"Wait!" I cried, the mist pushing in from the surrounding waters, rolling in unnaturally fast.

"Time waits for no one, sis. You should know that in your line of work. Every man's got his time, and it was and is my time to go."

"But you just got here!" I cried as the fog reached out tendrils, and one curled around Louie's wrist. It formed into a hand, the fingers lacing between his, and he clutched it back, the rest of the fog pushing at his back and starting to envelop him.

"The guys will take care of you," he said. "Try and take care of them back for me. We're all the same, after all."

"Wait!" I struggled to my feet, but my legs were asleep from the way I'd been sitting on them. The fog swallowed Louie whole then and the fire with it. I reached out and screamed in frustration, but then it felt like many hands grabbing me from behind, pulling, grasping, the whispers unintelligible filling my ears – feminine, masculine, overlapping, and babbling like water over stone. I fought to stay with my brother just a moment longer, but it was no use.

Those hands pulled me back into the vapor, those voices drowned out all sound, and as I was dragged mercilessly back into that warm cloud that felt like feathers from an angel's wing brushed my skin from every direction, the light receded from the fire, became diffuse, and winked out. Then there was only the warm, close, dark, and nothing else.

WHEN I OPENED MY EYES, it was to a dark so pressing, I couldn't immediately tell if I was awake or if I'd died myself.

I sat up sharply, my hands shoving into blankets and covers, a mattress that was almost too soft below me, and there was a nearby grunt in the dark.

I froze as someone big shifted next to me. An arm wrapped around my naked waist, and another snaked around from behind me and wrapped my chest, pulling me back down to lay awkwardly, half on the bed and half against a very warm and very solid chest.

"Relax." The voice was rich and dark, darker than the darkness of the room around us. "It was just a dream."

I scoffed, choked slightly on my bitter regret of not having more time, and said, "That was way more than just a dream."

The hands against me smoothed up and down my body, my back, over my nude hip, and I pushed up and flung a leg over the hips that belonged to the man I was in bed with.

I knew it was Saint. I could smell him, and after the last day or two of being pressed to him aboard his bike, his smell had become familiar to me. Woodsy, leather, and sunshine – the underlying tang of pure masculinity. Clean with just a hint of smoke from the occasional cigarette he smoked.

He let me straddle him in the dark and smoothed those rough hands over my hips and up my ribs. I arched back, feeling him grow hard against my pussy lips, which I ground against him to get him going.

The chill of that fog, of the spirit's hands that lingered through my clothes and against my skin, damp and with that otherworldly cold and clammy of beyond the grave – I wanted, no *needed*, something life-affirming.

I craved his warmth, the fire of his hands against my body, the warmth and heat of his cock inside me, and the magic we created when we fucked.

I needed it something fierce in that moment, and I was relieved and grateful that he seemingly had no designs on stopping me from taking what I wanted.

I rose up on my knees some and wrapped fingers around his thickening cock, and he gasped and moaned slightly, his hips jerking below me. I stroked him from root to tip and back down, giving my hand a little twist, relishing the hot, velvet texture of his flesh against my palm and fingers as I worked him.

"Not that I'm complaining, but what brought this on?" he demanded from the dark, grunting as I picked his cock up from his body and pressed it at my opening.

I was aroused, but it was the early stages of it yet, and I hadn't quite stretched with my arousal to fully accommodate him. I didn't care. Dropping over him and taking him into my body fully, if a little prematurely, the zing of pain associated with taking him before I was ready was erotic and arousing in its own right.

Saint grunted below me, and I moved, rolling my hips, my finger-tips brushing the nest of curls at the apex of my thighs, parting the hair, and finding my clit. I pressed fingertips into the throbbing bundle of nerves and struck a rhythm not only with the dance above him, moving him inside of me, but with my fingers against that sensitive spot, press-ing, circling, rubbing, the friction between the pads of my first three fingers and the hardening kernel of flesh, hungry and desperate for the attention-sparked fire in my veins, chasing back the chill of the grave.

Saints' rough hands found my hips, his fingers digging with a near-bruising force that just turned me on that much more. The sounds coming from him, the grunting, the impassioned breathing, the gasping and muttered words in their tone of aw and practically *worship*, goaded me into relaxing more fully.

I let my head fall back, my tits thrusting forward as Saint's arms stiffened and he held me aloft.

"Fuckin' touch that clit, baby. Come on, come for me," he urged, and I renewed the fervency with which I touched myself as *he* struck a hard and fast tempo from beneath me, thrusting up into me.

I felt my tits bounce with every contact our bodies made as I let myself fall to meet his upward thrusting. I bit my lip against the sharp but bittersweet pain of him bottoming out against my cervix. Some-times, I liked it. Sometimes, I didn't. And sometimes, like now, I was trapped somewhere between the two, undecided if it was good or if it was just too much.

I concentrated on my breathing, timing things, playing with my pussy, even as Saint worked to destroy it. I felt myself, so wet, the sound of his cock sliding in and out of me, the wet slap of our bodies connecting, all of it a dirty symphony of carnal delight that I couldn't get enough of.

"Oh, yeah," I gasped as that tingling started, making my pussy tighten around him.

"Oh, fuck yeah," he echoed, and I was pleased he felt it. That he felt what he did to me. "Come on, baby, do it for me, come for me. That's it." His voice was low and filled with a concentration that could only be him trying *not* to go until I got mine, and I appreciated that. That shit took restraint, and it was a restraint that most guys didn't fucking bother with these days.

I liked sex with Saint. I felt like a *partner* and not like a living sex doll with him, which was nice. It was really nice.

"Oh, yeah!" I knew I sounded breathy, I knew I sounded close because I *was* close. So, close. So very close! The heat building between my legs, the fire low in my belly stoked and all-consuming, rising higher and higher within me, splitting somewhere near my navel, both licks of flame curling and writhing, seemingly tweaking and tingling in my nipples from the inside. Reaching further and choking me off as lightning struck, forking up through my pussy, and down through my head, causing my heart to seize and my body to tighten, coiling like a spring. I was hanging on that beautiful shining precipice of looking at the starlight and *becoming* the starlight until, with a final inhalation of breath, the stars burst and shattered around me, diving at me, the shining particles sliding underneath my skin and amplifying me into a supernova of pleasure so fine that it became a decadent pain, a beautiful torture that I never, *ever* wanted to end.

CHAPTER EIGHTEEN

V elina...

Going undercover was a lot like fishing. Hours and hours spent in bars and watering holes around the city, where they tended to frequent, waiting to be in the right place at the right time.

Mission accomplished on that front – then it was all about patiently waiting as bait in the water to be noticed and thought tasty enough by one of them to get hit on or find a way in.

At least, that was how I thought things were going to go for me.

What *actually* happened wasn't that one of the *guys* saw me first. It was one of their ladies, or a small group of them that tended to hang around the guys to party, score free drugs, or to get laid, that picked up on my existence first.

"Hey!" she said, breasting boobily up to the bar next to me where I sat, chatting with the bartender.

"Hi!" I called back over the loud music.

"Didn't I see you over at the Snapping Turtle the other night?" she asked.

Shit-fire, motherfucker, I thought to myself and thought fast.

"Aw, yeah! I think that was me!" I called out. "What a coincidence!"

If there was anything I had learned through the clandestine time I had been spending with the Voodoo Bastards and Saint between job hunting for a cleaning job at the city's many hotels and looking for a cheap room or place to rent – it was that the women of a club were just as dangerous if not *more* dangerous than the men. Which... *duh.*

Women just went about things differently than men. Rather than overt violence, the danger with them lay in the *covert* violence of whispers and lies that they could and would talk about the other club girls or with throwing new meat to the fuckin' hyenas on a particularly bad night to make some other woman a target to save their own ass.

"Yeah!" she called back, happy that she'd recognized me, I guess, and then introduced herself. "They call me Singer!" she called over the noise.

"Are you?" I asked with a smile.

"What?" she called, looking perplexed.

"A singer!" I called back. "Do you sing?"

"Oh!" She leaned back and her laugh was lost under the noise and din of the bar. "No! I sew real good, and all the boys bring me their patches to sew onto their cuts!" she hollered back.

I feigned stupidity and asked, "Cuts? You mean their leather vest things?"

She laughed again and called out, "You don't normally hang around places like this, do you?"

"No!" I called back. "I just moved here, and I'm just going from place to place looking for a good time, I guess!"

"What's your name?" she called.

"Louise!" I called back.

"Well, welcome to New Orleans, Louise! Why don't you come hang with us?" she called.

And just like that, I'd found my in.

Singer was a pretty girl or had been before getting in with these guys. I mean, she probably still had hope – but I'd been rocked to my foundation when she'd said she was twenty-seven. I thought she was forty-two or somewhere around there, age-wise.

She took me over to a table of ladies near the pool tables in the bar, a knot of Bayou Brethren surrounding the billiards, leaning on cues, cracking jokes, and talking more than they were actually playing.

There, she introduced me to four other girls.

There was, of course, Singer herself, who was, again, twenty-seven and dressed like she was perpetually on spring break from Texas. She favored short shorts and cowgirl boots, with a sports bra peeking through her cropped and 1980s cut-and-tied stringed-out tee shirt. She was all pink and white, and Barbie sparkles and glitter. She kept her long blonde hair up in long pigtails with pink bows.

Singer was off and on with Basilisk, one of the men around the pool table who had his back to me, so I couldn't really tell you what he looked like for now, anyway.

Also at the table was Candy. Candy was in her late teens and shouldn't even be in this bar, but she was also heading the way of Singer in looking ancient for her actual age. She was rail thin, and her dyed black hair damaged. I was betting she was hooked on something by the glassiness of her eyes.

Sativa was a stripper, and she seemed the sharpest if not paranoid and angry. She was loud, from her voice to her looks. She wore an elaborate but cheap-looking wig, the purple and neon green vibrant and demanding your attention, fell down to her waist in these slick, shiny curls. It was as though she'd just pulled it fresh out of the packaging, and put it on, and left it – uninterested in making it look like anything, really, let alone real hair.

She wore a bodycon dress that was so tight, you could see her nipple piercings pressed to the thin material, and it clung so close to her skin in its gray-and-white snakeskin-printed pattern that you could see the ripples of cellulite on her over-pronounced ass. She was… a lot… her artificial eyelashes so thick I didn't know how she held her eyelids up, her thick lips painted with a dark purple lipstick, her eyeshadow purple and green like her wig. She had a shiny fake diamond piercing where Marilyn Monroe had her famous beauty mark and wore gladiator sandals in a champagne gold that wound up her thick legs.

I mean, she had *said* she was a stripper like she was waiting for me to judge her so she could make a big deal out of me being just another judgy white lady Karen, but I'd dodged that landmine – evading it cleanly. If she was a stripper, which I didn't doubt, it certainly wasn't at any high-class joint. She was way too chunky for that, but absolutely good on her for getting that bag. I was neither built for nor coordinated enough to ride so much as a fucking fire pole down from a second floor without hurting myself.

After Sativa was one of her stripper friends who went by the name of Vixen. Where Sativa looked like she never missed a meal, Vixen looked like she missed too many. She was rail thin, and I mean, *yikes*. She had no chest to speak of and wore what I had to assume was her stripper outfit bold as brass out in public. It was a white set of lingerie, or maybe more like a bikini. The top was very much a bathing suit top, the bottoms a thong, and tight to her like a rubber band – not leaving much, if anything, to the imagination.

She had on over the white suit with its gold bead accents, a bright, and I do mean *bright* orange – I didn't know what you would honestly call it. A dress? A swimsuit coverup? Which didn't honestly cover anything. It was like nylons or pantyhose material, and in these, sort of, completely holey oval shapes that were intentional but made the whole effect seem… ratty.

Her wig was better than Sativa's and a reddish brown, done to make it appear that she had conical fox ears pinned on top – the long silky rest of the wig falling straight to her flat ass. A fox's tail was safety pinned to the back of her outfit, and I guess I should have been grateful it was safety pinned and that she wasn't wearing one of those foxtail butt plug things you saw all over the internet.

She had bright orange ostrich feathers at the cuffs of her long sleeves, which were shedding all over the place, drifting down to where some of the other girls were having to fish bits of them out of their drinks before sipping. Ew.

Vixen wore contact lenses to make her brown eyes appear more bronze or gold, and she was quiet for the most part until Sativa got going. Then she was hyping up her friend, who would scream and yell across the bar to try and either start shit with one of the boys at the pool table in a friendly banter kind of way or to start shit with other patrons in a not-so-friendly type of way.

Sativa was one of those bitches who was constantly stirring the shit and looking to start some drama. I sincerely hoped that no one would take the fucking bait. If they did, I hoped they made her ass lick the fucking spoon.

Then there was the queen who reigned supreme at their table.

Midnight wasn't just some club girl. She was an old lady. Rebel's old lady, to be exact. He was the chapter president. But when Midnight got up from the table and went to the bathroom with Candy, Sativa jumped right on to talking shit.

"Girl, don't let her fool you. She ain't a queen except in her own imagination. Yeah, Rebel over there is the *chapter* president, but he ain't the *club* president. That's the man with the *real* power there."

"Who's that?" I asked innocently enough while I filed all of this new information away and sipped my beer in front of me. I was studiously staying away from the hard alcohol and trying to seem tipsy without letting on I was sharp.

"Lazarus," Singer answered, and she looked spooked or nervous. "Tiva the Diva hasn't even seen him," she said, rolling her eyes.

"Not yet," Sativa said, scoffing at Singer like she wasn't shit. "My milkshake brings all the boys to the yard, though, and he won't be able to resist." She snapped her fingers, the long talons of her bejeweled square-tipped nails clattering together with the lull between songs. "That's a fact!" she proclaimed as the bass hit for the next hard rock song that went right into it that came onto the jukebox.

"What the fuck you sayin' over there?" one of the men at the pool table demanded, looking our way.

"Ain't nothin' you have to worry about, sugar!" Sativa called back, her tone dripping with artificial honey. "This is just girl talk over here!"

Vixen laughed, and Singer and I exchanged a look and grinned, Singer rolling her eyes behind Sativa and Vixen's back.

"Who you got there with you?" another one of the men at the table demanded, looking right past the other women and directly at me.

He was no Saint, but he wasn't bad to look at, either.

He was blond, with hair between chin and shoulder length, a

goatee that was a little longer and unkempt than I tended to like, shot through with a few threads of silver starting to come in. He wore one of those sleeveless and close-fitting black athletic tees that hugged a strong body, but it was an all-natural one. One that bespoke work but not working out, if that makes sense. His gut was just barely starting to poke out over the waistband of his jeans, but all in all – yeah, he wasn't ugly like some of these other ones. When he smiled, he had all of his teeth, and they were clean, white, and, for the most part, straight.

"Depends. Who's asking?" I asked playfully, demurely hiding what I hoped came across as a flirtatious smile behind the rim of my glass as I made eyes at this guy over the rim.

He straightened up and set his pool cue across the table, seemingly abandoning his game now that I was in his sights.

"They call me Carver," he said. "What's your name?"

"Louise," I lied. "But my friends call me Louie."

His smile grew and he moved around the table to come over, dropping into the chair that Midnight had vacated next to mine.

"Well, I'm pleased to make your acquaintance, Louie. I think I might like to be your friend, too," he said.

I laughed lightheartedly and thought to myself, *I'll just bet you do.*

CHAPTER NINETEEN

S aint...

Fish on.

I stared at the two words on my screen and chuckled. She worked fast. I'd expected it to take longer. I looked up and over at Cypress, Bennie, and Collier. We were at Velina's apartment in California, packing up everything that even remotely looked like clothes or anything sentimental. The furniture would stay – the rest was going into bins and into the back of the club's crash truck. We'd store the shit in my attic for now or at the club. Whichever. It didn't matter to me...

Except it did.

I would rather store it at my place, the Bayou Baroness' words lingering in my ears about Velina and I being some kind of a good match.

I didn't think she was wrong – the only problem?

I was a saint in name only, and that name was tongue in cheek at best.

I was a jealous fucker, and I didn't know how well or how long I could deal with her cozying up with those sons of a bitches.

"Yo, Saint, I think we're done here," Collier called out, and I sighed, looking around. Everything was emptied – the cupboards, bookshelves, closets… everything that wasn't nailed down or was too bulky was left – so pretty much all the furniture. We took the bed. She would need that – but everything else? The couch, the small dining set? The old, outdated, too-small television?

Nah.

There was no need for any of it.

"Let's go," I said, putting on my sunglasses, and we left her tiny apartment behind.

It'd been a depressing place. Most of her books on her little shelf were text books… some true crime.

All of that had been packed, but the box truck still had room to spare, and the pickup we'd brought? No need for it at all.

She led a simple life, like she was afraid to put down roots, and I wondered about that. But that would be for a game of quid pro quo in person after we got back.

I didn't answer her text. I told her that as soon as she sent anything, to delete it. For the purposes of Velina's character, Louise, her daddy was alive and well and how my number was saved in her phone.

That was her story and she was to stick to it.

As for *my* phone? It was just Velina… and a picture I'd snapped in secret of her smiling as she skimmed the picture frames and art in a thrift.

I sighed and thought about that picture and had to admit, even if it was only to myself, I hardly knew her, but I was head over heels for her already.

Damn.

CHAPTER TWENTY

V elina...

I was sick to death of the roach-infested La Chiquita on Veterans and didn't want *any* of my shit anywhere near it to pick up any hitchhikers, so I was glad when Saint offered to store it at his place until we could figure out where I was going and what I would need.

This undercover shit was a pain in the ass, especially when you didn't have a whole alphabet soup of bureaus to finance it.

It had been easier than I cared to admit to find a job cleaning in New Orleans. I'd hired on at one of the fancy-pants hotels in the French Quarter, and it'd given me a couple of advantages. One, I was making some money, and two, after I got off work, I was already in bar central.

Finding housing was proving to be more difficult, but the club was helping me at least stay put here for the time being.

I'll tell you what, after doing biohazard cleaning, cleaning a hotel room was easy. Know what *wasn't* easy? Cleaning forty of them, one right after the other, especially considering some people were *fucking savages.*

The downside was having to do biohazard cleaning without any of the proper personal protection gear, which sometimes had to happen.

I had no idea why anyone would shit in a shower.

Fucking. Savages. I tell you.

As soon as I got in from my night with the Bayou Brethren, I texted Saint with *fish on*, to let him know I'd made contact and that I had wormed my way in. Probably a little too well, as Carver had so graciously given me a ride back to my hotel.

My car was here, so it was fine. The bus line was helpful in that it was pretty much a straight shot to where I needed to go in the heart of the Quarter for work, and the Quarter itself was imminently walkable.

There had been another thing I hadn't taken into consideration when it came for my bid for revenge, and that was I hadn't expected any of the Bayou Brethren to be any sort of *likable*.

Carver wasn't half-bad. An asshole, sure, but no worse than Saint in that regard. Still, he lacked Saint's innate charisma.

As for the women of the Bayou Brethren? I liked Singer, and I couldn't find any fault with Midnight yet. Vixen wasn't *terrible*, Candy held my pity, but Sativa? Sativa could fuck allll the way off. I couldn't *stand* her. If anything, she was going to be the hardest thing about the Brethren to deal with. Good fucking *God*, the drama!

I didn't expect a text back from Saint. I'd traded numbers with Carver, and had him saved in my phone as such. Same with Singer. I'd expected Singer to be the first one to text me, but I'd barely shut the door to my hotel room and latched it after sending the text off to Saint, when my phone buzzed in my hand.

I half expected it to *be* Saint with the timing of things, but no, it was Carver.

Be seeing you real soon, Louie. Tonight was a lot of fun.

I rolled my eyes.

For him, maybe, but it'd be a while before I could get Sativa's grating and annoying hollering out of my head.

Instead, I texted back the same thing I would have texted my brother, Louie, if I'd been talking to him.

You shouldn't text and drive!

I tossed my phone onto the made bed and went in to use the bathroom, brush my teeth, and just generally get ready for bed.

By the time I got back to it, I had a text waiting.

I'm riding, not driving, and at a stoplight. It's fine.

That made me smile. It was probably something Saint would have said, too, except Saint would have tacked on something insulting. Funny but insulting. It was one of the reasons I liked him. He didn't treat me fragile like a flower. No, he had more sense than that. He treated me fragile like a bomb.

I flopped down on the bed and texted back.

Fine, riding, driving, whatever – don't text and do it. It's dangerous.

I sighed and set the phone down by my hip, and stared at the water-stained ceiling. I missed him. Saint, not Carver. I realized as I was lying there, that this was going to be harder than I'd expected for all of the reasons I hadn't considered.

"Well, fuck me," I muttered to the cockroaches. "Ain't life just a fucking party all the time?"

"Hey, Louie!" Carver called out as I walked up. I'd been invited to a night out on him – *just* me and him. I didn't know how to feel about that. I hadn't realized how fucking *weird* it would be to play this other person. I was hoping that it would be a good way to get in with him enough to learn about the Bayou Brethren. At the very least, a good starting point would be to learn how he got in with them and just what the appeal was.

"Hey, you," I said and let him hug me.

We were on Bourbon, and I didn't know if any of the Voodoo Bastards lurked nearby.

Saint had said they were under a sort of de facto truce, but only because law enforcement was breathing down both clubs' necks, just looking for an excuse. Unfortunately, the fact that the Voodoo Bastards were the longer living and known quantity to the NOPD, they were pretty much on their ass more than the Bayou Brethren's even though it was one of the Voodoo Bastards who had died...

My brother.

My sweet, funny, kind, sometimes dopey, and all-the-time struggling little brother.

I forced a smile to my lips in spite of the fact that the emotions I was feeling didn't even come close to matching.

"Are you sure this is a good idea?" I asked, carefully trying to sound cautious and afraid.

"Why?" he asked, looking me over.

"I heard the girls talking and they said something about the Voodoo Bastards. I've seen them riding through here like all the time," I said, casting my line in hopes of hooking some information.

Carver barked a laugh and said, "Those fuckwits?" He shook his head. "Nah, we're fine. They're too pussy to do shit." His confidence was misplaced, and because I knew what I knew about the cops and the current situation, which I *wasn't* supposed to know – it came off more like bravado. Still, I played along, nodding and smiling.

I stayed silent, afraid to push too hard or too much on the subject too soon.

We walked along the street, and he said, "Let's go this way. There's a great café. Are you hungry?" he asked.

"Starving," I admitted.

He slung a leather-clad arm over my shoulders, and we struck out on the cracked and uneven sidewalk.

You had to be careful down here for more than a few reasons. The main one, it was the French Quarter and inherently dangerous just for that fact. Situational awareness was a must. There were tourists, sure, and roaming PD that you caught a glimpse of every once in a great while. But if you were paying attention, there were men like Carver out here, and headcases, and drunks, and worse than drunks – druggies.

The French Quarter had a totally different vibe during the day than it did at night, and you could *feel* the transition take over as the sun set behind the buildings and the shadows rose from the gutters and crept out of the tight alleyways.

It was like the darkness was more than just *dark* like something salacious and even malicious crept out of the sewers and alleyways with it.

I was no shrinking violet. I'd been through violence before – enough to know how to, and that I would like to, avoid it if I could.

Despite the dangers all around and the fact that I was essentially cozying up with a fucking mountain lion in Carver, I was glad for his presence and escort. As we walked, it only took a glance at the vest he wore for several onlookers to part like the Red Sea. If I looked behind us, those same onlookers looked either surprised, confused, and, in some cases, dubious at the patch on Carver's back. Likely that it *wasn't* Voodoo Bastards.

There were all sorts of MCs and riding clubs that went through here. I'd seen them a plenty during the day. All from parts unknown or far away – but always, *always* in packs of three or more. Never solo.

The only ones I'd seen who dared to walk around on their own were the Voodoo Bastards, and it made me wonder what Carver was playing at. Was he crazy, stupid, or was he making a statement walking through their territory bold as brass, a girl on his arm, like he owned these streets? I had a feeling it was the latter and that he was looking to piss some of Louie's brothers off.

I didn't know how I felt about being a prop in his peacocking charade. It told me one thing – these guys did not give a *fuck*. Not like the Bastards. They at least were keeping their women somewhere away from all of this madness. I'd had yet to meet more than just Alina, but from what she had told me over dinner that one night, she, Corliss, and Jessie-Lou were tight, and Sandrine was being brought into their little fold of opening up a witchy metaphysical gift shop in the Quarter.

From everything I'd gathered reading between the lines in the Bastards' presence – they were really trying to turn to more legitimate and less dangerous ventures.

Meanwhile, the Bayou Brethren were taking that almost personally, as though it somehow made the Bastards weak and thus the potential power plays for the Bastards' territory.

That was the explanation I'd been given in short, but the traded looks and glances between my three dinner companions made me suspect there was something more to the story. I'd been brazen and I'd asked. LaCroix had been the one to confess that there *was* something, but even the Bastards didn't know exactly what. Just that something about how things had been playing out with the Brethren had seemed way too personal to be just a power play for territory.

That was partially where I came in.

I was to keep my ear to the ground, report movements, and anything else I heard that could be pertinent.

It was a daunting task because I didn't know what was what and felt like no matter how big or small, I was going to have to remember and report just about *everything* that I heard. To that end, I had an empty stack of journals waiting back at the hotel.

I guess Louie writing letters long hand and sending them through the mail had sparked some ideas with Saint, except instead of snail mail, we would use a courier service. Faster that way and not out of place. Couriers came to and left the big fancy hotel I was working at all the time.

It was starting to feel like real covert spy shit, but if it brought some sense of justice or revenge for Louie's murder – I was all for it.

Nothing would bring him back, I knew that – dead was dead... but *damn*... I don't even know.

"Louie?" I came back to myself and realized I'd been staring vacantly at the menu. I looked up, over the top, and found Carver staring at me intently with eyebrows raised. I realized with a bit of startlement that the waitress was standing by our table, pen poised over her notepad expectantly.

"I'm sorry," I apologized with a shaky laugh. "It's been a long day, and I zoned out for a minute there. What's the question?"

"Drink, what would you like to drink?" Carver asked with a wry grin.

"Coffee?" I hazarded.

"We have all kinds, honey. Hot or iced?"

"Bless you," I said. "Iced."

A few more leading questions from her, and we had a whole order in – coffee for me, and a beer for Carver. Now all that was left to decide on was food.

This place specialized in breakfast all day long, and since I'd gone with coffee, I decided I might as well go all in. "Bananas Foster French Toast," I ordered when our waitress had returned.

Carver had ordered a burger – at a place famous for their all-day breakfast – but hey, to each their own.

The meal was alright. I learned a little more about Carver, who was refreshingly honest if, dare I say, *proud* about his outlaw four-time-felon status. Red flags, of course, went up when one of those felonies was casually revealed as an aggravated assault with a domestic violence enhancement against an ex-wife who I was assured deserved it.

Apparently, she'd been cheating while he'd been in jail or prison – that part was unclear – as even though he clearly knew the difference, he used them interchangeably. Of course, that made perfect sense if he didn't expect *me* to know the difference.

If he were talking to Velina, I would have been out of there so fast because I recognized it for the manipulation tactic that it was. Calling prison "jail" and the minimizing language he used over his offenses, which were all pretty much possession and possession with intent to distribute right up until the domestic.

The college-educated *real* me knew he was posturing. Talking himself up to look like a badass and a bad boy to appeal to who he thought he was talking to – a barely high school graduated, innocent little Louise Whittier who led a nomadic life, cleaning fancier hotels with a start in Los Angeles as she moved south to where she *really* wanted to be – New Orleans, or St. Augustine, or Savannah, or Charleston – she didn't know. She was just trying them all out, moving along in order as she pushed east. She planned to spend six months to a year in each city before moving on to the next and ultimately deciding which one suited her best.

That had been calculated to appeal to this lot – a woman with no family, innocent and moldable. It was as low-hanging fruit as it could get. Maybe too low if any of the Brethren had half a brain to see it, which is why I was treading carefully.

I laughed at some of his jokes that I would never actually find funny in a million years – at least no one with any actual empathy or smarts would, and agreed to accompany him to a bar further into the Quarter for adult beverages and to continue our talks and trading jokes, etc.

He actually would have been charming to me if he expressed any actual remorse for any of the things he had done. If he showed any actual desire to work on himself and to do or be better, but he was too narcissistic for that. Charming and sweet with his actions enough that if I'd been one iota less than who I was, I wouldn't so easily feel like he smelled like bad decisions.

He held doors, he wasn't too handsy, but he wasn't shy about touching me, either. A hand on the waist or on the back guiding me through doorways or around broken pieces of the sidewalk. He was gentlemanly in walking on the side of the street and mean mugging anyone who dared get up too close or in my business. Be it bumping into me rudely, to begging me for change.

He played white knight – but just like every woman knew, it was placating. It was a show because the more comfortable he became, the lower his hand would wander, the more familiar the touches, the closer he stood, and the tighter the space between us became, all signaling one thing. He wanted to bone, and he was overtly imposing his desire in such a way as to gaslight me into thinking it was what I wanted, too.

It didn't matter if I was ready or not.

Thing was, I would never *be* ready. Would I do it if I had to? Yes. If it managed to shoe-horn me into getting what I wanted and where I wanted to be – which was into their inner circle, then absolutely I would. I would loathe every damn second of it, though, and I would probably need to shower for days after to scrub the ick out from under my skin.

I wasn't looking forward to it, in case that wasn't clear, but I *was* expecting it.

I would have been stupid or naïve not to. This was the real world, not some episode of *Gangland Undercover*.

The bar wasn't what I had expected him to choose, and I wondered briefly as we passed through the stucco and exposed brick of the old structure that housed it, if this wasn't more of him trying to piss on Voodoo Bastards territory. It just sort of had that kind of vibe.

Lafitte's Blacksmith Shop was one of the oldest, if not *the* oldest, bars in the French Quarter. I didn't know the veracity of its claim to fame of being the site of the actual pirate Jean Laffite's blacksmith shop at one point in history. But you could feel the history here as though you peeled it back like a cloth over a doorway upon entry and stepped into another world.

"Wow," I said to Carver. "This is like its own cozy little world apart from ours in here."

"Oh, yeah?" he asked, as I did the insipid girly thing to do and wrapped both my arms around his one arm, threading my fingers through the spaces between his and cozying up to him even though every fiber of my being was trying to get me to put more distance between us, not less.

"Yeah," I said. "Do you think it's haunted?" We drew up to the bar as I asked, and the bartender must have overheard me, because he barked a laugh and answered before Carver could.

"Welcome to Lafitte's Blacksmith Shop, and yeah, sugar, it's haunted," he said in a thick, Louisiana drawl.

"What's the story?" I asked, thinking about my brother's brush with the supernatural down here.

"This here was the business front of one of New Orleans' most infamous residents – the Pirate Jean Laffite. He and his brother, Pierre, owned this place as a legal front to all of their very illegal dealings. It's said many a plan was hatched inside these walls to make those boys and their crew as rich as possible. Now, I ain't seen him myself, but some say you can see Jean over there by the fireplace lurkin' and plottin' if you're lucky."

He pointed past us, and I turned to observe a *very* old brick fireplace, a cheery blaze crackling in its depths despite the heat wafting in from outside the open archways lined with hewn wood shutters.

Also behind us was another couple waiting to order. I turned back with a smile, and the bartender grinned and asked, "What'll you have?"

Drinks in hand, we slid down the bar and sat on the stools. The bartender got busy with another couple, and Carver asked me, "You into all that spooky shit?"

"What, like ghosts and vampires?" I asked.

"Yeah." He grinned.

"Nah." I shook my head. "This place just has that kind of vibe, you know? I was just curious, that's all."

"I gotcha." He winked at me, and I laughed a little nervously.

"So," I said, trying to dredge up *anything* else to talk about. "Where are you originally from?"

His grin grew wider, and he said, "Well, I'm a Louisiana boy – born and bred."

"Yeah?" I asked. He didn't sound like it. If anything, he had the bland accent of nowhere, like I did.

"I know, I don't sound like it," he said.

I leaned back and smacked his arm lightly, saying, "Oh, my God! Get out of my head!"

We laughed, and he said, "No, I wanted to be different. I grew up in a place called Jennings, over there in Jefferson Davis Parrish. It's close to two hundred miles that way." He pointed in a vague direction and I just took his word for it.

"Small town?" I asked.

"Yeah." He nodded. "You could walk up to just about anyone on their porch and ask after somebody, and they'd tell you, 'aw yeah, I know 'im. They live over on such and such street and go there to the Baptist church' or whatever."

"Oh, wow! That's *definitely* small town!"

"It is," he said, nodding. "I was about thirteen when the biggest thing to ever happen in Jennings started to go down."

"What's that?" I asked.

"The Jennings 8," he said, and a chill went down my spine. "Bunch a girls who got themselves killed. Jennings' very own serial killer."

"What?" I asked and leaned back.

"Yeah. Doesn't surprise me, really. There's fuck else to do in that town except for the occasional cookout and a whole lotta Bible thumping."

"Wait," I leaned back and eyed him critically, "When did this all start?"

"Two thousand and five," he said.

I did the math and blinked.

"You're thirty-two?" I asked.

"Just turned thirty-three," he said with a grin.

"Stop!" I cried.

How was he only thirty-three?

"What?" he asked and started to laugh.

"I thought you were around my age!" I lied.

"What?" his eyes crossed.

"Yeah," I said, and he laughed for real then.

"I guess you're only as old as you feel," he said.

It was like the air was sucked out of the room the moment one of their booted feet crossed the threshold into the establishment from the street. You felt their presence before you had the chance to look in their direction. Their command of presence a powerful thing. The din of scattered conversations within the small bar dropped to a smattering of low talk and nervous whispers as the three men moved into the small room and bellied up to the bar beside us.

"What'll I get you gents?" the bartender asked, and I twisted in my seat to look up into Saint's brooding dark eyes.

"Tequilla, top shelf, neat," he said without looking at the bartender, his eyes boring into mine.

I felt small in that moment. So incredibly small. I shrank in my seat with the feeling even as Chainsaw and Axeman put in their orders for an absinthe and a Sazerac Sunset, respectively.

Saint's eyes flickered from mine to Carver's and back to mine, a faint smile tugging at his lips.

"You ever want to hook up with a *real* man, you just let me know, sweetheart," Saint said to me, and he flicked out one of those white business cards with just a phone number printed across its front.

I scoffed, took the card, and ripped it up, throwing the pieces like confetti into the air.

He barked a laugh, Carver stiff at my back, and I turned back around. Carver looked at me impassively, and I rolled my eyes.

"Rude," I said, and he smirked.

The three Voodoo Bastards moved off to a table by the street, and I sighed.

"Guess that's our cue to leave," I said, and Carver shook his head.

"Finish your drink," he said, and he sounded impressed but also… there was something else there. Something underneath. A hard layer of underlying steel to his tone.

"O-okay," I stammered because that was what Louise would do.

He was trying to be hard, but it didn't come as naturally to Carver as it did to Saint. Saint sent shivers down my spine and I couldn't help but *want* to obey him when he gave an order like that. Carver, I almost wanted to laugh, but that wouldn't do. That's what Velina would do, and I wasn't Velina right now. I was Louie…

Louie.

Louie.

CHAPTER TWENTY-ONE

*S*aint...

We got the call from Lafitte's that a Bayou Brethren was cozied up with some broad at the bar. I was both hoping it was and wasn't Velina.

Chainsaw, Axeman, and I got on our bikes and headed out that way. Lafitte's was *our* bar. No, it wasn't what you would consider a biker bar, but we were getting too long in the tooth to live it up and throw down on the regular, and Lafitte's had a low-key kind of vibe that we liked. It was chill, and it was where *we* liked to chill. The Bayou Bitches knew that, and the silent challenge couldn't go unanswered, even if we were all under scrutiny from the PD.

Ye haw, fuck the law, I thought as we pulled up against the curb, wedging our bikes into some back-in angle parking in a gap left between two cars that would barely fit a fuckin' Mini Cooper.

We all silently checked with each other and, after some quick, curt nods, went up the rest of the block on Philips to the corners it shared with Bourbon.

Lafitte's wasn't much to look at, all things considered. A squat, stucco-and-exposed-brick building with open doorways or large windows to the street lined to either side with rough-hewn shutters that were as big as doors and served as 'em when the place was shut and locked.

Gas lamps flickered, and the hurricane lamps and fireplace were lit within. I caught the bartender's eye as we stepped in and threw him some chin. He threw me some back, subtly, and jerked his head to the side in the direction of our offender. I scanned the bar, and my eyes fell on Velina as she smiled and tried to look interested in whatever the blond fucker from the Brethren was talking about.

I wandered right up to the bar and looked over, her keen green eyes meeting mine. She raised her eyebrows almost imperceptibly, and I smirked.

She gave me what I could only call a warning look, and my smirk turned into a grin.

"You, uh, ever want a *real* man? Look me up," I told her – or something to that effect anyway. I handed her one of my cards.

Brazenly and never losing eye contact with me, she tore it up and threw it over me like a baptism in stupid.

"Thanks, but *no, thanks*," she said flatly and spun on her bar stool to turn back to her date.

I laughed and we took our drinks to our table while I fucking *seethed*. Not at Velina, but at the motherfucker she was with. His fuckin' *audacity* at being here, of all the fuckin' bars in the Quarter. His audacity at bringing *her* here. For all he knew, she was an innocent and not a part of the life at all. He damn sure didn't give a shit about her well-being, just about scoring another point in all this made-up bullshit drama against the Voodoo Bastards.

It chapped my ass, man. Enough that I couldn't help myself in staring them down the entire rest of the fuckin' time they were there.

When they finally got up and left, we watched them go, the juvenile with Velina reaching a hand back to flip our table the bird as they exited the building. Chainsaw and Axeman rose, chairs scraping, and I shook my head and barked, "Sit down, boys! Here ain't the time nor the place."

They sank back into their seats, and Chainsaw said, "I'm suddenly a lot less worried about *her* and how she's going to pull this off."

"Can't say I disagree with that sentiment," Axe said with a wolfish grin.

"Glad you two knuckleheads are so confident," I said, scowling.

"I wouldn't go *that* far," Chainsaw declared. "Just less worried than I was."

I nodded and tossed back the rest of my tequila, which turned to the bitter ash of damnation in my mouth.

I had it bad for Velina.

There was no denying that now – not when I wanted to rip that motherfucker's head off his shoulders and shit down his neck just for touching her back possessively to steer her out of the bar.

"Where 're you goin?" Chainsaw demanded when I stood up with some finality.

"Home," I said and he and Axe exchanged a look.

"For real home, or..." I looked back at them both, and Axe raised his eyebrows in a silent, *you good?*

"For real. Home," I said, and I went out into the revelry on Bourbon, dodging drunken partiers and heading for the bikes.

I got on mine and fished out my keys, sighing.

I didn't go home. I headed in that direction for Metairie but found myself taking the turn into the parking lot of the garish yellow building that housed the La Chiquita Motel.

I parked way in the back, up under the shadow of a pair of palm trees against the cinderblock wall, and sat on my bike for a while, thinking about nothing and everything all at once.

What if she brought him back here? What if he followed her up?

I'd kill him.

I'd have to.

I couldn't fathom him touching her like I did. I couldn't picture her moving underneath him the way she moved under me without this *incendiary rage* building until I felt like my ribs fucking cracked trying to contain it in my chest.

I lit a cigarette, drew in a lungful of rich tobacco smoke, and breathed it out through my nose – a dragon, lurking in the dark, standing watch over his treasure – but she wasn't here. At least, not yet.

I wondered briefly how long I would be waiting when I heard the distant roar of pipes.

I couldn't tell you how I knew it was them, I just did. Sure enough, the headlamp on his rig swept the lot, and he pulled in a smooth arc into one of the open spots in front of Velina's room. She hopped off the bike and handed him his helmet. He took it, leaning it against his hip.

I couldn't hear their discussion, but she was all smiles, and so was he. So whatever it was, it was lighthearted and not bad.

Why did that run across my soul like the business side of a fuckin' cheese grater?

I held still so as not to give away my position as he pulled her in and laid one on her, a kiss goodbye.

Fuck.

I felt my palms itch with the urge to fuckin' slap him.

Velina practically skipped to the fuckin' stairwell and took the stairs like a gazelle to the second floor, walking along and stopping against the railing to wave goodbye at the fuckstick as he backed out of his space – even going so far as to blow him a kiss as he put it in gear and took off back toward Veterans.

As soon as she was clear, her shoulders sagged, and she huffed a sigh out into the humid night air.

I got off my bike and went for the stairs on this end, taking them up to her floor two at a time.

She was just sliding her key card into the slot above the door handle when I crashed into her from behind, shoving her in through the door and kicking it shut behind us. I spun her in my arms, captured her chin in my hand, and forced her head up to accept my lips as they crashed into hers.

She made a little shout of fear, and it thrilled me, but not nearly as much as it did when she recognized who it was that had her and how she *melted* into my arms. Her tongue plunged into my mouth, and she kissed me back with every bit of passion I put behind my own lips. My hands smoothed over her clothed body, annoyed at the rough denim under them rather than the silky soft smooth feel of her skin.

"Saint!" she gasped my name, tearing her mouth from mine. "You scared the life out of me!"

"You should always have your key out and ready," I growled into her ear. "This could have been anyone."

"Noted," she said flatly. "But it isn't, and I'm glad you're here."

Her arms went around me, and I held her tight, lifting her, her legs automatically going around my hips as she clung to me, and I took her to the bed.

All conscious thought fled and wonder took its place as our clothes came off, our lips finding skin, and the kissing turned into a deeper exploration of one another.

By the time I nestled my shoulders between her thighs, holding her open for me, there was only one place left for me to kiss.

I slid a fingertip along her slit, her panting and moaning music to my ears. It was almost too easy how my middle finger slid up inside her, and I fucking *loved* how she arched against the bed for me, pressing her body down into my hand, eager for more.

I locked my lips around her clit, and teased the little kernel of flesh standing tight and erect with her pleasure with the tip of my tongue. She tasted sweeter than honey, rich with desire, and the way her hallowed green eyes looked down the length of her body into mine, framed by the peaks of her pert nipples, through the chasm of the valley of her breasts – fuck, I *burned* that shit into my memory.

She was like fluid fire, the way she moved, the way she burned against my palms and my tongue. I smoothed my hands over her silky skin, back and forth, up and down her beautiful curves. She was amazing. She was pure magic if you believed in such things.

I didn't. At least I hadn't... not until I'd held her in my arms. Not until she'd kissed me and bewitched me better than any hoodoo woman or swamp witch could.

I brought her, screaming, with my hand and my mouth, teasing the most intimate parts of hers, making her melt, making her mine, and it was a wonder that any woman as strong-willed and ornery as she was could submit so completely.

She did, though – beautifully.

She panted as I climbed her body with gentle presses of my lips, cock straining so hard I thought I was liable to split the skin. It was almost too sensitive as I slicked the head of my dick through her wetness against her soft velvet folds. It was even harder holding back when she looked at me with such perfect trust in her eyes to make her feel good.

"Please," she begged me quietly, her breath panting, her voice breathy, her arms twining around my neck and dragging my mouth to hers.

I kissed her deeply as I slipped inside her, and it was something else – something I had no words for. A sensation like no other. A feeling like I'd tasted something before, but not to this degree. The smell of some wonderful confection that you'd only ever just scented on the wind, and this was your first real taste of it.

It tasted like *home*. She felt like *home* to me. It was the only explanation I had for it. Like arriving at a comfortable destination, at once familiar and sweet after spending eons on the road, riding under a hot sun, the grit of sand scouring your exposed skin.

Sliding into her was *soothing* in a way I just didn't have any words for.

It hit me that I wasn't *jealous* that she'd been with that fucker – no, I'd been *scared* for her. I hated the thought of any harm coming to her – more than she'd already endured – which, by the judge of it, had been a lot.

I held onto her, moved inside her with care, and kissed her carefully. Drawing back, her eyes fluttered open, and there was a hidden question in their depths. One I tried my best to answer with actions, not words.

I was sure she'd been paid enough lip service for one night. I wasn't about to pay her anymore. No, I would *show her* instead.

I would show her all night if that's what it took.

CHAPTER TWENTY-TWO

Velina...

I lay against Saint's side, my head on his chest, listening to his heartbeat. My fingers absently played with a curl of his long hair as I stared into space in what could only be described as a blissed-out coma but for the thoughts twisting and spiraling in my head.

"Make it make sense," I whispered, and he jolted slightly underneath me, as though he'd been on the verge of sleep. He traced blunt fingertips, rough with the trade work he did, along my back, and I shivered with delight at the careful touch.

"Make what make sense, baby?" he asked me, and I couldn't help the faint smile that graced my lips. I liked the way that sounded when he was referring to me... *baby*...

"Tell me again how all of this started," I said.

He sighed, kissed my forehead, and said, "We honestly don't rightly know. It all sort of started when they started gathering numbers. We didn't care. They can do what they want – just not inside the city limits. That's our territory."

"Okay," I said carefully, tone neutral and vague.

"Then they started fuckin' with Cypress. Like *really* fuckin' with him, out there in the swamps. He's a gator fisherman by trade. Whole family is from his daddy to his grandpappy to his great-grandpappy before him. Hell, probably even before that, if we're honest. The Gaudet family can trace their lineage all the way back to the original trappers who settled this area when it was still being discovered." I smiled as his hands went up, and he put air quotes around "discovered."

"Cy comes in and he and his daddy find out someone's been poaching their lines. That's big money out this way and just something you don't fuckin' do. Spits on just about any code of honor an Acadian has. Come to find out, it's these Bayou Bitches poaching the lines and trying to declare turf war on us when all Cy and his daddy was doing was fishing their family lands and swamps the way they done since time immemorial."

"Okay," I said quietly. "Then what?"

"Then we hear they're setting up shop out at this place called Swamp Daddy's, just inside the New Orleans city limits. So, we got an issue with that – obviously. We had some business to take care of in the city lockup, so we decided hell, we might as well kill two birds with one stone and went out there and started some shit. Harmless shit, you know? 'Get the fuck outta our town,' some crash, bang, boom – a couple punches, a few broken bottles, and a bar fight later, we figure they got the message. Right?"

"Right," I said, snuggling a little closer as the air conditioning kicked on in here.

Saint held me tighter and rubbed up and down my back, the other hand idly tracing fingertips up and down my arm, tickling a line from elbow to wrist, all the way up the back of my hand along the back of my middle finger to the very tip and back down. Over and over, making me melt.

"Anyway, they kept beefing with Cypress out there in the swamp, but then they really fucked up. They went after him at home, except it wasn't technically *his* home. He lived there alright, but he lived there with his sister Jessie-Lou and his nephew Tate. They bit off more than they could chew with Jessie-Lou."

I laughed at his unintentional rhyme.

"Still, in the end, one of them got themselves perished, and they did but fuckin' great at pissing us the fuck off to the point we needed to send a bigger message."

"So, what happened then?"

"Well, we had beef with Swamp Daddy's at that point because they wouldn't back the fuck down on letting the Bayou boys in and even went so far as to side with them and ban our boys for life over that little tiff with Cy's poachers. So, we took care of it."

"Define, *took care of it.*"

"A bigger boom, when no one was there. No more Swamp Daddy's, no more problem."

"*Jesus,*" I said. "You guys!"

He shrugged underneath me a bit. "No one got physically hurt," he reasoned, and I just tried to get my head around it.

"Still, you blew it up."

"Yup."

"The whole thing."

"Yup. Five-alarm blaze."

"That's unhinged," I argued.

He didn't disagree, just said with a straight face, "Yup."

Mind. Boggled.

He cracked a smile and chuckled at the expression on my face.

"And that was worth shooting up your clubhouse in retaliation?" I asked softly.

"Yeah," he said and didn't sound at all happy – which, why would he be? Louie was gone, and for what?

"We figure they're big mad over Jessie-Lou taking out their little wrecking crew sent to beat down her brother, but legit, she was just defending herself and her son. So, what is there to get pissed off for?"

"They're like some diabolical super villain group out of a comic book series," I agreed, and he huffed a laugh.

"Best description if I've ever heard one."

"And no one knows what got them so hard for you guys in the first place?" I asked.

"The only way I can figure it, it's all about the power. We just had a sort of blowout not long ago in and among ourselves." He swallowed hard. "A restructuring of the club, so-to-speak. These boys whipped up fast and outta nowhere. I guess they thought the blood in the water was some sort of chum, and the fuckin' bottom feeder sharks that they are, they saw an easy meal."

"Louie told me some things about that," I said softly.

"Oh, yeah?" he asked, and the way he almost imperceptibly tensed beneath me, I knew I was telling him something he wanted to hear.

"Again, your secrets are safe with me," I said softly. "We're on the same team."

He massaged up and down my back, thinking on it quietly, and finally said, "I like the sound of that – and you're right. I'm on your side, so I need you to listen to me." He tipped my chin gently to make me look up at him and locked eyes with mine.

"Whatever Louie told you, whatever you might hear when you're with me or around the club – when it comes to the cops and shit? *No, you didn't*, you get me?"

I nodded. "I have no idea what you're talking about."

He smiled then.

"Good girl."

I laughed at that, and I admit, it was a bit nervously because, after all, that did things to me. Entirely too many things, too many feelings, and all of them ones that I *liked*.

"What'd ol' Louie tell you?"

"That the club had mutinied on the old president, and for good reason. That you all performed a sort of coup because the old president was out of his mind and playing entirely too fast and loose with things, dragging all of you into a hell of a mess of legal trouble and deeper into illegal things."

"That was part of it," he agreed carefully.

"He also said that he was being a greedy fucker, keeping the lion's share of things for himself and letting none of it trickle down through the rest of the club."

"That was another big one," he said. "Probably the biggest."

"He said you all had big dreams of a better life. One that was less risk, more reward."

Saint nodded carefully.

"We did what we did to get what we wanted," he said. "The

biggest problem being, Ruth was getting everything that *he* wanted and then some – the rest of us not so much. We were supposed to be brothers, and he talked a good game to that end, but he never *showed* it. Not once. He was living high off the hog while the rest of us struggled. Lost a home, lost a parent to some stupid shit, if only their meds could be afforded. Ruthless didn't treat us like brothers. He treated us like peasants fighting for scraps from his table."

"Louie said something to that effect, too. Said he saw it. How Ruth treated the club like his mom treated him. With family like that, who needs enemies?"

Saint grunted.

"Something had to give. It wasn't what we were supposed to be about. He was adding motherfuckers to our ranks willy-nilly and ignoring the bylaws about it having to be a *unanimous vote*. It was bullshit, but he didn't care. All he cared about was loyalty – and by loyalty, he meant us putting our asses on the line to face prison time while he hid behind the curtain, the great and powerful Wizard of—"

"Fraud," I said. "Oz was nothing but a huckster – a fraud."

"That's right," he said.

"So, the distillery, the gift shop, they're not just to launder money?" I asked.

He chuckled.

"No, they're to *make* money. Clean money from the word go."

"And the other things you do?" I asked.

"What is it you think we do?" he asked.

"That, Louie would never say… just *things*. I imagine anything from drugs and guns to human trafficking and protection rackets."

"Truth between us?" he asked.

"I thought we were doing pretty good with it. Why stop now?" I asked.

He chuckled and said, "Fuckin' touché *again*."

I giggled and stared up at him, patiently waiting him out while he made up his mind.

"Some of those things, yes, but definitely not *all* of them. The Russians were a big problem with human trafficking around these parts, and we helped nip that one in the bud, and all agreed – *fuck that shit.*"

"That's a relief and definitely good to know," I murmured.

"We do some other… imports and exports, but mostly it's the absolute latter. Some places around here pay us handsomely to keep the peace, so-to-speak."

"That's wild."

"That's the life, sometimes…"

"And now you want to give it all up?"

"No," he said. "We just would really like to scale back. Ain't none of us getting any younger."

"No, I suppose not," I agreed.

We were quiet for a time, laying with each other, just touching and thinking. Lost inside our own heads for a bit.

"You're awfully quiet," he murmured a time later.

"It's a lot of food for thought," I whispered.

"It is," he agreed.

"So, I guess now is a good time to say that I'm still here, I'm still in, and that I'm supposed to accompany Carver to a cookout in the swamp on my next Sunday to me."

"Sunday to you?"

"Yeah, I don't get Sundays off, but I get two days off in a row, so *my* Sunday." I rolled my eyes. "Try to keep up."

He laughed, shook his head slightly and growled out, "Watch the attitude, baby. I'll fuck it right out of you."

I grinned. "Don't threaten me with a good time."

He sat up, gripping my upper arms and thrusting me down, back flat to the mattress, his mouth crushing back down over mine.

My heart raced and started to soar – because, Lord, this man was intoxicating. The only man I'd ever met who could make me drunk off pleasure alone.

CHAPTER TWENTY-THREE

S aint...

I lay with her in the dark, her body snug and warm against mine, and I couldn't stop myself from caressing her smooth skin. Up and down her back, her arm, over her hip, the round globe of her ass... she was perfection. Her body tight from work and regular exercising, but not a gym rat. She didn't strike me as a gym rat. More a hiker, a nature buff. I liked that about her.

I liked a lot of things about her – her feisty attitude, her loyalty, her steadfast conviction. She was perfect, but whether she was perfect for me or not was irrelevant. I wondered if I was perfect for *her.*

It was a weird thought. I didn't think like that about anyone. I didn't fuckin' *care.* Until now... I guess that meant something.

Not sure what – okay, that was a lie. I knew exactly what it meant. It meant she was the one.

I knew it down to my fuckin' bones. The Bayou Baroness knew it and had all but said as much. The ride I was on with Velina was the wildest I'd ever taken, and I couldn't help but think or feel like it was also the ride with the highest fuckin' stakes that I'd ever taken in my fuckin' life.

I didn't sleep. I couldn't. My thoughts were wide-ranging and fuckin' wild, and I didn't know what to do with them except think them through and wait for my lady to stir.

She was down for the count. Well-fucked, and I held a silent pride in the fact that I'd been the one to satisfy her so completely.

The sun was up, and it was creeping in toward late morning when her breathing lost its steady cadence, and she sucked in a sharp breath. She grew taut beside me, stretching like a cat and shuddering with her muscle tension in this adorable way that had me fuckin' smitten all over again.

"Morning, kitten," I murmured, and she made a face.

"Bleh, coffee first, then pet names."

I rumbled a laugh and gave her a little squeeze, and she cuddled back up to me. I absently kissed the top of her head, and she melted into me.

Perfect.

"So, what's on your agenda today?" she asked.

"I slept like shit last night," I told her honestly. "Probably go back to my place, get a shower, fix something to eat, and try to get some real shut-eye. What about you?"

"No plans," she said quietly.

"Come with me," I said spur of the moment. "I'm only a few blocks away from your hotel."

"Yeah?" she asked. "I thought it was farther – took you forever to get to the café."

I chuckled. "I was being an asshole."

"Figures," she said with a sigh and without surprise. "Yeah, I'm down," she said, finally pushing off me. "Let me grab a shower and get dressed."

"Sounds good," I said.

One of the things I loved about her was that she didn't keep me waiting. She took a five-to-ten-minute what I liked to call a *tactical shower*. Washing up the necessities with speed without lingering. She dried off just as efficiently, dressed and pulled her hair up into a clip without bothering to dry it.

I wasn't even dressed all the way before the shower shut off, and I wasn't even halfway through my first cigarette of the morning when she came back into the borrowed room we'd landed in at Cy's borrowed pad.

"You ready?" she asked me.

"Whenever you are," I said, straightening up.

I had some shit back at my place that I thought she might like. Photos and shit like that. I figured she could look through 'em all while I fixed us something to eat.

I went out to my bike first, scanning the street and over the bayou, looking for trouble. We were technically in Bayou Brethren territory, and it never hurt to check. Seeing nothing and no one, I called out to her to come on out. We rode back over to my place, and I pulled us into the garage, the door trundling closed behind us and closing us in.

"Never pictured you for living in a small house in fucking *suburbia*," she said with her special brand of sarcasm, dismounting the bike.

"It was my mom's house before it was mine," I said. "Same house I grew up in."

"It's in really good shape," she said, impressed.

"Yeah, well, you saw LaCroix's place – the one out on the barge. He built that shit mostly by himself, and Hex *did* build his place and Bennie's. We got some talented guys."

"Never said otherwise," she said with a smile. It was a genuine and kind thing, full of a soft pride.

"Louie was getting good at helping out," I said. "Really took a shine to learning all sorts of things. Got good with his hands. Was always eager to help."

"He seemed like a good soul," she said, and she looked tired, sad.

"Yeah, well, it's part of why I wanted to bring you here," I said, heaving myself off my bike's seat. "C'mon."

I led her into the kitchen off the garage and told her to sit at the kitchen counter. She did as I asked beautifully, and I wondered at that. She was so obedient with me when it was just us like this. She was definitely the same vein of deviant in the bedroom that I was. Seemed to delight in ceding control as much as I delighted in taking it.

She hopped up on one of the stools at the kitchen island, and I went into my small den, hanging my cut off the back of the chair in there and sliding a box off the top of one of the bookshelves. I plucked a couple of thick albums off the shelf below it and headed back into the kitchen with both.

"I never really liked digital photos. I take 'em, sure – who doesn't? But I found this app that allows you to get something like eighty-five free prints per month and all you have to do is pay like ten bucks or less for shipping. The photos are actually decent quality, and they print the coordinates and shit right on the back of where and when and what time the picture was taken – all that shit. So, I started using it and keeping these."

I set the box in front of her and the album beside it.

"These are newer," I said, flipping off the lid of the box. "These are older," I said, tapping the albums. "Knock yourself out."

"Is Louie in here?" she asked.

"All through 'em, I'm sure. Lots of his story in there. You want to know, just ask. I'm going to fix us something to eat."

She stared at the photo on the top of the box and looked up at me.

"Thanks," she barely breathed as if it was hard for her to draw breath around the emotion swelling in her breast to get the word out.

I leaned down and kissed her, a hard smack of lips.

"Don't mention it," I told her.

She started sorting through the pictures, carefully lifting each one out of the box and studying it before laying it face down beside it.

"Where was this?" she asked, holding up a picture of me standing with Marlin and Cutter of the Kraken out there in sunny Ft. Royal, Florida.

"Those are some buddies of ours out there in Florida on the Gulf side. They came on out this way to handle some business and we struck up a friendship a few years back. They did things the right way."

I told her about how the Kraken had called up to let us know they were gonna be in our territory. How they'd put some respect on our name and how we'd been more than willing to extend our hospitality. That was how shit was *supposed* to work. Respect. Respect was everything in this life. The only currency worth a damn and in the absence of respect, fear would fuckin' do.

"They had a problem that just so happened to coincide with a problem we were havin' – well, not a *problem* per se, but it was still a sort of enemy of my enemy kind of a thing," I said as I ran a knife through a bundle of fresh basil from the fridge.

Velina rolled her eyes. "Gee, where have I heard *that one* before?"

I chuckled and set to work smashing and peeling some garlic.

The recipe wasn't anything super fancy, just your basic pasta sauce loaded with garlic and fresh basil – all of it from scratch. Easy peasy for an Italian boy like me.

"Oh, wow." She lingered on a photograph and smiled reverently at it. I peeked over the top at one of Louie's smiling face, standing with a beer in one hand, his other lifted in a bicep curl.

"That's a good one," I said.

"It really is," she agreed.

"Set it aside. You should keep it."

"Really?" she asked.

"Yeah. We'll get you an album and some frames just for Louie."

"I'd hit the thrift store for that project," she said.

I smiled and mixed and stirred, waiting patiently for things to start to bubble and simmer on the stove.

"I don't recognize these guys. They must be from before."

She slid a photo across to me, and I tapped the chunky one in the middle.

"That's Ruthless. He mostly liked to be called Baby Ruth," I said.

"Like the candy bar?" I asked.

I chuckled darkly. "Like he used to take a Louisville Slugger to some kneecaps, and he thought it was funny to be known as the Babe Ruth of bikers."

"Eee." She made a face. "He really was ruthless."

"He never let a motherfucker forget it, either," I said quietly.

I'd been one of the guys to dispatch him out there in the swamp. Four of us had shot him all to hell and gone and left him for the gators. Body was never found – which is how we liked it. Wasn't unusual around these parts. Oeople disappeared into the swamps all the time.

She studied his picture and went through several more in the box.

"What's wrong with his eye?" she asked.

"He was blind in it."

"Really?" she asked. "I thought you couldn't ride if you were blind in one eye."

"You're not supposed to, but it's possible. He was legally blind in it, but he could sort of see out of it – enough that he kept riding. He compensated for it. You can."

"I didn't know that," she said. "I thought the government just wouldn't give you the endorsement or whatever."

I laughed. "Darlin', who the fuck *cares* what the government has to say? Ye haw, fuck the law," I reminded her.

She laughed then and shook her head.

"Irreverent much?" she asked.

I shrugged, and she continued to go through photos, studying them and asking about brothers past who were gone. Either died or, in one or two cases, left the club. It was rare, but it *did* happen.

Some were put out, *out bad,* and that was a whole other rabbit hole or warren of conversation.

We looked through photos, ate the decadent pasta lunch I'd fixed, and eventually found ourselves back in the bedroom – which I didn't mind. I rather liked having Velina in my bed.

I slept, she watched some television, and eventually, when I woke late that night, she was gone – a note left on the nightstand on the side of the bed she'd occupied.

Didn't want to wake you. Carver's picking me up on the early side on Friday morning – which is my Sunday. I have to catch up on laundry and other shit on my Saturday. I'm walking back to the hotel.

Miss you already.

Yeah, okay, that was weird to say. Sappy and weird. Sorry.

Later,

v

I dug the sappy and weird, because honestly?
Same.

CHAPTER TWENTY-FOUR

Velina...

I'd gotten through my work week and hadn't gotten to see Saint since our little tryst the week before. He had to work, and our schedules were at odds. It was what it was.

Carver had picked me up bright and early, as promised... well, early for *him*, I imagine, as the hour was still in the single digits – if barely when he'd shown up.

"So, who all is supposed to be there!" I called out at one of the final stop lights before we hit the open freeway out to wherever it was that we were going.

"Everybody!" Carver called back as the light changed, and he twisted down on the throttle to take the on-ramp. I held on, the wind hot but still cooler than the stagnancy of being still.

I smiled in spite of myself. While I definitely preferred riding with Saint, I found myself loving riding more and more just for the sake of riding. It was a thrill, the wind and the environment whipping past and underneath us. I think it may very well be one of the closest things that you could get to flying.

I held on to Carver with my knees, flung my arms out and my head back, and just *soared* over the open road, knowing that this was very likely going to be the highlight of my day.

Lord knows Saint had left me deliciously sore between my legs, sore enough and satisfied enough that I wouldn't be interested in sex for a while. I felt fine now, but for the first couple days back to work, I had to think of him with every step I took.

I was hoping to avoid having to do Carver, hoping it was still early enough yet that he wouldn't press it, which I just didn't know. Depending on how things went today, Carver may expect it.

I would have to think fast if it came up.

He'd already greeted me with an enthusiastic hug that was more about feeling me up and a kiss that crammed his tongue practically to my tonsils. Yeah, it was par for the course, but after spending the time with Saint that I had? Talk about a major turn-off.

I let the wind carry all that bullshit off me and left it behind in the city. Peeling out of my life as Velina to leave Louie shiny and new at my surface. Slipping skins and changing personalities and headspaces as thoroughly as I could before we reached our destination.

I had no idea where we were going. Just out in the swamp along some lake or bayou somewhere. To some property owned by Rebel, the chapter president.

I'd asked about that the day before with Saint, trying to make sense of the rank and file. He said he didn't understand what I was saying when I said that Rebel was apparently just the chapter president and that there was a bigger dog or club president above him. He said the only way he'd traditionally heard of that happening was if there were multiple chapters to a club. That some of the bigger clubs had chapter presidents, but that the original chapter's president sort of acted as a de facto *club* president to the whole lot – but that was only with big charters.

Charters like the Sacred Hearts.

Small outfits of one-chapter clubs like the Voodoo Bastards or the Bayou Brethren only had a chapter president who was also the club's president.

It was news to him that there was some other big cheese in the picture and it seemed to rankle him. It certainly ruffled his feathers enough to send off a text to LaCroix and to Hex.

When Carver and I pulled up at the spot that was supposed to be the big meet or whatever, I was low-key shocked at how many bikes were parked in the grass leading down to the lake.

"I thought it was club only," I said, and Carver grinned at me as he reached out to help me with the D-ring buckle holding his helmet onto my head. It wasn't easy, like a trident clip, to get on and off.

"We're bigger 'n you think," he said.

"Clearly," I agreed, mollified.

"Getting bigger every day," he said. "Just stick with me or with Singer and Midnight. It's all good, baby."

I was relieved to hear at least two familiar names of the feminine persuasion.

Of course, Sativa was there and loud as ever. There were a lot more unfamiliar faces than there were familiar, and it wasn't long before Carver was pulled away, leaving me with Singer and Midnight and a bevy of other girls.

"Wow, this is quite a crowd!" I cried, hugging Singer to me. She seemed really happy to see me.

"Come grab a beer, honey! Sit with us," Midnight urged. "Ignore them other bitches. They're just club sluts 'n hanger ons."

A redhead gave a dirty look over her shoulder, and Midnight snapped at her, "Don't look at me in that tone of voice!"

The redhead tossed her hair down her back and turned back around quickly, and Midnight shook her head.

"You better watch your man," she said to me. "These bitches are hungry, thirsty, and everything in between."

"Oh, I'm not worried," I said, laughing. "I don't know that things are *that* serious," I murmured, and Singer put a hand on my arm, looking worried.

"Don't let anyone hear you say that too loud," she said. "They'll think you're fair game, and trust me. You don't want that."

I blinked and glanced from her to Midnight, who nodded.

"She's right, honey. Any brother asks, you belong to Carver."

"Okay..." I drawled and took the beer that Midnight held out, taking a drink of the foam that tried to escape the neck of the bottle and shaking some off the back of my hand that'd managed its jailbreak successfully.

"So, who is everyone?" I asked Singer, and she smiled.

"Well, that one there is my man, Basilisk," she said, pointing and I smiled.

"Oh yeah?" He had been at the bar the night we'd met; I just hadn't talked to him.

"Yeah." She smiled fondly, but it held an edge of something. It was... brittle... and it sent up a red warning flare to my mind.

Trouble in paradise, I thought, and it wasn't a question.

There were at least seventeen fully patched brothers, with a few more yet to attend. Beyond that, the club had something like six prospects. Six. Which according to Saint and his rundown of how things were *supposed* to work the day before, was a wildly unprecedented number to have.

One to three was usually the norm.

Then there were the guys wandering around in hang-around gear, and there were *a lot* more than just a few of those, too. Probably something like twenty more.

Add all of the scantily clad women – some of whom definitely looked like fucking crackwhores and more than a few women with wild and feral children running underfoot, shooting at everyone with super soakers, and the gathering was barely controlled chaos and mayhem.

"Which one is Lazarus?" I asked, craning my neck and looking around. "Isn't he supposed to be here?"

"Oh, he's here. He's in the house with Rebel talkin' club business. Don't you worry. The *king* will be out before long." I was low-key surprised at the contempt in Midnight's tone.

"You don't like him?" I asked.

"Doesn't matter what I do and do not like, darlin' – just matters that I lie back and spread my legs when Rebel wants it."

Okay, once again, trouble in paradise, I mused silently.

"You need to vent, I'm here to listen," I offered, and Midnight sniffed, her eyes watering, and waved me and Singer both off.

"Reb's just being a special kind of asshole, lately," she complained.

"I'm sorry," I said lamely, for lack of anything better to say.

"It's all good," she said. "He ain't gonna listen to nobody but Laz, and I can't help but worry. They're fixin' to find out."

"Let's hope not," Singer said, and I smiled at her.

She was in a pink bikini top that was barely a set of strings and two triangles that barely covered her nipples. You could see the strings of a matching pair of g-string bottoms poking out over the low-cut rise of her acid-washed short cutoff shorts, with the rhinestone embellishments in the shape of the fleur-de-lis on the back pockets.

The whole outfit was topped off, or would that be bottomed out, by a pair of gladiator sparkly white stripper platform heels.

"What you talking about, Stripper Barbie?" Sativa demanded, flouncing into the conversation like she was somehow above Midnight, which just made Midnight grit her teeth and look away from the fat *actual* stripper.

Singer laughed and said, "I'm a stripper just like you, but I ain't got the tits to be Barbie."

"Girl, what 'choo talkin' about you a *stripper just like me?*" Sativa demanded, putting a shitty whiny pedantic accent on the "just like me" part, implying Singer was some kind of whiny cunt – which, *whoa*, talk about out of bounds! Singer was as sweet as could be and didn't start shit with nobody.

"There ain't nobody like me!" I perked up in my seat by Midnight as Sativa advanced on Singer. I was about to open my mouth when Midnight held out a hand in front of me and gave me a stern and silent look to keep my mouth shut.

"I didn't mean nothin' by it," Singer quailed, and her face just dropped. It made me angrier on her behalf.

"You got somethin' to say?" I *did* perk up then, dragging my eyes from Singer back to Sativa, who had rounded on me.

"Plenty," I said, and I left it at that.

"Whatever, *Consuela*," she sneered. Good to know she was a racist piece of shit on top of being just, well, a general piece of shit. "You think you better than us even though you scrub toilets for a living?" She rolled her eyes, which were green today from the contact lenses she wore, and she tossed her fake-ass purple braids over her shoulder. I rolled mine right back.

I swear to God, someone needed to take her down a notch, and if she wanted that person to be me – so be it.

"Feelin' froggy, just fuckin' jump already," I said, staring her down and standing my ground.

Midnight cackled beside me and clapped.

"And *that*'s what makes her ol' lady material while you're just another fuckin' slut of a club girl. Get you fuckin' gone, *tramp*!"

Sativa stared at Midnight aghast.

"Prospect!" Midnight crowed, and one came jogging up.

"Get her outta my sight," she demanded, and the nameless prospect took Sativa by the arm and hauled her away. One of the brothers stopped him and asked something while Sativa dissolved into tears, and the prospect pointed back our way.

"Say somethin'!" Midnight called. "I dare yah!"

The brother made a face, took Sativa under his wing, and led her further away.

"Thanks, y'all," Singer said, dropping into a camp chair on the other side of me from Midnight.

"Pfft! Don't take her shit," Midnight declared. "You could learn a thing or two from ol' Louie here."

"I ain't never had someone stand up for me like that before," she said, and the look on her face as she looked at me? It broke my heart.

"You don't need anyone to stand up for you, girl. Y' need to stand up for yourself," Midnight declared and took a drink of her beer.

"I hate to say it, but there's definitely something to what Midnight is saying," I said. "There are times no one will be there to stand up for you, and the only person you have to stand up for you is yourself."

"Spoken like a bitch who's lived it," Midnight said.

"I grew up with three siblings, a drunk for a dad, and a pushover of a mom," I said with a shrug. "It was me against the world."

I took a drink off my own beer, and Carver wandered over a little while later. "Boy, I'm impressed," he said. "Not many can make *Sativa* cry." He grinned at me, and I shrugged.

"Bitch deserved it," I said.

"Ain't nobody can stand her ass," Midnight agreed.

"Told you, you'd fit right in," Carver said with a wink and I grinned.

The food was good, and the music, when it got going, was amazing. A live band made up of locals playing zydeco late into the night. Rebel never did appear, nor did the mysterious Lazarus, and I was frustrated by that.

I knew that Saint was curious about the Bayou Brethren's structure, and by default, that made *me* curious. I wanted to know what made this Lazarus guy so special.

Carver was getting friendlier and friendlier as the day and then eventual night wore on, and the liquor flowed. He wasn't quite *drunk*, but he had certainly imbibed too much to be good to ride for the next good bit.

We danced under the bare bulbs strung between trees as the band played on a raised dais of plywood over pallets. The dance floor was likewise – plywood duct-taped together and just laid on the dry and brittle grass and silty fine dirt – and a cloud kicked up and poofed out from around the dance floor edges as the plywood flexed.

I spun under Carver's arm, and he pulled me in, a hand to my ass. I knew, heart sinking, that the jig was up and that he would be expecting some tonight.

I would try to dodge with the excuse that I was on my period and that I didn't fuck while I was on the rag – which was true. I didn't. Loathed it, in fact. Just never could get down with the mess or the smell like old iron and pennies left to rot in an old tin can.

Bleh.

"How about you and I find someplace just to ourselves?" he whispered in my ear.

I chuckled and said back, "I wish." *I didn't. I really didn't.* "But I'm on the rag, and I just *can't* while I am."

"I don't mind," he said with a wolfish grin. I smiled back and tried to look apologetic.

"*I* do," I said. He dropped it, and there it was…

"You got a mouth. How about you take care of your man. I'll get you later, baby. I promise."

Fuck.

Did I want to? No. Did I want to blow my cover? Hell no. If there was a lesser of two evils when it came to blowing, I would blow him – but *fuck.*

Talk about taking one for the fucking team, I thought to myself. Though I wanted to grind my teeth, I didn't want to risk giving my true feelings away. Instead, I plastered on an uncomfortable grin and said, "Sure."

He chuckled low in my ear, kissed my temple, and said, "You really are a dream come true, you know?"

"I'm the best, alright," I said, rolling my eyes. He laughed and practically hauled me off the dance floor double-time.

Shit.

We kissed, stopping and starting in our beeline across the lawn to "work each other up" although I'm telling you – I was straight faking it until I made it here.

I don't want to do this, I don't want to do this, I don't want to do this, repeating over and over in my head as the kissing got hotter, the petting got heavier, and at the same time... at the same time, I had to know. I had this morbid need to know, a fascination, a need to...

I swiped my hand over the front of Carver's jeans and felt him hard and ready through them, and yep, nope, he was thick, maybe, but he was nowhere near Saint's length.

Why am I not surprised? I thought to myself.

"Where should we go?" I whispered the question against his mouth.

"Porch, there's a couch in the shadows, that end." He jerked his head, and I nodded and we went that way.

The couch was right up by the front door, and technically, only half of it was in shadow, the end of the couch furthest from the door – but it was blessedly unoccupied. Carver dropped down onto it, and hey, at least he was nice enough to throw one of the cushions onto the ground between his feet for me to kneel on.

Fuck me, I thought. *Fuck me. Suck it up.* My hands went automatically to his belt, fingers stiff and numb with how much I didn't want to do this, but there was no going back now.

I was painted into a corner, and I knew it.

"What if someone sees?" I tried, and he grinned at me, teeth white in the dark. Almost like the Cheshire cat – just a toothy grin, nothing else.

"Let 'em," he said, and he brought himself out of his pants.

He wasn't long, but he was uncomfortably thick.

Suck it up, Louise, I thought and intrepidly, I went down on him.

Loathing crept up my throat from the pit of my stomach with the bitter tang of bile, and I told myself repeatedly, *You will not throw up. You will not throw up. You will not throw up.*

I did it. I did what needed doing, even though I felt sick about it. I gagged more than a few times, but I got the job done. I would be damned if I would swallow. Instead, I pulled myself to the railing, spit, and quietly tried my damnedest to keep from retching.

It was as I turned back, Carver tucking himself away with satisfaction into his pants, that the front door opened, and Rebel stepped out, and then another man behind him. I felt myself pale as the light caught the side of a familiar face, albeit one I'd only ever seen in photographs.

His face was scarred and pitted on one side, the eye he'd been blind in gone for good, and the majority of the scarring hidden by a leather patch.

"Well, well, well," Baby Ruthless said. "What do we have here? Y'all having yourselves a little fun?"

I stared up, aghast, and Carver laughed. "Just finished, actually."

"Well, ain't that nice?" Ruth said, and he turned to follow Rebel down the front porch steps, lighting up a cigar clenched between his teeth. In the glow of his lighter, I read his name flash on the front of his leather cut. *LAZARUS* picked out against the dirty white background in hunter-green thread.

Son of a bitch…

CHAPTER TWENTY-FIVE

S aint...
The pounding on my front door was insistent, and the way it went on said that it was likely the fucking cops. Wouldn't have been the first time.

"Alright, alright, alright!" I barked, my head throbbing in time with each *whump* against the wood. It wasn't until I was throwing back the locks that I heard the weeping.

I ripped open the door, and Velina threw herself into my arms.

I didn't hesitate. I swept her into the foyer and looked outside to make sure nothing was trying to come up on her heels. There was nothing and no one out on the darkened street.

"Baby, what's wrong? What's happened?" I demanded.

"I'm gonna be sick!" she cried, and I thrust her into the half bath off the front hallway, where she went to her knees in front of the toilet and let loose.

I kneeled beside her, my knees crackling with my damnably getting older and rough treatment of my body, as I smoothed back her hair and let her hurl.

"What's up, baby girl?" I asked soothingly, smoothing a hand over and over her hair.

"I came as soon as I could," she said between dry heaves, and I continued to sooth her.

"Shhh, shhh, easy now, just breathe. Go on now, deep breaths, baby." I flipped on the cold water and pulled the hand towel out of the ring into the sink's bowl to wet it.

She reached out, still retching, but nothing coming up, she depressed the lever on the toilet. The thing flushed, the water swirled, dragging down her sick with it into the rest of the sewage and muck unseen.

"Slow down, take it easy," I said, pushing to my feet to ring out the towel. I got back down on my knees for her and pressed the cold cloth to the back of her neck, blotting the sides of her face, her mouth – I somehow didn't think this was food poisoning or even some kind of a stomach bug.

If I had to guess…

"I had to blow him. I'm so sorry," she blurted, and looked like she was going to be sick again.

"Well, if this is how you react, I promise to never make you blow me," I said.

"Fuck you," she moaned into the toilet, spitting again, but she was wheezing out a laugh.

"Not why I'm here. Definitely why I'm sick," she said.

"Fair," I said. "Why *are* you here?" I asked. "They moving on us?"

"Yes – I mean, no – I mean, I don't know what was discussed. I'm here because *who*." She heaved again and wasn't making much sense, but I waited her visceral reactions out.

She was one of those ones who once she started heaving, it was hard to make it stop.

I thought about that, and it put me on my ass a bit.

This woman cleaned up dead bodies and some of the foulest shit you'd ever fuckin' heard of in your fuckin' life and didn't bat an eye. Yet one blowjob later, she was here heaving her fuckin' guts out like it was the most disgusting thing she'd ever encountered in her life.

She was emotional. A total wreck… *shit*. She hadn't even fuckin' cried this hard or this much when she'd found out her brother was *dead*.

She was trying to get whatever it was out, but suddenly, it didn't fuckin' matter. None of it did. The only thing that mattered to me was that she wasn't alright, and I would do anything, and I do mean *anything*, to calm her down and make whatever it was okay again for her.

I sat on the floor of the john, gathered her up into my lap, and held her tight while she tried to get herself together when she finally choked out her story. About the fuckstick she was with ignoring her boundaries and telling her she had a mouth, about the blowjob on the front porch, and finally, about Ruthless.

"You're sure?" I asked.

"Absolutely," she said. "His face is all fucked up on the one side with the bad eye. He has an eyepatch there now."

"Jesus Christ," I muttered. Of course it would be fucked up. One of our bullets caught him in the fuckin' face.

"You guys were right," she said. "It's personal. He's coming for you. I don't know what they have planned next, but they were in that house all fucking day."

She shuddered in my grasp and clung to me. She had a right to be scared.

"I've gotta call LaCroix and Hex," I told her.

"Do it," she said. "I came as soon as I could, as soon as he dropped me off. I made sure he was gone, and I walked here. I don't think I was followed, but you really never can tell. Y'all motherfuckers are slicker than owl shit," she complained, and I barked a bitter laugh at that one.

"I've got to grab my phone," I said, and she nodded and drew back from me. "You're staying here tonight. Call in tomorrow. You're sick." I stared her down, and she nodded at that too. I'd half expected her to argue with me, but she didn't.

I grabbed my phone and shot a text that I would call as soon as I got Velina into my shower. I went back to her, stuffing my phone into my back pocket, and reached a hand down, hoisting her up onto her feet.

"Come on." I led her to the master bath off my bedroom and started the shower for her.

"Oh, my God, I love you," she said weakly, and I smiled. I knew she probably didn't mean it like that, but it was nice to hear anyway.

"C'mere, baby. I've got you," I said, and I helped her out of her clothes a little at a time, going slow and making sure she was alright every step of the way.

Once she was safely ensconced within the glass shower doors and soaking under the hot water with every bit of soap and shampoo and whatever else she could get into at her fingertips, I told her I'd be right out in the bedroom and to take her time.

I slipped out and called Hex first because he was the brains of this outfit and would be the one to figure out or know what to do when it came down to the nitty-gritty.

"What the hell is going on, now?" he answered by way of greeting.

"Velina says she saw Ruthless," I told him.

"How?" he demanded. "How can she be sure?"

"Let her go through some old photos of mine looking for her brother. She saw some of Ruth and had a whole damn chat about him."

Silence on the other end of the line.

"Hex?"

"Bring her to the clubhouse," he said finally judiciously.

"Nah," I said. "You wanna do this, you an' LaCroix come here. She took one for the team tonight in a big way. She's not fit to head anywhere."

"What do you mean, 'took one for the team?'" Hex demanded.

I told him. He was silent for a short time and finally said, "LaCroix's at Alina's apartment. I'll swing by and collect him, and we'll be on our way."

"Thanks, man. She should be out of the shower by the time you both get here."

"Copy that. See you soon," he said and ended the call.

I stood in my bedroom and sighed. I felt like shit. While I'd taken into consideration that she'd have to possibly blow or fuck one of those douchebags, I had deluded myself into thinking that she was made of fire and steel. But even steel forged in fire had to be tempered correctly. Otherwise, it could be fragile. I was afraid we'd overestimated her ability, and she had snapped.

I couldn't even imagine what it would be like to be in her head-space right now. To give pleasure to a man who was complicit if he hadn't outright pulled the trigger on my own flesh and blood?

"Velina," I called, and she called back softly, "Yeah?"

"Can I come in?" I asked.

"Yeah, of course," she said. "It's your fucking house."

I cracked up a bit and got my shit together before stepping back into the bathroom to check on her.

She was still stood up, which was good. Her forehead leaned against the cool tile as the water poured over her back and body, washing her sins down the drain. Except to my mind, she hadn't committed any and let any motherfucker even try and judge her in my presence. I'd tear them a new asshole.

"Hex and LaCroix are on their way. They want to talk," I said.

"Oh, goodie," she muttered and tipped her head back to take the water full in the face. I turned to the sink and loaded my toothbrush with paste for her. She jumped when I popped the seal on the glass shower door, and it clacked. I handed her the toothbrush. She didn't say a word, just stuck it in her mouth and started scrubbing with a muttered word that was probably something like "thanks."

"Don't mention it," I said. "Go on and finish up, baby. I'm going to find you something to put on and lay it on the bed.

"K," she said, and I went back out again, digging through one of my drawers for a clean tee.

I found one that was on the bigger side even for me and hoped it would cover her satisfactorily. Her boxes of shit were in my spare bedroom, and they included clothes and shit – but I didn't know what was what or where anything was, so I didn't bother to go digging. It wasn't entirely important right now.

What was important was getting her tucked into my bed, cozy, and with something fortifying be it tea or a stiff drink, and making sure she was taken care of.

I didn't doubt for a minute that she saw what she said she saw. I just wanted to fucking know *how?*

How had that slippery fuckin' snake even begun to survive that?

I went back to the bathroom door just as she shut off the tap. "You want tea, coffee, something stronger?" I asked her.

"Tea would be good," she said and looked surprised.

"Okay, shirts on the bed, tuck yourself in. I'm going to the kitchen, and to open up for the boys. Be back soon."

"Okay," she agreed and she looked unnerved somehow.

I asked her, "What is it?"

"I don't think I've ever been taken care of like this in my life," she said, and I leaned a shoulder against the bathroom doorway as she worked on drying off and wrapped the towel around her.

"Need another for your hair?" I asked, and she nodded.

"Behind you on the shelf."

She took down another towel to wrap her hair in, and by the time she threw her head back and stood up from where she doubled over to wrap it, I was already striding for the kitchen.

Everyone deserved to be taken care of at some fuckin' point in their life, but from the way she talked, being a middle child like she was and so independent… I had to imagine she'd been skipped quite a bit when it came to any sort of love and care going back as far as she could remember.

While it didn't surprise me, it sort of hit differently. It was probably some of the reason she was so selfless. She knew a certain level of neglect and didn't want anyone to feel that way from her.

I went into the kitchen and switched on the electric kettle to get some hot water going.

I went with an herbal tea, one that my mother swore by to settle the stomach.

The water was just coming to a boil when I heard the bikes outside. I went to the front door and opened up, letting Hex and LaCroix slide by me into the house.

"Tells me what you think of this woman that you'd insist on us coming here," LaCroix said.

"What's that supposed to mean?" I asked.

"You don't let anyone around your place," Hex said affably, and I frowned.

"You're right on that," I said. "Hope y'all have never taken offense, though."

"Nah," LaCroix said. "But the Bayou Baroness was right once again."

"Maybe," I said and left it at that. I wasn't willing to concede anything where that woman was concerned. She just… she creeped me the hell out.

I crossed myself and went about fixing Velina's tea. LaCroix and Hex exchanged a look and a pair of grins but didn't say nothin' about it.

"So, if it is ol' Ruthless, how d'you reckon he survived that shit?" Hex asked, pulling himself up onto my kitchen's island to sit.

"Your guess is as good as mine," I said. "Get off my counter." He grinned but slid his ass off my kitchen counter and planted his booted feet for the drop.

"Where is she?" LaCroix asked.

"My room. Gimme a sec to fix this an' I'll take you back."

"She real upset?" LaCroix asked.

"She'll be fine," I answered without answering. "She's strong."

The boys followed me back and we found Velina tucked into my bed, the television on, and her vacantly staring as she flipped through a streaming service looking for something to watch.

"Hey." I handed her the mug of tea, and she took it, wrapping her hands around it and breathing in the steam, the muscles in her face relaxing some as it touched her skin.

I sat down on the edge of the bed and put my hand on her upraised knee, giving it a squeeze over the blankets that she was tucked up under.

"Hey," she said somberly, looking up at LaCroix and Hex.

"You sure it was him?" LaCroix asked, cutting right to the chase like LaCroix was want to do.

"I'm sure," she said. "You got my phone?" She looked up at me.

"Yeah, I think you left it on the bathroom counter. Just a sec." I went and got it for her.

"I didn't think y'all would believe me, so I did my best. I'm not sure if I got him on camera, though."

She pulled up her gallery, and a five-minute or so video of her and some Bayou Bitch threading their way across a lawn to a row of bikes played. There was a bonfire and lights strung over yonder but not a whole lot of light to speak of for the camera to work with.

The footage was almost dizzying in a covertly taken, found-footage movie kind of a way. Couldn't say much for the camera work, but she'd taken a huge fuckin' risk to get it.

The chatter was overlapping, nothing real discernible there, but then it happened – an outburst of laughter and it was a familiar laugh.

Hex, LaCroix, and I all looked at each other at that sound.

"What?" she asked.

"That's Ruthless, alright," Hex said grimly.

"Know that laugh anywhere," I said.

"There!" She paused the screen and flashed it in our direction. On it – at a crazy angle or so – was Ruthless, an eyepatch over his eye, face lit by his lighter as he sucked on one of his customary cigars to get it re-lit.

"I'll be a son of a bitch," Hex declared.

"You send that to Saint for me, would you, sweetheart?"

"Yeah," she said and set to work clipping it down to get it through to me in a text.

"I'm callin' all the boys to the yard," LaCroix told me. "Best you get ready to head into church."

"I'd expect nothing less at this revelation," I said as the text came through from Velina.

"What about me?" Velina asked.

"Rest," I ordered. "I'll be back as soon as I can."

She nodded but looked troubled.

"See you out front," Hex declared, and he and LaCroix filed out of my bedroom.

"Be right there," I told their retreating backs, and I dropped onto the edge of the bed to pull my boots on.

"Are you sure about me staying here without you?" Velina asked softly.

"I'm sure. I'd rather you here than at the roach motel," I said. "Just in case dipshit comes back around."

"He won't," she said with a sigh.

"Never know," I said.

"You worried?" She was trying to make a self-deprecating joke, but I wouldn't let her get away with it. I stared her down. She lost the smirk, her face going lax and then solemn.

"Yes," I said, no joke or humor in my tone. "Against all odds, I actually like you – like *really* like you. I think I'd lose my shit if anything worse happened to you."

She swallowed hard, her eyes growing misty with unshed tears.

She didn't speak, and that was a first. I didn't think it was possible to render Velina Young speechless. It certainly wasn't easy. She was just like her brother in that regard.

I leaned in and captured her mouth with mine. Her hand went to the side of my face, her fingers tangling in my hair, her thumb stroking over my beard, and in that moment, I ached something fierce to just *stay...* but duty called.

I pulled back and told her, "Rest. Get some sleep. I'll be back to you just as soon as I can."

She nodded carefully and let me go. I could tell she was still emotional, the emotions she typically hid from the surface of her thoughts and expressions so carefully, sliding behind her eyes like a reader board in the middle of Times Square, telegraphing just about every feeling loud and clear.

She didn't want me to go, and I got that. It made it that much harder to do it.

"Ride careful," she murmured as I stepped out of my bedroom door to head down the hallway.

"You know it," I tossed back over my shoulder.

LaCroix and Hex both looked over from where they smoked at the end of my driveway when I came out the front door.

I hadn't bothered to pull into the garage when I'd gotten home this time, so my bike was sitting out on the concrete slab of the driveway, theirs parked right behind it in a typical pyramid formation.

"She all good?" Hex asked, concerned.

"A little rattled," I said. "But she's strong. A little rest, and she'll be her feisty self."

"Good," LaCroix said, flicking the butt of his black Djarum into the street. He didn't smoke more than weed very often, and neither did Hex. So if the cigarettes or cigars, or hell, even cloves were out, it meant they were thinking and thinking hard on things.

We rode on over to the club, most of the boys already there.

"On a scale of one to fucked, how fucked are we?" Chainsaw demanded as we walked in the door.

"I wouldn't say 'fucked' but tonight's been a revelation," LaCroix said.

"We ain't fucked, but we're definitely in a game of chess, and the pieces been moving across the board without us," Hex declared.

"Collier and Cypress better hurry the fuck up," Chainsaw grumbled.

"Axe'll be here any second," Bennie threw in.

"Ditch your phones, head into the chapel," LaCroix ordered, and he didn't have to tell us twice. We tossed our phones into the basket on the bar, and I went behind it to pour myself a shot of tequila.

"Go easy on the drinkin' boys," Hex cautioned.

"Just the one," I assured him.

I poured a solid count into a glass, took it with me into the chapel, and took my place at the table. It was a fine quality sipping tequila, and I had no intention of doing anything other than savoring it. The occasion certainly called for a fuckin' drink. I tell you what...

It didn't take but twenty minutes or so for the rest of the boys to arrive and likewise post up in their positions around the table.

"Where's the fire at?" Collier asked.

"Saint is gonna bring his phone in here, show y'all something. I don't want a fuckin' one of you to say a goddamned thing until all of you have seen it, and he gets it back outta here. Am I clear?"

"Crystal fuckin' clear, but you wanna give us a heads-up on what's on it? Because not gonna lie, you're freakin' me out – *me*, if you can believe it." Axeman stared LaCroix down, his face stony.

"You'll see soon enough," LaCroix said, and he threw me a jut of his chin and a toss of his head to go do what needed doing.

I returned and played the clip from Velina to each of my brothers in turn.

"No fuckin' way," Bennie muttered, and LaCroix gave him a hard look.

Bennie handed the phone back to me and held up his hands in surrender. LaCroix still stared him down for a few more heartbeats before turning those creepy tattooed eyes of his, looking at each of the faces around the table in turn.

Chainsaw harrumphed and grunted, handing me back the phone. With a wave of his hand, LaCroix sent me back out to the bar with it. I dropped it in the basket and returned to the chapel to a stony silence. I shut the door behind me.

"How in the fuck did that slimy giant rat get outta the swamp after we filled his ass full of holes, I'll never know. But there he is, plain as day, and a whole lot of shit is startin' to make sense," Hex said finally.

"What the fuck do we do now?" Cypress asked, then lit off in a string of Cajun-French that sounded a whole lot like he was cursing the situation up one side and down the other.

"Better settle in, boys," LaCroix said grimly. "We ain't leavin' until we have some solutions lined up."

I sighed. I knew he was right, but damn if I didn't just want to go home to the woman in my bed and make sure she was alright.

CHAPTER TWENTY-SIX

Velina...

I sucked in a sharp breath and instinctively cringed from the warm touch that roused me.

"Hey, all good, it's just me. I'm home."

The two words at the end felt... strange, falling from his lips. Like they were weighted with something more, a deeper meaning, than just the average.

"Welcome back," I said tiredly, and he slid a hand under the covers, grazing those rough fingertips along the back of my thigh. I pushed up onto my elbows from where I lay on my stomach in the warm nest of blankets, the ceiling fan spinning crazily above me, pushing the cool air from the house's air conditioner down like the wind over the arctic tundra.

"Is everything okay?" I asked. "Did I miss something important?"

"Everything's okay," he murmured. "You haven't missed anything, I promise."

The last was said on a grin and held an edge of a chuckle on the lilt of his words.

"Mm." I settled back down and relaxed into the mattress, which was a hell of a lot more comfortable than the one at the La Chiquita – which might as well have been a plank of wood.

His hand moved from fingertips to the flat of his palm as he smoothed up and down the back of my leg and up onto my ass, kneading and massaging.

I groaned.

"You trying to start something?" I asked, and cracked one eye to look at him, head turned to the side and the other half of my face buried in the firm but soft cloud of his pillow.

"You want me to stop?" he asked.

"No," I said, maybe a little too quickly, and he barked a laugh.

"What, you thinking I'm not going to find you as beautiful or something?" he asked, and his tone held an edge of carefulness to it.

I pushed up and arched an eyebrow.

"I wasn't aware that you found me beautiful in the first place," I said. "Easy, maybe, but not beautiful."

Smack!

I yelped as he rubbed over the spot on my ass he'd just slapped.

"Don't you ever talk about yourself like that, little girl," he cautioned.

I rolled my eyes. "Yes, Daddy."

Smack!

I writhed a little, biting my bottom lip, as he rubbed the smarting glow out of my ass cheek with a patient hand.

"Next time, it'll be my belt," he warned.

Oh, God… yes please, I thought, then it hit me. Old childhood memories of my dad in one of his drunken rages, ripping his belt from the loops, the lash of it against my skin as I threw up hands and just screamed for him to stop… but he never stopped. Not until I lay zebra striped and sometimes bloody.

I still had a few scars.

We all did. Every one of us kids. A lot of us, you just couldn't see them.

…like Louie.

"Hey, come back here," Saint ordered gently, and I shuddered, popping from my reverie like Sleeping Beauty waking from her prince's kiss.

"No belts," he said judiciously. "Crops? Floggers?" He tilted his head, and I swallowed hard.

"I don't like stingy," I mentioned, and he nodded. "Floggers for fun, crops for punishment, then."

"Are we negotiating the terms of our relationship?" I asked. I know I made it sound like the very thought that he could want me was a joke in and of itself.

"Would it be so terrible?" he asked, and I felt surprisingly vulnerable in that moment.

I sat up, and I couldn't help the look of soft surprise coming over my face as I twisted my body beneath the sheets and blankets lithely to sit properly and face him. He didn't let go, his hand traveling over the soft, smooth skin of my ass, and my hip, coming to rest atop my thigh as I moved. God, the look on his face was serene as he stared vacantly and just seemed to enjoy the feel of me moving beneath his hand. He kneaded the muscle atop my leg, just this side of too hard, as I brought my eyes up, roving over his handsome face, searching for the truth, I guess. I was so often used to being lied to and led on, I was having a hard time believing this was real and not some dream.

Was I even awake? I wondered silently.

I stilled when I realized he was dead fuckin' serious.

"You can't be serious," I said, and he barked a laugh.

"As a heart attack," he said evenly and moved his hand up and down my leg in a light caress. *I couldn't get enough.* I couldn't get enough of the sensation of his rough hand over my soft skin. I couldn't help myself. I closed my eyes and relished in the warmth of it, the roughness and the sensation of it, the contrast between the light touch and sand papery feel.

"I didn't factor in on staying," I murmured. "I was just here for a good time, not a long time. I-I didn't know what I was going to do after all of this. I mean—"

"Quit it," he said. "You were never here for a good time, baby. I think what we have here is a failure to communicate."

I opened my eyes and stared at him, stony-faced for a moment.

"What do you mean?" I asked.

"I don't fuck for fun," he said carefully. "It's just never been me – never has been. I know it's part of the biker lifestyle or whatever, but I play to win, I guess. I play for keeps." His hand slid up under the shirt he'd given me to wear and cupped my breast.

I gasped as he played with my nipple between forefinger and thumb, squeezing it in a light pinch to get the blood flowing to it, rolling it back and forth. He set off a wave of sensation that swept through me gently, washing the thoughts right out of my head like a rogue wave sweeping the shells and sea glass I'd gathered right off the shore and back into the sea.

"I can't think when you do that," I whispered carefully.

"Seems to me, you think too much," he murmured, and he brought his mouth carefully closer to mine, whispering the last just over my lips.

I gasped, and he murmured, "I'm going to kiss you, then I'm going to love you into a goddamned coma if I have to. You're going to rest."

"Oh, am I?" I asked weakly, and he chuckled a sinister and dark little laugh.

His voice dropped into something low and soothing as he said, "Why you gotta be so stubborn, huh? Why not let someone take care of you for once?"

"No one's ever taken care of me," I confessed. "I've only ever really taken care of myself."

"Doesn't have to be that way anymore," he whispered, and his lips touched mine. I kissed slowly, and it felt... different... like I approached things with more trepidation.

I'd had what he was offering dangled in front of me more times than I could count. The promise of love and affection, and all the trappings of a relationship – but without any of the actual *partnership* that I craved.

No, it'd always been them wanting me to give my all while they barely tried, and this? This felt like he wanted more than that. I had longed for something like it to be offered, and I mean truly offered, for so long I didn't trust it. I failed to believe it could be real. *Yay, trust issues.*

"What's the matter?" he asked, drawing back, his thumb stroking my cheek.

I closed my eyes, leaned into the light touch, and asked timidly, "Is this for real, or am I just dreaming?"

He chuckled and asked me, "Why would you be dreaming?"

"It doesn't feel real," I answered automatically.

"Aw," he chided. "It's traumatized..." He was teasing, but he was also right. Still, it was a welcome respite from the heavy emotions settling onto my heart.

"Quit it." I laughed, I couldn't help it.

"It's true," he said. "When have I not been a man of my word?" he asked.

"That's very true," I murmured. "You sure you want something with me, though? I can be a real pain in the ass."

"I think I can keep you in line." He winked at me, those deep, soulful brown eyes holding a trickle of mirth, and I couldn't help but smile, laugh, and shake my head.

"How do you do that?" I asked, easing into the idea of staying, not just for revenge, but because... *I was wanted here...*

Holy shit.

I didn't think I had ever felt like I was actually and truly wanted *anywhere* I'd ever been before. I'd only ever just existed in a place...

"Do what?" he asked.

"Make everything a sarcastic joke but make it feel real at the same time?" I asked.

"I could ask you the same thing," he said, tracing along my hairline, moving my bangs across my forehead, and tucking some of the longer strands behind my right ear.

"What are you doing to me?" I asked softly, closing my eyes, almost afraid to look him in the eyes when I asked.

He put his lips next to my ear and practically growled, "Loving you."

There was nothing light, sarcastic, or joking about those two words. They were as stark and real as they got as he moved over me, laying me back in his bed. He had one knee between mine over the blankets, and with one hand, he reached up behind his head, grasping his tee and pulling, the material sliding over him and off his body, revealing a light tank under it.

He pulled that off, too, in much the same way, his tanned shoulders revealed, the muscles moving provocatively beneath the skin as he tossed both shirts away, to the bedroom floor.

I don't know what it was for me, but a man's shoulders really did it for me. Like it was my favorite part to look at, and turned me the fuck on.

Weird thing to be attracted to, I know, but I couldn't help it.

He stood long enough to lose the jeans and to move my covers, while I definitely helped things along by grasping the hem of my borrowed shirt, peeling out of it, up over my head. It joined his clothes abandoned and forlorn on his bedroom floor, which, to my mind, was a good a place as any for them now.

He got back up between my thighs, and I parted my knees to welcome him. Everything about this sexual encounter with him was different from the ones before. It was as though this one was filled to bursting with promise, with meaning, with a depth I'd never explored with anyone before, preferring many, if not all, of my sexual encounters to remain... frivolous.

There was nothing at all frivolous about the look in his eyes, the stony concentration in his face, as he palmed my hips and smoothed those rough hands over my skin, all the way up to palm my generous tits and play the nipples until he had me giggling and writhing against him from the sensations he wrought through me.

He lifted my hips with one hand, lining himself up with my pussy with the other, and holding me aloft just so, slid into me to the root. I gasped, his cock filling me, but also just long enough to bottom out against my cervix. The alluring mix of pleasure with that sweet, sharp pain at my end made me pant.

He put my legs up along his chest, holding me up across my thighs, below my knees, as he drove into me tighter, harder, in these short strokes that took my breath away from something like seventy percent pleasure and thirty percent pain. A sweet pain, a beautiful torture. I arched, and he thrust. It was the *perfect* angle, hitting all of the right places, making me cry out with the delight of it.

His intense look of concentration was broken only by the smile that graced his lips, teeth white, framed by his golden tanned skin and dark beard as I made the sound. He took pleasure from my pleasure, and it only compounded the blissful feelings spreading through my veins, as though my blood sang and was quickened by moonlight as it flowed through my veins.

His touch held the fire of the sun, and I could almost feel it. This overwhelming sense of belonging to one another, and yet like the sun and the moon, separated by time and space, a tragic love story of long-distance longing, but never having quite found each other to touch.

It was like that, except the longing was over, and we were touching. Oh, by God, how we *touched*. So close, yet so far away – two beings becoming as close as we could without the true ability to become one. Sparks flying, the cataclysm of our energies nigh as we attained unearthly heights, and I didn't know what to do.

I was afraid. Unsure if we would collide in our passions in such a way to tear our known world asunder or to make something incredible. Something new. With every thrust, it was like the strike of the hammer against the working. The passion between us our forge, and it remained yet to be seen after the quench if we would be formed into something indestructible or indescribably delicate.

With a final stroke, sparks flew, flitting along every nerve as I flew apart with them. He gripped my hips and bowed over me, arms slipping under me, wrapping me up, caging me under the shelter of his much larger body. I was vaguely aware, as I floated aimlessly and beautifully on the sensations pulsing through me, that he twitched inside me, coming as I had come, and I loved the feeling of it beyond all words, thoughts, or feelings.

I kissed his shoulder, the side of his neck, his bearded chin, and laughed. Finally, his mouth found mine, and we just *melded*. Welded together body and soul into something much stronger than even the sum of our equal, and yet still physically divided parts.

CHAPTER TWENTY-SEVEN

S aint...

I touched her all over, holding her close in the dark. The birds were beginning to chirp outside the window, and pretty soon, dawn would be pressing at the glass and the curtains. She was sleeping soundly in my arms. Still, I just couldn't stop touching her – stroking her soft skin, massaging her scalp through her thick, luxurious hair while her warm breath coated my chest at even intervals.

God, she felt phenomenal, and I still wondered how I'd gotten so completely entangled with her. I honestly couldn't say if it was any one thing. She had a will of iron, a heart of gold, and those green eyes of hers might as well have been silvered glass, although it was a mirror made of some kind of magic.

I didn't see myself reflected in them as I was now. I saw something more – the man she needed, the man I always wanted to be, but the world just wouldn't fuckin' seem to let me.

She gave me warmth and a glimpse of the life we were all fighting for right now.

Reflected in her eyes when I looked at her was a sort of peace that I'd been desperate for, and laying in my arms like this? One I'd never known... until now.

It was something big and overwhelming, which made the heart race and the mind silent, and the breath still into something deep and even in a silent whisper.

Fuck.

She was poetry in a way that I couldn't grasp intellectually, but on a spiritual level, it moved me. Incredibly. Irrevocably.

I closed my eyes and tried to sleep, but with her against me, draped over me, I found it hard to concentrate on anything but the feel of her.

Still, I managed to drift, and yet even with her in my arms, I still only dreamed of her.

I woke to sunlight streaming through the crack between the curtains, which put it at late morning, maybe early afternoon. I grunted and turned my head to get the beam out of my eyes and realized pretty quickly, I was in bed alone, but that the house was far from empty.

A clatter of dishes came from out in the house and I sat up, frowning. The smells hit me next. She was cooking, I think – or at least what passed for it.

"Shit, shit, shit, shit, shit!" she whisper-shouted, and I rounded the corner to a kitchen rapidly filling with smoke just as the fucking smoke alarms went the fuck off.

"Just what in the *hell* are you doing?" I asked, but I couldn't stop myself from laughing as she waved oven mitts in front of the oven and looked up like she'd been caught.

"Trying to cook your breakfast, but it's been a while! Okay?" she cried. I went in, rescuing the pot holders from her hands and fishing the broiler pan with some more-than-crisp bacon out of the oven.

"Who the fuck cooks bacon in the oven anyway?" I asked, setting it down on the cutting board before going for the detector in the dining room and pulling it down from over the archway leading to the kitchen. I pulled the batteries, and it stopped its screeching.

I tossed both the detector and the batteries onto the table and turned around to look at Velina, who was hugging herself in nothing but my tee shirt in the smoky kitchen, her butt leaned against the kitchen's farm sink, her arms crossed under her breasts.

Fuck, she was sexy without even trying.

"I appreciate the gesture, but why don't you let me take over?" I said with a grin. She threw up her hands and gesticulated wildly around her at the trainwreck that was my kitchen.

"Have at," she said, and she took a seat at the kitchen's island. Properly, unlike Hex. Pulling out one of the stools tucked under its edge and hopping up on it.

"Thanks," I said, and I set about attempting to figure out what she'd been trying to accomplish so that I could do it correctly.

"Pancakes and bacon?" I asked.

"I mean, that's what I was going for," she said, and she was smiling, but high spots of color that could only be embarrassment rode on her cheeks.

"I got you," I said.

"*My hero.*" She rolled her eyes and I laughed. I couldn't help it. She had that dry, sarcastic humor that I liked.

"If you were hungry, you could have just woke me up," I said, and she put her chin in her hand.

"That would sort of defeat the whole purpose of trying to do something nice for you," she complained.

"Now why you feel the need to go and do something like that?" I asked, and I was only half-joking. It was sweet, and I knew she wasn't in the habit of being sweet.

"You've been nice to me," she said softly and fixed me with those green eyes of hers.

"I like you," I said. Winking, I added, "Probably against my better judgment."

She cracked a smile and laughed a bit herself, bowing her head and shaking it. She said, "Yeah, well, that makes two of us."

"You doing better?" I asked, after a long silent pause during which I cleaned up some of her mess and tried to carry on with achieving her goal of fixing us some pancakes. Her batter looked sound and was from scratch. I didn't have any mix or anything around here so...

"I'm okay," she said, and I gave her a look that said, *you can't bull-shit a bullshitter.*

"I wasn't okay last night," she said defensively. "But I'm okay *now.* Thanks."

"You got us some valuable information, baby. For that, we thank you, but I don't know if it's a good idea you continue."

She perked up. "What do you mean? I'm not done yet. I can't be done. I've hardly even started!"

I stared at her until she settled back down into her seat, her hands smoothing back and forth over the stone counter. She looked chagrinned.

"You scared the shit out of me last night, and Ruth? Knowing Ruthless is in play is a big deal. He's a different animal. If he found out you were feeding us information, *shit.*" I shook my head. "He and his boys would do things to you that would make you *wish* for death."

"Speaking from experience?" she accused, and her passion, which was one of the things I liked about her, was about to get the better of her.

I sniffed, set down the bowl and whisk from pouring batter into the pan, and leaned on the edge of the counter, staring her down unequivocally.

"Yes," I told her simply.

She stared back for several heartbeats, doing the calculations, and then asked, "Like what?"

I shook my head, and she raised her eyebrows at me.

"I'm a big girl and capable of mathing out my own risks," she said.

"Strap you to a pool table and take turns on you until you literally fuckin' died, maybe," I told her. "You don't die fast enough. They might start using things to get you to bleed and get the job done faster."

"Jesus," she said. "I've survived the whole gang rape thing before, but that last part is a whole new horror show."

I froze at her frank confession. She'd made it to me once before, but that was *before…* you know? Now, things were different.

"I'm not going to ask," I said quietly. "But if you ever want something done about that…"

She waved me off.

"I didn't even bother to report it. There was no point. The system isn't built for women like me."

"What's that supposed to mean?" I cocked my head.

"Poor," she said with a shrug. "It was back in high school – a bunch of rich white boys."

"You're white," I said.

"I'm not rich," she countered.

"Touché," I conceded and she nodded.

"I let it go," she said. "I was just trying to get the point across that I'm tougher than you think."

I considered her and glanced down at the bubbling pancakes, but not quite there yet for flipping.

"Baby, I know you're plenty tough. I just don't want or need you taking any more damage than absolutely necessary."

"You know I like it when you call me baby?" she asked, and she was staring at her hands.

"Yeah?" I asked softly.

"Yeah, anyone else, and I would probably hate it, but you… I don't know. Sort of warms me from the inside out."

I flipped the pancakes in the pan and nodded absently.

"I don't want you to get hurt any more than you've already been," I repeated.

"I'm a big girl," she said.

"I know," I answered, but that still didn't stop me from wanting to protect her.

We were silent. I dished up some of the food and salvaged the mostly unburnt pieces of bacon, grateful we hadn't had a fire, just a shit ton of smoke, and I slid a plate across to her, going around the island to take up the seat beside her.

"Next time, you should bite it off," I grated, and she snorted.

"Believe me, I thought about it," she said. "I mean, I want to say he's not a bad guy – but we both know that's kind of bullshit." She sighed. "In another life, he might have been the kind of guy that I *did* go for, but I'd like to think I'm not that dumb." She eyed me then, and I chuckled.

"We may both ride motorcycles and do some fucked-up shit by society's standards, but the Voodoo Bastards aren't anything like the Bayou Brethren, babe."

"Aren't you, though?" she asked softly.

"In some ways, maybe too alike – but people change, and we've been trying like hell *to* change."

"Why?" she asked softly. "I mean, I get the whole getting older, yadda, yadda, yadda – but what *really* made you guys hit the pause button?" she asked.

"I'm pretty sure I've told you this already," I said. "But for real, it was the club out in Florida when they came around these parts on some business several years back. Those of us not entirely blinded by Ruth's bullshit looked at them and saw something we wanted. The more that time went on, the more we figured out – Ruth's way was *not the way*. That it would never pay off in the dividends we were hoping to achieve."

"And what would those be?" she asked softly.

"Work with the purpose of working for ourselves, earning enough wealth that we could ride more than work, attract and keep quality women," I eyed her. "Such as yourself. We want to build our little self-made empires with…" I trailed off, thought about it, and simplified it. "Just a life that no one could take from us, and that was our own."

"That sounds like the American Dream," she said with a slight shrug, taking a bite of her food.

"Yeah, well, we all know the American Dream is more like a night-mare for us fuckin' peasants on the ground."

"I know that's right," she said softly, rolling her eyes before drop-ping them to her plate.

"We're almost there," I said. "Or, we *were*."

"No," she said. "We *are*."

"We?" I asked, arching an eyebrow. She reached over with her free hand and laced her fingers through mine.

"We," she said. "I'm in this to win this, just the same as you. I have no reason to disbelieve what any of you have said. Everything has matched up with what Louie told me of you all, to a tee. You've only ever been kind to me with actions, even if we do rag on each other with words."

She smiled at that. I had to smile, too.

"I wouldn't have it any other way," I said.

"Me either," she told me, and I raised the back of her hand to my lips and kissed it.

"We've got this," she assured me, and I nodded.

"I believe you're right," I said, even if I was a little lacking on feeling it at the moment.

CHAPTER TWENTY-EIGHT

Velina...

When I went into work for what was supposed to be my Tuesday, it was to, predictably, a pink slip for no calling and no showing on what was supposed to be my Monday. I barely, by the grace of whatever God there is, sweet-talked my way out of it by gaslighting them into believing that I really *did* believe that today was my Monday and that I had been so sick that I'd missed a whole day of existence.

I didn't think my manager *really* bought it, but they didn't want to fire me, either. Partially because I had been so reliable up to that point. So, the pink slip turned from a *you're fired*, into my first write-up, which was a *"three strikes, you're out"* kind of a thing that rinsed and repeated with every new year. The reset button hits January first.

As far as policies went, it was a pretty fair one, but if I were being perfectly honest, I didn't picture myself working here for terribly much longer. This job really was just to maintain my cover with the Bayou Brethren, and given certain... revelations that I'd made, according to Saint, it wasn't something I was going to have to keep doing for very much longer.

I didn't know what the Voodoo Bastards had planned, and I didn't want to know. That whole *club business is none of your business* when it came to the club's women was looking mighty fine by way of plausible deniability right now.

They didn't want their women involved insomuch as they didn't want us to be questioned when it came to any alphabet soup of federal or local law enforcement. We only knew as much as we needed to when it came to getting the boys lawyers and who to call when some shit *did* happen to go down.

We were, in essence, their fallback plan, and even though I low-key hated it and would rather be part of the initial plans in some ways, I had to respect their setup in that it *did* try to keep us girls out of trouble. I wasn't cut out for prison life.

I worked the remainder of that week in a state of honest nausea with having to keep up appearances like I had a *great* time blowing dipshit in the dark of some stranger's front porch for all eyes to see in the middle of some swamp property out along some bayou I couldn't name. There were so fucking many of them out here that it annoyed me to no end that I hadn't been able to keep track to tell the boys. Of course, with the tracker app on my phone, I hadn't needed to. They'd been able to pinpoint the location.

I agreed to meet up with Carver and a group of the other Brethren and some of their girls in the French Quarter after work on my Friday to have some drinks and to do some dancing or whatever, but man, I wasn't feeling it. My feet hurt, and I was fucking *tired*.

Not only that, but I didn't know what it was about it that week, but there had been a rash of violence and fucked-up shit going on in and around the Quarter. The vibe as I stepped out of work onto the darkening street was something... *different* than usual, but then again, it could have just been the weather.

The sky hung low with clouds that were pregnant with rain, and the air was somehow thicker than usual.

I had, of course, texted Saint with the knowledge of where I would be, and we had that other failsafe by way of the location-sharing app that was running in the background on my phone. I was running at all times to where he could see where I was, and I him if we needed to.

I looked at it before I left my job, and it showed him in the Ninth Ward, where the clubhouse was located.

In reality, I knew it was only minutes away – but on the map, it looked like it could take light years for Saint to get to me.

That was okay, though.

I reminded myself under no uncertain terms that I was a strong, powerful, and wholly independent woman, and there wasn't a person alive I could rely on to keep me safe but me. I didn't need no man, but the scared little girl part of me, in the deepest recesses of my being, certainly *wanted* Saint at my side.

Shit, if any of my siblings could see me now, they would say I was the *biggest* moron for putting myself into one of the un-safest positions that I possibly could by still pretending to be Louise, a.k.a. Louie, with this band of fucking jackals riding their big boy trikes and bikes.

I couldn't argue the point. They'd have been right, but it was also still the right thing to do.

I walked swiftly down the sidewalk, fists buried in the pockets of my jean jacket, my purse slung over my chest across my body underneath it to keep it as un-snatchable as possible. It'd been a wild week of assaults and robberies splashed across headlines. Most unrelated to each other, it would seem.

There was a pack of internet "pranksters" who found it funny to punch random women in the face for no apparent reason. Incels, if you asked me. The dipshittery started in New York but had quickly gone viral, and now there were videos and cases popping up all over the continental United States. With New Orleans and the French Quarter being so tourist heavy – it'd taken hold here pretty quickly. But it was a strong likelihood it was tourists rather than locals when it came to that shit.

The robberies, on the other hand, were *definitely* a local outfit – they just didn't know who.

I'd asked Saint about it one night on one of our now nightly phone calls about what would happen if the Voodoo Bastards saw something like that. With the money that a lot of local businesses paid, he'd said that the Bastards would have curb-stomped the individual responsible.

I had filed the information away because I planned on bringing it up tonight – to see what Carver or the Bayou Brethren's answer would be.

Thunder rumbled, and the wind picked up, smelling green and wet from the direction of the river. I hurried my pace, as lightning flashed and skirted quickly under the awning of the bar where I was supposed to meet everyone, when the heavens opened up in an absolute deluge.

"Holy shit," I heard behind me, and a laugh. I turned and came face-to-face with none other than *Lazarus*... which was what he was calling himself now. I got the joke, I just didn't think it was funny. Judging by the look in his one eye as he looked at me, it wasn't meant to be funny.

"Made it in the nick of time, huh?" I asked, forcing a genial laugh.

"I'd say," he said and turned sideways in the doorway so that I could squeeze by.

"Carver here yet?" I asked.

"Oh, a bunch of us are," he answered casually. "I'm Lazarus, and who might you be?"

I smiled a little wider. "I'm Louise, but everyone calls me Louie," I answered. He scrutinized my face, like he found something familiar about it but couldn't place it. I cursed my attempt at being funny without being funny when it came to my choice of cover name and hoped that he didn't put two and two together about my eyes like most of the Bastards had on second look.

"Pleasure to meet you, Louie," he said, and captured my hand, brushing lips across the knuckles. It made my skin absolutely crawl all the way up past my elbow.

I laughed nervously, and he said, "You go on in past the bar and into that back room an' you'll find us." He stepped out of the doorway, out under the awning, moving to the side as far as he could before lighting up his cigar... right next to the *no smoking* sign posted against the front of the building.

"Thanks!" I called and slipped further into the gloom of the bar, away from the blush of cooler humidity from the rain falling from the sky.

I lingered a moment, just inside the doorway, outside of Lazarus' sight, and watched the rain fall, the drops bouncing off the street in what my mother had called "ponies" when I was growing up.

It was one of those deep and torrential rains I had always thought of as a cleansing rain and the winds that accompanied it? Well, they felt like the winds of change.

I was hoping they were, at least. Come what may, it felt like it was needed.

I found a knot of Bayou Brethren and their girls in the back room with the billiard tables. There were only two pool tables and both were occupied by Bayou Brethren. There was money on the games, which made me nervous. One of the most common motives behind fighting and murder was money. Add alcohol, the chances of either happening increased exponentially.

I tried not to think too deep into it and instead completed my assessment of the room. High bar tables lined the perimeter of it, and what girls were present lounged on the tall stools tucked up under them. Sativa was present and accounted for, which was annoying but not unexpected.

I scanned the other faces and found Singer, her man, Basilisk, and, of course, Carver, who spotted me and lit up. It took everything in me to force a thousand-watt smile while my gut wrenched just at the sight of him.

"Hey!" I called cheerfully, let him wrap his arms around me, and returned his kiss with what I hoped was the right amount of enthusiasm.

"Hey, baby," he said and gripped my ass, giving it a painful squeeze and a shake. "Mm! Can't wait to get some of that later tonight," he growled next to my ear, and I laughed like that sounded good when it honestly sounded anything but. I didn't know how I was going to get out of it this time, but I was sure that something would occur to me.

Saint and I had talked about it, and we'd agreed. I'd already gone just as far as things needed to go for me. That if my dot arrived anywhere that wasn't for commercial use, or if it arrived at my hotel, and he didn't get a text in the next ten minutes after my landing there, that he was coming and bringing hell with him.

He and his brothers had all agreed. Carver would be the first of many, and that they would pick them off one at a time.

That was my new mission – to gather intel on as many of their movements and personal lives as possible, but not to the detriment of my bodily autonomy. Never again on that front.

I would do what I had to, but the assurance that the boys on my team were done with me having to go that far warmed me. For the first time in my life, I felt like someone had my back.

After a lifetime of going under the bus, I felt like, for the first time ever, I was in the driver's seat.

"Carver, your shot!" one of the other Brethren hollered, and Carver winked one of his blue eyes at me and turned me loose over near Singer.

"Hey, girl, how you doing?" I asked, sliding up onto a vacant stool on the other side of her from Basilisk. If I had to guess, he got his name from the stone-faced stare he tended to give people.

"Hey," she said back and her smile was a brittle one.

"You good?" I asked.

"Yeah! Yeah!" She forced a smile, and I caught Basilisk looking at her in a way that I didn't like.

When you know, you know, and it was totally apparent – they were having some sort of problem. I was curious but wisely kept my mouth shut. I'd get it from her sooner rather than later.

I was right on the money when Singer got up and said, "I gotta use the bathroom, and Louie needs a drink. We'll be right back."

"Hurry it up," Basilisk said, and I smiled and nodded, gesturing to Carver at the far pool table that I was going with Singer and pantomiming I was getting a drink. He waved me off and leaned in to listen to something that Spite, one of the Bayou Brethren's enforcers, was saying.

Those two were something... Spite and Malice were their road names, over some card game that involved two decks of cards to play. As far as I'd heard, the names were fitting as the two of them were absolutely chock full of both spite *and* malice, and tended to do some seriously heinous shit just for the fun of it.

I wouldn't be surprised if one or the both of them were active serial killers. There were rumors about screwed-up issues from early childhood – as in the serial killer trifecta of bed wetting, harming small animals, and starting fires.

I didn't doubt it. Each one of them on their own gave me the creeps. Both of them together gave me the full-on heebs.

I let Singer lead me out of the back room and down the narrow hall to the ladies' room, where there was, of course, a line. We stood in it, and I asked her, "Girl, are you good?"

"Yes… no… I don't know," she said and hugged herself.

"What's going on?" I asked gently.

"You know I got a past, right? Like heavy drug use in my teens, a bad eating disorder, shit like that."

"I didn't, but it's okay. We all have our histories," I said.

"Basilisk keeps wanting me to get on E when we fuck, and I just don't want to even go down that road. I've been there, and I don't want to go there again. I've worked really, really, hard to stay clean, and I don't want to risk it, you know?"

"No, yeah, I know! I totally get that. Is he just not taking 'no' for an answer?" I asked.

"No – I mean, he's taking the 'no' but he's not happy about it and is being a real dick, making me feel bad about it."

"Honey, no! You have no reason to feel bad. You're doing what's right for you!" I put my hand to her shoulder and gave her a reassuring squeeze. "You don't need that shit to have fun," I said. "He can do what he wants. He's a big boy, but Jesus. He needs to leave you the fuck out of it."

"I just don't want to slip up, you know? I worked really hard to get out of that life, and I know this one ain't so great, shaking my ass on a stage, but for the first time ever, I'm making good money, *enough* money. I ain't gonna be able to do it forever, and I'm trying to make enough that I ain't gotta, you know? I don't want to go back to turning tricks and starving half to death just to get my next fix."

I nodded and hugged her tight.

"You stick to your guns, okay? Don't give in. You got a plan, and you stick to it. There's nothing wrong or dumb about making a better life for yourself."

"Thanks," she said and sniffed, knuckling under her eyes to keep her mascara from blurring.

"Any time, and if he keeps getting up your ass about it, there's nothing wrong with walking away. You don't need that shit."

"Aw, hon, pretty of you to say and think so, but that's not how this life works, you know? You don't get to walk away. Once you become an ol' lady, they *own you*."

I was going to say something, but the line moved, and Singer and I were next, the stalls opening up for us. I went pee, even though I didn't really *need* to. It just seemed like a good idea, considering that before long, I would have to and I didn't want to have to wait forever in line again.

The rest of the night went... okay. It seemed like everyone was in some type of mood, and chaos was the order of the day. Everyone was just getting mad at each other and picking fights over things for no reason. Most disturbing of all, there was Lazarus, sitting back in the corner, egging it on and instigating things just to watch the chaos ensue and his own people burn like it was top-tier amusement.

I didn't find anything about cruelty for the sake of cruelty fun or funny. It wasn't my scene, and the heat and crush of bodies, along with the curtain of pouring rain out there, made the bar seem more claustrophobic than usual.

In short, it was not a good time. Then the fight started, and, of course, it was Sativa and some unknown – probably a tourist.

The fists were flying, the hair was being pulled, and her weave was taking a big hit, all with the Bayou Brethren circling and *cheering*. Some of them even going as far as to place bets while the bar's bouncers tried to wade through the crush of bodies to break it up and throw the two women out.

I'd had enough by that point, and even though Carver had a hold of me, I decided it was time for me to exit stage left.

"Hey, babe, I've gotta use the bathroom!" I called, and it took like three tries to get through to him and to get him to let me go so I could.

Bathroom, my ass. I immediately skirted the small back room like I was headed in that direction, but then ducked into the crowd and made for the fucking door, leaving the whole damn mess behind me.

I'd rather get drenched and drop a gear and disappear as Saint liked to say. Even if the only gear I had to drop was putting my Crocs in sports mode… you know, if I actually wore those hideous things.

I ducked out the front door to the bar and caught sight of a few Bayou Brethren smoking where Lazarus had been. I turned the other direction and dashed up the street and around the corner, vaguely in the direction that I needed to go.

I knew that Carver was probably going to be pissed and that I would need to come up with some kind of an excuse, but *ugh*, yuck.

I was soaked within seconds and dialing Saint as I walked, trying to keep an eye out so I wasn't spotted.

"Hey you, are y' okay?" he asked as soon as he picked up.

"Hey, yeah, it's just pouring, and I'm trying to get away from the bullshit. I just don't have it in me to put up with it anymore tonight."

"Where you at? I'll come get you," he said.

"Uhhhh, close to – shit, hang on, I can't see the sign. It's pissing down out here."

"You know what, never mind. Just find you some cover, and I'll come to your location in the app. We'll see how accurate it is."

"Sounds good," I said, relieved, and kept walking, looking for something sufficiently crowded to blend in but not so crowded as to be stupidly overwhelming.

"Coffee shop," I said. "I see a coffee shop."

"Good, go in and try to dry out, get you some caffeine, and I'll be there as soon as I can. Look for Hex's truck. You know what it looks like?"

"Yeah, vaguely," I said.

"Call you when we get close," he said.

"Thanks," I shot back, and we didn't bother with any other pleasantries. I was over today. I just wanted to go home… which was *not* my hotel room. It was wherever I could get dry and cuddle up with Saint.

I melded into the crowd at the coffee shop, and by the time I reached the counter, Carver was blowing up my phone. I rejected the calls and sent him a text, saying I was sick, really wasn't feeling well, the whole vibe was off, and I just needed to go.

He kept blowing up my phone with calls until I knuckled under and answered.

He was *not* happy, but he wasn't *exactly* being a dick about it. I told him that by the time I was done nearly shitting myself to death in the bathroom, everyone was so thoroughly engrossed in the drama with Sativa that I had just planned to catch up with him once I was back home and had the time to get cleaned up.

Was it my finest moment pretending I'd just sharted to make my escape? No. Was it effective? Hell yes. He thanked me sarcastically for the overshare and swore as he was hanging up on me, so yeah, he was pissed. What a fucking gentleman. Your woman is sick, and *that's* your answer? You're pissed off because you were gonna get laid, and now you can't?

I pictured Louie and Carver parting ways and in the *very* near future.

I sat at a little two-person table, jotting down my notes on what I'd learned about who that night – which was more than you would expect. I swear to God, these guys thought their women were idiots, and to be fair, some of them really *were*. *Lookin' at you, Sativa.*

Then there were the ones like Singer, and I felt genuinely bad for her. I couldn't imagine fighting as hard as she had to overcome her host of problems only to end up with a guy who wasn't only totally unsupportive of her sobriety but was actively trying to *break it*.

My heart broke for her, especially considering that while she didn't seem like the absolute brightest bulb in the string, she was actually *trying*. Not only that, she also seemed so incredibly innocent. Still! Despite all of the shit that she'd clearly been through.

My phone started to buzz across the table, and I looked up and out the fogging window to watch a big Dodge Ram pickup creep by. I snatched my shit and dashed out into the lessening rain and up to it, knocking on the passenger glass and startling the shit out of Hex, who was in the passenger seat. The locks popped, and I dove up and into the back seat of the truck to the sound of Saint laughing his ass off, losing his shit, and hollering between his gasping breaths, "You should have seen the look on your face, man! You screamed like a little fuckin' girl!"

"Man, what would you fuckin' do?" Hex demanded, but he was laughing too. It was worlds away from the vibe I'd left behind. I started laughing. I couldn't help it, and it was good. Cleansing. In a way that the rain drumming on the truck outside just couldn't seem to get right.

CHAPTER TWENTY-NINE

S aint...

"That's fucked up," Jessie-Lou said, taking a pull off her beer. We were back at the club, the couches from the front back here in the back bay, and sat down around the firepit which we had going. It was cozy, and Velina was drying out. I had her boots and socks off, her feet in my lap, rubbing them as she talked about her night.

"I know, right?" she said. "I can't imagine working that hard to pull yourself out of an active addiction, to get yourself right and put yourself through shaking your naked ass in front of strangers night after night with a goal in mind, only to have the dude that supposedly loves you try and tear it all down because he wants an adventure in getting his dick wet."

She rolled her eyes and some of us laughed at her phrasing, but definitely none of us were laughing at Singer's situation.

"For real," Chainsaw agreed.

For once, we were all here. Every brother and ol' lady alike. We were keeping it low-key around here, and no one else was fuckin' invited. Some day, we might get back to partying and having outsiders hang with us or whatever – but now? No. No fuckin' way. We didn't trust anyone who was outside the club, and with good reason.

It'd been entirely too easy to get Velina close to the Brethren – and that'd been one of our biggest arguments when it came down to it when Ruth was in charge. The more people you had hangin' around and the faster you added to the club, the more likely you were inviting a fat rat into the fuckin' pantry.

Ain't none of us wanted to go down on the kinds of charges we were racking up, but he just wouldn't fuckin' listen.

"So, how'd you get yourself out of hanging with those losers tonight?" LaCroix asked, and it was a good question.

"Oh, trust me, Carver wasn't fuckin' happy. But ain't nobody down to go down on a woman who's confessed that she sharted and was on her way home to clean herself up."

"You did what?" Bennie demanded, but all of us were too busy falling out laughing, including Velina, who was giggling too hard for her to reiterate what she'd just said. Not that she needed to – we all heard it, loud and clear.

"That shit's too stupid to make up," Corliss said from Hex's lap.

"I was banking on that," Velina said.

"Well, well fuckin' played," Hex crowed, saluting her with his beer.

"That's wild," Sandy said, taking a drink from where she sat at Bennie's feet on the area rug that we'd thrown down back here over the concrete.

Bennie had been arguing with her off and on over the last half an hour. He kept trying to get her up off the floor, and I had to admit, it *did not* look comfortable, but she kept insisting she was fine.

He started in again, and it was Velina who rolled her eyes and called out to Sandrine, "Oh for fuck's sake, will you just let the man love and take care of you?"

Sandy stopped, whatever she was going to say dying on her lips, and looked from Velina to Bennie. Without another word of protest, she got up off the ground and curled up in the battered recliner with her man. Both of them were small enough they fit in the damn thing, which had been built for a man of considerable bulk.

It used to be Ruth's makeshift throne around here.

Somebody'd dredged it out of the back corner of the garage some-where when we'd been scrounging for extra seating to accommodate everyone back here comfortably.

I was impressed at how Velina was getting along with everyone, despite only really having spent time with me, Hex, LaCroix, and out of the women, just Alina to this point. Alina had clearly liked her and put in a good word with Cor, Jessie-Lou, and Sandrine.

They were all working together to open a witchy-themed gift shop down in the Quarter, an unexpected opportunity arising from Sandy's boss wanting to retire. They were trying to take over her space, where a witchy-vibed shop already resided and was closed down, making the transition and the space their own. They'd been working on it pretty steady with the help of some of the brothers in their spare time surrounding us, still trying to get the permits and shit to make the distillery dream a reality.

That was on the verge of happening, too. All our plans were right there within reach, on the cusp of being a reality when here we all were, hunkered down in the thick cinderblock walls of our fuckin' clubhouse like fuckin' refugees, while the Bayou Fucksticks were out there running amok in our city like they owned it.

Let 'em think so. We were coming, and we had every intention of bringing hell with us before we finalized anything.

We didn't want to give these assholes any hard targets, so it was all a part of the fucking plan at this point.

We were just biding our time. No need to rush anything. Rushing is how you got caught. Rushing is how you made mistakes... like we'd rushed to get the hell out of Dodge after dispatching Ruth.

Biggest mistake we'd ever made to date as far as I was concerned, but killing him ain't come easy to any of us.

"You good?" I murmured to Velina during a lull in conversation and storytelling while people emptied bladders and got refills on their drinks and shit.

"Yeah, just tired. It's been a hell of a week with everything going on. Not just the dipshits, either, but the news and the crazy shit going on in the Quarter. It's been just crazy high stress staying on high alert like all the time, you know?"

"Yeah, I get that," I said, grinning.

"Sorry," she said, blushing.

"For what?" I asked.

"I get the feeling I just sounded like a civilian or whatever right there."

I laughed. "Citizen, and yeah, a little."

"It's not so different at the end of the day," Jessie-Lou said. "Bein' a woman or bein' in this life. Either way, you're always lookin' over your shoulder and wonderin' what's next."

Velina was staring into the fire, sort of vacantly, but she was listening. Jessie-Lou had pretty much been born into the life. Her daddy was an outlaw – out poaching to make ends meet some years and rogue fishin' out in the Gulf. Her people didn't have much love for the government – just a bunch of rules and regulations that made an already tough life even harder if you asked them.

"She's right," I conceded when Velina looked to me and raised a brow.

"Yee haw, fuck the law," Collier said and gave Jessie-Lou's knee a double squeeze from the camp chair beside hers.

"Sometimes I wonder what it's like bein' so blissfully unaware, you know? How people can go to work with the same job and not two or three, an' make enough to live off of comfortably. Y'know?"

"We'll get there, baby," Collier said. "I promise."

"Oh, I know," she said with a little half-smile.

"Just gotta work for it, they say," Velina said. "Has a lot to do with luck, too, and the station you were born into."

"There's more 'n one world out there," I said with a heavy sigh.

"I didn't use to think so, but coming down here has definitely opened my eyes," she said.

"New Orleans is the kind of city that'll do that for you," Hex declared, coming back into the conversation and dropping back into his seat. Cor slid into his lap and sighed.

"She either opens up her arms and welcomes you wholeheartedly, or she chews you up and spits you right the fuck out – that's for sure," Jessie-Lou declared, saluting Hex with her drink.

"Depends on the kind of person you are," I said, knowing exactly what they were talkin' about as one of the lifelong, born-and-raised residents of the city herself. No offense to Jessie-Lou, she was as Cajun through and through – Acadian to the bitter last, but she was Louisiana born – not city born like I was. There was a difference.

"You come to this city and have a deep vibe like you've been here before, or that you belong, she welcomes you," I explained to Velina's questioning look. "You one of the people who come here, and the vibe of the city scares you or gives you the creeps – you might as well just leave. She ain't ever gonna love you. You aren't her people."

"I don't know exactly which category I belong in," Velina said truthfully.

"How's that?" Jessie-Lou asked.

"Like, don't get me wrong, this is a cool city, and I get it. I feel like I belong here on a good day, but at the same time, it just has a different vibe from day to night, man. Like I don't even know."

We all sort of waited her out while she gathered her thoughts on the subject.

"Like, you go into the Quarter during the day, it's fine, it's a tourist trap – whatever. It's all well and good, but you can *fucking feel* the change as the sun starts to set. It's not like the vibe just instantly shifts. It's like this slow and creeping thing that comes up out of the sewers or oozes out of the alleyways, and the vibe at night is totally different to the one during the day. I hate being out during the shift. Like out at daylight, fine. Out at night? Also, fine. During the in-between times? No, thank you."

"Oh, see, now me? I *love* the shift," Sandrine said. "That's when you see and feel things. It's especially wild around Halloween."

"What do you mean?" Velina asked.

"I've seen people walking down the street at the shift, and like, the rest of the people don't even realize they're doing it. They just sort of part like the Red Sea and make way for them. Like these are perfectly ordinary looking people, but they give off some kind of an aura or whatever that makes people move."

"Yeah, those people ain't alive no more," Jessie-Lou said, laughing.

"What, like they're ghosts?" Velina asked, but she wasn't laughing. She was genuinely curious.

"Ghosts, vampires, maybe. Roux Garou. Hard to tell. They just ain't real or alive anymore. This city, she holds onto things. Like echoes from the past. Just how she is."

We all sat with that for a moment, and ain't none of us could argue.

"You need anything?" I asked Velina after a little while.

"Honestly, I think bed. Can I stay at your place?" she asked.

"Fuck yeah. Anybody got a cage willing to give us a ride?" I asked.

"Yeah, the weather's shit for riding," Chainsaw said, and we all looked out the big open bay door which we kept open for the smoke to escape.

It was still coming down out there like it would never end.

"Right on," I said.

CHAPTER THIRTY

Velina...
Chainsaw gave us a ride back to Saint's, and Saint had to direct him. It was a reminder of how Saint really didn't let anyone fully into his life, let alone his space, and I didn't know how, with how... adversarial our beginnings, I had made the cut, but I was grateful.

When we got in, we took a hot shower together, kissed and fooled around, but I had to tap out and confess I was still sore from the last round we'd had together just the day before yesterday. He stopped, just like that. Pulled me close and kissed my forehead and touched me until I whimpered and moaned, and then he slowed down with even that.

He was a soothing presence that made my mind go blissfully silent. When I was like this with him, everything was alright. I felt safe, protected, and loved. It was a wholly new and unique experience for me. One that I craved and wished I could hold on to for as long as possible.

We fell asleep watching a horror flick, and it was nice – but all too soon, my phone was going off with its alarm, and I was going to be late for work if I didn't *hurry*.

I was already on thin ice, so I hauled ass to get ready. Saint gave me a ride in his truck – even though it was dangerous as all get out to potentially be seen.

We risked it, and I managed to get through the day, even though Carver was being a total asshole, blowing up my phone and still bitching about how I'd "ditched" him the night before. Which, yes, I had, but Louie was *sick* – so fuck him.

I sparred with him a while, back and forth, texting between rooms, but eventually it just became this vicious cycle. Louie and I were tired of it, so we just stopped responding.

When I got back to my motel at the end of the long day, I was unnerved enough that I requested to change rooms for safety. They had no problem and moved me right away. The girl at the desk sympathetic.

I told Saint what I was doing via text, and all he asked was if he needed to take care of it. I told him no, not yet. I didn't feel like my work was done, and he simply came back with an *okay*.

I moved my stuff to a decent room around the corner. A little more decent than the one that I'd just vacated, which honestly wasn't saying much.

I showered, settled in, and with a sigh of relief, turned on the television to the nightly news. I pulled my book off the nightstand, but I didn't open it, not yet.

I woke to the blaring music of my ringtone and the glow of the bedside lamp and television. I didn't even remember falling asleep. I answered the phone when I saw it was Singer, and she sniffled on the other end of the line and warbled out, "Louie?"

"Hey, yeah, it's me. What's wrong?" I asked.

"He hit me, and I don't know what to do," she said mournfully. I sat up more fully.

"Okay, where are you at?" I asked gently. "I'll come help."

"I'm at home," she said.

"Okay, can you text me the address?" I asked.

"Yeah," she said and sobbed.

"Okay, do that, I'm going to get dressed, and I'll be right over. Is he still there?"

"No, he took off," she answered.

"Okay, okay, I'm on my way. Just hang on," I said.

"Okay," she said.

"I'm going to hang up now."

"Okay."

I immediately texted Saint with the news and Singer's address. I knew he was likely to be asleep, but he messaged me back to be careful, and that he would be keeping an eye on me on the tracker app.

I texted back.

Don't you ever sleep?

When you're not with me, and I can't get you off my mind? No.

Oh.

I pushed the thoughts and feelings those words evoked to the side in my panic to get to Singer. I was worried about her. I pulled up on a crowded street in an older, rundown neighborhood in some ward. I didn't know them all yet. It could have been closer to the Ninth, but I couldn't be sure. I just didn't know my way around that intimately yet.

It took me a while to find parking up the way, and I practically *ran* down the cracked and tree-root-lifted sidewalk to the door marked with her number. I knocked swiftly. She opened up, and my heart broke for her.

"Oh, honey," I said quietly. "Come on, let's get you cleaned up."

She hugged me and wept into my shoulder. I couldn't help but feel my heart dropping to pieces for her. Her one eye was swollen shut, and she had a cut above it through her eyebrow. Hell, the whole one side of her face was swollen and raw, and I had to imagine he had her down on the floor as he'd pounded his fist into the side of her face mercilessly.

Her tiny little apartment's living space was a mess of scattered items and broken things, from the coffee table to knickknacks, books from her small bookshelf scattered from where she'd been knocked into it.

"Come on into the kitchen, baby, and let me have a better look. Do you have any first aid stuff?"

"Under the bathroom sink," she said and sniffed.

"Okay, come on." I shut the front door to her apartment behind me and let her lean on me as we carefully picked our way through the carnage to her little kitchenette table. I pulled out a chair for her, lowered her into it, and said, "Wait here. I'll be right back."

I went in search of her bathroom and found it in the hallway. Under the sink, I found some useful things. A first aid kit, hydrogen peroxide, antiseptic, and the like. The first aid kit looked like it had never been used except for maybe a few Band-Aids, but still, she had a couple of boxes of those, and that was a good supplement.

I'd seen women take beatings the likes of hers before, and I had to wonder if it wasn't best to get her to a doctor or hospital for imaging. She could have some facial bone fractures, and those were honestly nothing to play with.

I went back out to the kitchen, where she sat in her cream satin nightgown and teal satin robe with cherry blossoms and cranes printed on it. I pulled a chair around to sit across from her.

"This looks bad," I said, tsking as I gently tucked some of her wild blonde mane behind her ear to get a better look at the damage to her face.

"Yeah?" she sniffed.

"You definitely won't be working for a while, but I'm more afraid there might be fractures under here. I really think that we should get you in for some X-rays."

"No," she said sharply. "No doctors. A doctor would call the cops, and you don't call the cops on these guys. I'm not gonna rat. I don't want to die." She burst into tears, and I sighed.

I hugged her and soothed her as best I could and finally said, "Let's not worry about it unless the pain gets too bad or there are changes to your vision. Right now, let's just focus on getting you cleaned and bandaged up, huh?"

"Okay," she said weakly. So I did just that, carefully cleaning off the worst of the blood and swabbing the cuts with antiseptic and bandaging them up.

"What happened?" I asked her evenly when she'd finally calmed down, half afraid I would get her worked up all over again when I didn't want to.

She sniffed and said, "He wanted me to take a hit of MOLL-E

before we got busy, you know? I said no, and he got pissed off. Started bitching about how I always had to be such a drag and how I had no sense of adventure or whatever. I told him no, that I did, I just didn't want to risk my sobriety. I just didn't want to do any drugs, and he got mad." Her voice broke. "He hit me. Said no dumb bitch stripper was gonna talk back to him, and he-he…"

"Did he rape you?" I asked quietly, and her broken sobbing was all the answer that I needed. I took a deep breath and hugged her, rubbing over her back and just being a shoulder that she could cry on.

"It's not so bad," she said soggily a few minutes later. "I've had worse." She sniffed, and I understood the need to compartmentalize things like that. To minimize them in order to just *deal* with them in any way that could make the horrors small enough to fit in the boxes and vaults in the darkened recesses of your mind to forget them.

Still, her attempt at rationalizing this just made things exponentially *more* horrifying for me as her witness.

"He'll never do this again," I promised, and she let out a broken and bitter laugh.

"You can't promise that, Louie. You can't."

"I *can*," I said. "What's more, you're going to help me."

"I told you, I'm not going to the cops," she said. I shook my head.

"No cops. They're fucking useless around here, anyway," I said. "I'm going to trust you with something," I said, making the decision. "Listen carefully…"

I told her.

All of it.

About Louie, my brother, and the Voodoo Bastards. About who I really was and what I was doing, and most importantly *why* I was doing it.

"You're crazy," she said in a horrified whisper, her one blue eye wide and showing so much white.

I nodded.

"So I've been told," I agreed.

"Why are you telling me this?" she asked, a fresh track of tears leaking down her cheeks.

"Because you've worked way too hard to get where you are to stay with someone who's gonna treat you like this," I said.

"And *they* don't?" she asked incredulously.

I stared her in the eyes, my face as solemn as I could make it, and didn't say a word. I just shook my head slowly and with conviction.

Her face crumpled in confusion.

"If I get them to help you get away from here, all it will cost you is information," I said.

"I don't wanna start over again," she said, and her expression grew stricken. I felt monumentally guilty about putting this on her, but...

"Please help me help you," I begged. "You're not trapped, I promise. I know it feels that way right now, but I *promise*, I'm trying to help you. When I said he will never do this shit to you again, I meant it – but I need your help, too."

"How?" she asked. "How can you expect me to do this, any of this?"

"Let's get you in a shower and changed out of these bloody clothes," I said.

She looked down at herself and said, "Damn, this was my favorite set. It made me feel pretty."

"Don't fret," I said. "I can get the blood out. I'm trusting you, so please, please, *please*. I'm going to need you to trust *me*."

She sniffed, nodded, and said, "O-o-okay."

I got her into her shower and stood at her bathroom sink, blotting the blood out of her pajamas, pouring hydrogen peroxide on them, and letting the stains foam and foam, blotting, and repeating, until barely a whisper of discoloration remained.

We got Singer into a fresh set of clean clothes following the shower – a pair of leggings and an oversized shirt. Something comfortable and covering for now.

I helped her into bed, tucked her in, and said, "You don't have to make any big decisions right now, but soon, okay? Let me get this place cleaned up. You rest right now. Try to get a little sleep on it."

"What are you going to do?" she asked.

I swallowed hard.

"I'm going to call my man – my *real* man – and work something out. Don't you worry," I said, and vaguely *I* worried. I worried that Saint was going to be fucking pissed at me for letting the cat out of the bag, but I really wanted to help Singer out. At the same time, I knew she could help *us* out.

I was looking at a monumental shortcut here – she already knew so much about all of them. Their movements, their hiding places, all of it. It was really just about tapping that fine feminine rage every woman harbored within herself and turning it loose into the ether.

I thought I could get there, but it was iffy. She was scared, like really scared, and I understood that I was too. I was going out on a *major* limb here, but I was hoping that we could help each other. I really wanted to get her out. Get her somewhere where she could keep moving forward, up, and *out* – find the life she *wanted* and leave all this stupid shit behind.

I didn't know how to connect the dots, but I was hoping like hell that Saint *would*.

As soon as she was resting and I was alone, standing in the wreckage of her apartment, I made the call… hoping against hope that all the pieces would fit.

CHAPTER THIRTY-ONE

S aint...

"Yeah, I need some help," I said over the line to LaCroix on the other end.

"What's up? Velina, okay?"

"Yeah, she's good. She's real good. She may have just seized us a real opportunity here, but it's gonna take some leverage," I said.

"What's that?" LaCroix asked.

I explained the situation. About how one of the Bayou Brethren had beat the fuckin' brakes off of his woman, done her down and dirty – all because she wouldn't get doped up for his pleasure. About how she was in recovery and how Velina had taken a liking to her. About how Velina was sure she wanted out and how, if we provided a clear path out of Dodge and got her set up somewhere, how she may be willing to trade us pertinent information on the Bayou Bitches in exchange.

LaCroix listened on the other end of the line and was quiet for a minute.

"Let me call the Florida boys and see if they might be willing to take in a stray," he said, and I felt a slow grin overtake the lower half of my face.

"You read my fuckin' mind," I said.

If anyone was going to be sympathetic to the cause of keeping someone who wanted to stay clean, *clean*, it was the boys of the Kraken MC. They'd helped their little lost chick who'd gotten sucked into the worst of the underworld of human trafficking get clean when those evil fucks had been using heroin as a means to keep the girls in their clutches docile.

If anyone could help shelter this chick from that life, it would be them.

"Get over to 'em, take Chainsaw with you. He should be up by now."

"Will do," I said, and just as soon as I got off the phone with LaCroix, I dialed Chainsaw up.

"*Fuck*," he swore. "I got a big oak to help take down around some powerlines over in Plaquemine Parrish today." He sighed. "Where you wanna meet up?" he asked.

"Café du Monde on Veterans Boulevard," I said. "Metairie."

"Yeah, yeah, I know where it is. Be there as soon as I can."

"Thanks," I said.

We met up and headed to the pin on the map where Velina was. When I texted that we'd arrived, she was waiting on the front porch of a dilapidated little one-story apartment building set in a strip along the road. We found street parking around the corner and took ourselves quickly into the place.

"Where's she at?" Chainsaw asked, and Velina shook her head.

"Resting," she said. "I'm cleaning up the wreckage in here. Have a seat." She indicated the living room, where a broom and dustpan rested against one of the chairs, while the trash can from the kitchen rested next to a broken coffee table with its lid off.

"Jesus, he put her through the coffee table?" Chainsaw asked.

"Yep," she said, her face carefully schooled into something neutral, which told me she was masking a fine burning rage. Only way a fire of that magnitude was stoked in a woman was when some seriously foul shit went down.

"Raped her too, I reckon," I said, and nothing about her expression really changed as she took up the broom and swept in short strokes over the area rug to gather up some of the shattered glass and broken pieces of whoever this girl's life was.

"Yep," was all she said in the same tightly restrained tone.

"Shit," Chainsaw swore softly. "She gonna be okay?" he asked.

Velina leveled him with a look and told him what the girl had said to her. "She said it wasn't the worst thing to ever happen to her."

Chainsaw and I exchanged a look.

"And she's willing to help us out?" I asked.

Velina took a deep breath and let it out slowly. "I really hope so," she said. "She's scared as hell, and I can't say I blame her."

"Motherfucker," Chainsaw muttered and hung his head.

She didn't know... I'd gathered what she'd told me on the phone was what she *would like* to happen, and it was all totally within reason and doable.

"LaCroix put in a call for us. We're just waiting to hear back, but I'm sure what you want is totally within the realm of possibility," I said.

"What does *she* want?" Chainsaw asked, referring to the woman in the other room whose place we stood in, his hands on his hips.

"To stay clean," Velina said. "To make enough money she doesn't have to fucking strip anymore if she doesn't want to. She wants some fucking *peace.*"

"Easy, there darlin'," Chainsaw said. "We're on the same side."

"No, I know," Velina said, stopping her sweeping and sighing, pinching the bridge of her nose.

"We'll make it happen," I said. "We just need to hear what she's got to say and go from there."

Velina nodded, and Chainsaw and I set about helping out in cleaning up, mostly by taking the wrecked coffee table out of the picture and out the door in the back. There was a small parking lot back here with a dumpster in the back corner.

We made quick work, just in case Singer's man decided he wanted to put in an "I'm sorry" appearance. We'd much rather get the drop on him rather than the other way around.

By the time we were done with cleanup and Velina had made coffee, we heard stirring in the back bedroom. Chainsaw and I took seats in the living room while Velina finished up in the kitchen. This beat-to-fuck-ing-hell blonde woman came moving slowly down the hall, hugging herself. She froze at the sight of me and Chainsaw and called, "Louie?"

Velina came around out of the kitchen with a couple coffee mugs and handed one to each of us boys before going over to the girl.

"It's okay," she soothed. "That one there is my man, Saint, and that's Chainsaw," she told her.

"Um, hi," the blonde said, trembling in fear.

"Hi," Chainsaw and I said in unison.

"Come sit down, sweetheart," Chainsaw said, gesturing at the chair open beside us.

She crept into the room like a frightened cat and looked like hell, her pretty face swollen and fucked up with a big Quasimodo shiner on one side.

"I'm Temperance," she said. "I mean, that's my real name... ironic, I know."

Velina smiled and said, "I like that much better than Singer."

She went back to the kitchen as Temperance tucked herself into the chair and drew her knees up to her chest.

"So, um, what happens now?" she asked.

"You give us information, and we get you out," I said.

"Just like that?" she asked.

"Just like that," Chainsaw affirmed.

She looked terrified, and Velina asked, "How do you take your coffee, honey?"

"There's flavored creamer in the fridge," Temperance answered.

We were all silent for a time while Velina fixed up a cup of Joe for Temperance and herself.

When she brought it out to her, Temperance took it with shaking hands, damn near sloshing hot coffee out of the mug.

"Easy, you're okay. We're not gonna hurt you," Chainsaw said gently and I swallowed a mouthful of coffee, unsure of what to say that would help.

"So how does this work?" she asked. "I tell you a whole bunch of things about the Bayou Brethren, and you do what? Use it to kill them?"

"That's about the right of it," I told her.

She sniffed and looked into her cup as though it held the answers there.

"You're asking me to sign people's death warrant, you know that, right?"

"Can I ask you something?" Chainsaw asked in a conciliatory tone.

She looked to him, her battered face pathetic, and nodded once.

"What have these people done for you? Hmm?" he asked.

She stared, her blue eye rapt on him, and blinked slowly, the wheels in her head turning.

"That's what I thought," he said quietly, leaning back in his seat.

She looked ill, and I hated it for her – but the truth fuckin' hurt sometimes. I just hoped it hurt enough to motivate her into doing something about it.

This was one hell of a gamble, a hell of a play.

My phone rang, and I answered it.

"Yeah," I said.

"A couple of the Kraken boys are on their way out here to collect the girl," LaCroix said. "Have her pack some bags. If she's got a cage, have Velina drive it and her here to the club, pull around back. We'll get her all taken care of."

"Copy that," I said and hung up.

"That was LaCroix," I said.

"Yeah, no, I heard," Temperance said. "Who are the Kraken?" she asked.

"Club out of Florida," I answered. "We help each other out from time to time. They're willing to help us out and take you someplace safe. Take you on out there to Ft. Royal, Florida – start a new life for yourself. All you have to do is tell us what you know about the fuck-tards who did this to you, and you're home free."

"How can I trust you?" she asked quietly.

"Short answer? You got any other choice?" I asked.

"You're not trusting them," Velina intervened. "You're trusting me... or Louie. We're the same people. You know?" she said.

"I mean, I don't know," she whispered. "You've been lying to me this whole time!" She was getting upset, but she wasn't wrong.

"Either way, you can't stay here. That asshole is liable to come back. Go pack yourself a couple of bags. We'll get you out," Chainsaw said.

"You've got your choice between him and us," Velina said. "And I promise, we haven't hurt you, and we're not going to. Neither are the Kraken. For real, we help you, then you help us, okay?"

Temperance stared at Velina, and it was my turn to intercede.

"Do what he says, honey. We'll get you out first, then worry about the rest."

"You have until you finish your coffee to decide," Velina said, seeing she was overwhelmed.

"Thanks," she said, and the confusion was apparent. She was struggling, but I felt good about things. Like we were winning.

We all worked on drinking our coffee, finishing in silence. Velina gathered our cups and took them to the kitchen to wash and dry them by hand.

Chainsaw went back with Temperance to stand at her door and make sure she didn't pull anything like send a text or make a call. Velina and I waited in the living room when a knock fell at the door. I stepped quietly and carefully into the hallway out of sight with a soft nod at my girl to get it.

She nodded back, and adrenaline spiked. I pulled out my collapsible baton from its spot on my belt and put a finger to my lips as I looked down the hallway at Chainsaw to signal him to keep quiet and to keep Temperance quiet.

We had no idea who was on the other side of that door...

CHAPTER THIRTY-TWO

Velina...

The knocking came again, more insistent this time, and I looked back over my shoulder as I reached the door. Saint gave me a single nod before melting back into the shadows of the hallway, and heart pounding in my chest, I opened the door.

Basilisk stared at me with his stony, ever-present non-expression and demanded, "What the fuck are you doing here?"

"Taking care of Singer since you worked her over," I said flatly. "She doesn't want to see you." I tried to slam the door, but he stuck his steel-toe boot in it and shoved it open and me off it with one great shove.

I mean, dude was strong like an ox, stubborn like a bull. I let him cross the threshold and slammed the door behind him.

"I *said* she doesn't want to see you!" I shouted. "Now, get out!"

"Fuck you, bitch!" he growled and grabbed me by the chin, throwing me down on the floor in front of the couch.

I laughed at him. I wanted him to turn his back to the hallway, and it worked like a charm. He rounded on me, and there was nothing stony about his look now. He looked positively *crazed*, like he was definitely on something.

"What you laughing at, huh?" he demanded, looming over me menacingly. I couldn't help it. I just laughed harder as Saint appeared behind him in the mouth of the hallway. By the time he whipped out his wrist and the collapsible baton made its rasping and click as it tele-scoped out and locked into place – it was too late for Basilisk.

He turned just in time to take Saint's first swing right in the cheekbone.

He went down like a ton of bricks and Saint just kept right on swinging. I scrambled past them both and into the hall, where I caught Temperance, who had escaped from Chainsaw. I hollered at Chainsaw to go, to make sure Saint was going to be okay, and hugged Temper-ance tight while the boys dealt with Basilisk.

She cried and whimpered with every meaty thwack and blow that landed, and I forced her to look at me. I said savagely, "I told you. He would never fucking hurt you again."

She stared at me, eye wide with shock, and swallowed whatever she'd been about to say or scream next and just crumpled into my arms and wept, her whole body sagging with relief.

By the time my boys were done beating him to death, we were firmly in my wheelhouse.

It was time to clean a crime scene.

CHAPTER THIRTY-THREE

S aint...

I stood up, panting, covered in blood spatter and cast off, the dipshit motherfucker who'd put his hands on my woman deader 'n shit in the middle of the living room area rug in front of me. I turned to look back in the hallway where Velina stood, turned back in my direction, holding the weeping blonde in her arms, hiding her away from the carnage.

My woman looked me dead in the fucking eye and said the hottest shit I'd ever heard come out of a woman's mouth, "My turn."

She then proceeded to rattle off a list of shit she would need to help clean this place up like we'd never fuckin' been here.

I nodded and stepped away, getting on the horn.

"We've got a situation," I said. "The good news? One down – however many of these motherfuckers to go."

It was a hell of a whirlwind after that.

Bennie and Hex showed up, and Velina sent her friend packing with Bennie and Chainsaw. Hex stayed.

We had the keys to Temperance's car and would use it to handle things – buying ourselves a little insurance with any of the evidence left behind in her car rather than in Hex's truck.

Shitty? Yeah, but honestly, I didn't think we'd need it. Still better to have insurance than not.

Velina went through that place top to fucking bottom, cleaning up while Hex and I rolled the motherfucker up in the living room rug, duct-taping that shit as secure as we could get it.

She didn't miss a thing and imparted all sorts of useful information every step of the way to make us more efficient in our, ah, *future endeavors*. Which, as far as I was concerned, we had just kicked off with the disappearance of Basilisk here, and his woman.

We waited for the wee hours of the morning and loaded the rolled-up carpet into the trunk of Temperance's battered old beater car and drove him on out to the smokehouse. It was just me and Velina at that point. Hex had gone and taken my bike out of there. We didn't go back. The apartment was scrubbed clean, and clearly, with the missing furniture and rug, something had gone down – but good luck finding any evidence, fuckers.

After that, we went to the club and stashed the car in the garage, pulling it into a back corner and covering it up with a tarp until we could sort that out.

By the time we were done, Temperance was already on the road to Florida with the boys from the Kraken, and had imparted enough information to LaCroix and Axeman to set up for our next target.

I was tapping out, though. I burned my clothes in the burn barrel back at the club. Velina said to me, "Give me that," and held her hand out for my cut.

"You know what it means I should hand this to you and trust you with it?" I asked.

"I know," she said.

I handed it to her in front of everyone, and she set to work on it. No, we weren't supposed to clean our cuts – but I wasn't about to hold onto one full of fuckin' evidence by way of blood spatter from the motherfuckin' worm I'd beat to death, either. Discretion being the better part of valor – I let her handle it.

"You come in handy, huh?" Cypress asked my woman as he watched her work with a bottle of hydrogen peroxide, an old rag cut from an old tee, and a cheap toothbrush.

"Guess so," she said.

We were both exhausted by the time we went to collect her car and headed home.

"I hope the couples that murder together and clean up the scene of the crime together stay together," she said flatly once we were in the shower.

I laughed, and she gave me a weak smile before twining her arms around my neck and hugging to me tightly.

I held her and kissed her temple, burying my hand in the back of her hair.

I had to remember she was used to cleaning up the aftermath of violence of that level, but she wasn't necessarily used to seeing it first-hand or the body.

"You alright?" I asked her.

"Drained," she said. "Exhausted… but yeah, I'm alright."

We stood under the hot shower spray for a time and just held onto each other in silence.

"I scare you?" I asked, worried.

"No," she said.

"No?" I asked.

She shook her head and turned it so she could rest her ear against my chest.

"I don't think you'd ever do it to me," she said. "If you did, I'd kill you."

I chuckled at that for a couple reasons. One, the thought of hurting her was ludicrous to me. Two, even if I hypothetically could hurt her– I highly doubted she could kill me. Many had tried and failed, but I supposed stranger things could happen.

"I don't doubt that you would," I said. "But I would never. I'd as soon as cut off my own arm."

She cuddled into me, looked up, and said, "Kiss me. I just want to forget the last several hours."

"You're speaking my language," I purred, and I met her mouth with mine. God, she tasted good. So fine, so pure, but with that edge of darkness like a bittersweet dark chocolate. She'd certainly had her soul stained with violence long before she'd met me, but this had been a different animal. This time, she'd dipped her toes into the darkness all by herself, with no help, and I couldn't help but wonder if it'd been enough to satiate her appetite for revenge or if it'd just been an appetizer.

It was a conversation for another time, another day – another life, maybe, once we'd gotten through this.

We were just getting started, and I hoped like a motherfucker we would all make it through. That Velina would be able to hold on with me, become something stronger for it, more self-assured, *my dark queen,*

The kiss turned fervent, more passionate, *life-affirming,* and our hands couldn't stop their wandering over slick, hot skin. It was starting to get hard to tell whether the steam clouding my small bathroom was generated entirely by the hot water or if it was coming from us. From the connection we had, from the bond we'd quenched in blood, that'd become something stronger than iron, stronger than steel.

Soul deep, our passions ran, and I couldn't keep myself from growing hard against her, where she pressed her lithe tight body to mine with its epic curves and so-soft skin.

She was a masterpiece for the senses, and I couldn't get enough of her if I tried.

I kissed all the way down her body, kneeling on the shower floor and nuzzling her stomach, pressing her against the stone tiles of the wall, and draping her one leg over my shoulder. She yipped and tangled her fingers in my hair as I went for my prize and delved my tongue at the cleft of her sex.

Her yip of startlement at being put off balance turned into a throaty moan that ended on a strangled gasp as she tried to hold her composure, but I was determined she lose it. I wanted her to come against my mouth, standing in the shower, as the hot water beat against my back and poured across my skin.

I wasn't worried about her staying warm. I would work that out just fine with my mouth on her, my hands on her, and, if need be, my fingers inside of her.

"Mm, yeah!" She gripped my hair tightly at the roots and pulled me tighter against her body, encouraging me to give her what she needed, and it was *so* fucking *hot.*

I teased and tantalized, sucked, and slicked my tongue against that sweet bundle of nerves that would send fireworks through her veins, and I rolled my eyes up the length of her body to watch her.

Her breasts heaved with every breath, her head leaned back against the tile, and her eyelashes made dark crescents against her lightly tanned face as she lost herself in the exquisite torture of my touch.

The sight of her pleasure, the sound of her moaning and panting, the feel of her hot, smooth skin under my hands, lips, and tongue, the scent of her, the intoxicating flavor of her passion – again, she was a living *masterpiece,* and it was something thrilling to be able to mold her with my attentions into something of starlight and madness. It made me hard to the point of aching, and I couldn't resist fisting myself and stroking as I ate her out and worked at wrenching an orgasm from her.

She rode my face in the shower, and I had to let my cock go to steady myself, one hand on her outer thigh of the leg draped down my back, the other between her thighs, middle finger deeply entrenched in her tight wet pussy, the delicate tissues squeezing around my invading fingers as she built closer and closer to that ultimate goal.

I fucking loved how tight she got when she was about to come. Loved how she pulled my face where she wanted it, how she writhed and practically humped my tongue to get herself there as much as to let me get her where she wanted to go.

She panted and moaned, cried out, and then stiffened against me, her pussy throbbing, squeezing down and releasing in the rhythm of the heavens as starlight touched her veins and she practically glowed with the exquisite sensations racing along every nerve ending like fire across water.

God, she was fucking perfect.

CHAPTER THIRTY-FOUR

Velina...

I gasped and panted, my body trembling finely as both the wall and Saint held me up, but as good as that had felt, it wasn't enough. His fingers inside me just *weren't enough.*

"Fuck me," I begged.

He laughed and asked me, "That good?"

"God, please fuck me!" I begged, and I put down my leg and turned, bending over to give him access to my pussy.

He growled in appreciation and lapped at my sex from behind, sucking on my pussy lips and licking me from clit to taint. All it served to do was drive me even more fucking *feral* for him. I pushed back and whined.

It wasn't enough. I didn't know if it could ever be enough. I was so fucking *desperate* to have his cock inside me, and I was half afraid that even that wouldn't fulfill the desire raging through me, burning me up from the inside out.

"Please," I begged. "Please, put it inside me!"

"You craving that cock, baby girl?" he asked me in that low, rough tone that sent shivers all through me in an aftershock from the first orgasm.

"Please," I begged. "Please don't tease me."

He chuckled low and dark, and pressed into me while I pressed back onto him. He grunted and took in a deep breath through clenched teeth behind me, smoothing a hand through the water trickling down my skin.

"God, I fucking love how tight you are for me," he said. "Brace yourself, both hands against that wall. Do it," he ordered, and I pressed my hands flat against the wall in front of me as he gripped my hips in his big hands.

"Fuck yes," he hissed as he drew back and thrust forward. He was *not* gentle about it, but that was good. It was so very fucking good because I didn't want gentle. I wanted him to fuck me so hard I felt it for *days* after. I wanted the roughest fuck of my life. I wanted that sweet pain to let me know I was *alive,* and God, did I beg him to do it.

I panted, I demanded, *"Harder!"* with every slapping report our bodies made. I loved how it felt, the head of his cock punishing my cervix deep inside me. I relished the bruising force with which he took me, and I couldn't get enough of it.

It was decadent, it was dark, and it was also sickly sweet, the smell of roses hanging in the night air of a poisoned garden. The tang of a rich soil and the palate of a dark tiramisu melting across the tongue. It was fire and ice, it was night and day, it burned, and it chilled me to the bone the power he held in his hands, against my skin, that he thrust into me with, making me melt and harden like wax on the skin.

Fuck, it was fine, and *fuck,* I couldn't get enough of him.

His touch, his scent like good tequila and cypress wood, an unknown spice and something rich, like sable soft fur that caressed the inside of your skull. Impossible, but there, a sensation that made no sense but drove me absolutely wild all the same.

I pressed my hands into the shower wall as he gave no mercy as he drove into me, and I didn't want it, mercy, that is. I most definitely wanted everything he was giving me and more. The dark part of me that was alright with the murder, mayhem, and cleanup of the scene of the crime somehow, someway, wanted *more.* My thirst for blood had been stoked rather than slaked.

There was some part of me that was rising like a phoenix from the ashes of my broken childhood, from the bonds of rules set forth by a society that didn't give a rat's ass about me, and it felt *freeing*. As freeing as anything I'd ever felt before, and it was a gift beyond words and beyond measure given to me by the man who fulfilled every one of my darkest desires without judgment. If anything, he lifted me up and made all things possible, and I loved him for that.

I loved him for freeing me so completely, for loving me so savagely, and for protecting me with everything that he had.

I would let him do whatever he wanted to me and submit wholly to his will, if he just promised to hold me close like he was so want to do forever.

I wailed as he unmade me in the shower all over again with his cock, trembling finely and nearly falling as the orgasm rocked me, but he wouldn't let me fall. Catching me around the waist and keeping me on my feet as he laughed as my body failed me with how he'd broken me apart, and I couldn't help but laugh too, in joy and delight, in perfect love and perfect trust, knowing that Saint had me.

"Who's next?" I asked quietly as we lay cuddled and satiated in the dark later that night.

"Mm?" he asked groggily.

"What's next?" I asked, changing my phrasing ever so slightly, suddenly embarrassed somehow with how I wanted to just keep going through every last one of the ones responsible for killing my brother.

"What's next is getting you outta that fuckin' hotel and getting you home," he said. "As for *who's* next... easiest one to pick off is gonna be the fuckstick that had you blow him, so we want to make sure Louie is good and gone before that goes down."

I thought about that for a little bit and asked, "Do you think Singer is going to be okay?"

"Yeah," he said. "I know so. The Kraken are good people, baby. They'll get her set up to where she can thrive soon enough. With her man good and gone and her good and gone and her apartment the way it looks? I'll bet before long, there'll be a manhunt for him, and they'll be out combing the swamps for *her* body."

"Ooo, I didn't even think of that," I said, and he chuckled and kissed the top of my head.

"It definitely looks like some shit went down at her place, and ain't nobody going to assume that *she* took *him* out. Honestly, it's all about making her car disappear altogether – and that's easy enough. We can lose it through one of the junkyards around here or push it off into one of the bayous or swamps. It'll never be found. Won't nobody look too hard for her. She'll just go down as another missing person."

"It's sad when you think about it, but you're right," I murmured.

"Give it some time. We'll get on out that way, just the two of us, and see how she's doing. Would you like that?"

"Honestly?" I asked. "Yeah. I would. I really would. She was the best out of all of them and wasn't really like them," I said. "You know?"

"Yeah, I got that. She seemed like a nice girl who just lost her way, only to find it again to fall in with the wrong people determined to pull her off the path all over again."

"Yeah," I said. "*Exactly.*"

"It is sad," Saint agreed. "But you did good. If anything, you saved that girl today." He heaved a big sigh, and we were quiet for a time.

"You're a good person," I said, starting to grow drowsy, all the adrenaline having worn off.

"To you, maybe," he said. "To the next guy, I might as well be the devil incarnate."

"If they'd stayed in their lane, you wouldn't have to be," I said, and he chuckled and kissed my forehead.

"Now you're gettin' it, baby. Now you're gettin' it."

I slept, something deep and dark and dreamless. More like a coma than just a sleep – the mental and emotional exhaustion creeping in.

While I didn't feel *good* about what'd been done in Temperance's apartment that day, I didn't feel like any of it was *wrong*. Except for the part where the man who was supposed to love her had beaten her and hurt her – no bad had happened there. No bad, only justice… which I knew the point would be argued by some.

That vigilantism wasn't justice, but honestly? For men and women like the rest of the Voodoo Bastards. Like my little brother Louie, and like me – it was the only kind of justice we got.

CHAPTER THIRTY-FIVE

S aint...

"You ready to do this?" Axe asked me, and I grinned
savagely.

"Fuck yeah," I said.

It'd been a few weeks, maybe even a couple of months since we'd
disposed of Basilisk and had rushed Temperance out of town.

Velina had resumed playing Louie, and it was for the best, honestly.
She was able to keep her ear to the ground and still move in the Bayou
Brethren's circles, even if it was more on the periphery than before.

She'd played things careful, keeping things to text with Carver and
playing the game of a girl with her feelings hurt after the way he'd
treated her surrounding her supposedly being sick and "ditching" him
at the bar.

They'd taken a break, and he'd kept trying, while she'd kept
stringing him along, acting skittish, and only agreeing to meet with
him publicly in the Quarter, and not allowing him to pick her up or
drop her off.

She played it like he needed to rebuild trust with her and gave him
the illusion that she'd give up her pussy at the end of the fucked-up
rainbow, and he bought it. Which is right where we wanted him.

Tonight was the night that she would lead him right to us and that she planned to retire Louie altogether.

We had plenty else to go on for the rest of the club by way of the information Temperance had been imparting.

We'd spent the last several weeks compiling her info, doing reconnaissance, pinning photos to boards, and mapping movements.

We weren't just sourcing the information from Temperance, either. We'd greased some palms in the city and had more help than the Brethren reckoned. A lot of the bars in the Quarter were sick of them coming in and starting shit and were more than willing to help us out to get rid of the problem. We knew that would only be a matter of time, but the waiting was killer by the same token.

Axe and I lounged on our bikes, waiting for Velina's signal that they were leaving the bar and heading for her hotel room. She'd moved from the LaChiquita into my house with me, but we still rented a room at a cheaper, even less savory place on the edge of the Ninth.

Yes, it was further from her cover job cleaning hotel rooms in the Quarter, but at the same time, it was closer to *us* and our stomping grounds. It also was in a hood where no one would call in gunfire, nor would anyone ask questions. It was a place where everyone minded their own fucking business.

She'd used the excuse of an outrageous rate hike to make the move, and the dipshit she was going with had bought it all hook, line, and sinker.

I got the text and sat up. "They're on their way this way."

Axe smiled and cracked his knuckles. We were waiting and watching. It wouldn't be long, now.

We let ourselves into the room next door to the one Velina had and waited. Our bikes were in a parking lot over the low cinderblock wall separating the properties. Conveniently, the wall was high enough to keep the bikes hidden from the parking lot. There was only one angle you could approach from where they would be visible, and Velina and her quarry would, one hundred percent, be coming in from the opposite direction, so it was good.

We heard a bike outside, and Axe peeked out the curtain and said, "Yeah, it's them." We kept our fucking mouths shut.

Game. Set. Match, motherfucker, I thought, and we both waited at the door adjoining the two rooms, listening intently.

The main door to the outside opened, and I heard Velina's familiar giggle. My blood pressure spiked when those giggles I so coveted were accompanied by the sounds of kissing and masculine laughter.

Axe put a hand on my shoulder, and I scowled at him. He took it off, holding it up in surrender, and gave me a look like *okay, I just needed to make sure.*

We waited until the bed squeaked under their combined weight before slipping through the conjoined door.

Velina was straddling him, and she pushed up off his chest with her hands, tearing her mouth from his and sitting up.

I put the plastic bag over his head and kneeled, pulling it tight over his face.

He bucked and fought, and Velina stared down at him dispassionately. No, that wasn't right. To stare at him dispassionately would imply that she had any kind of emotion on her face, which she didn't. She just stared with a blank expression and rode him as he clutched at his face and scrabbled at his throat while Axe took up position.

Dude wasn't completely dumb. He opened his mouth wide and punched a hole in the bag with his finger. I ripped it off his head just in time for Axe to press the barrel of his gun to the guy's forehead.

He held up his hands in surrender, and Velina sat back on him.

"Not so happy to see them, huh?" she asked.

"You *fucking bitch.*" His tone was full of a venom, and I knocked the taste right out of his mouth with a swift punch to his jaw.

"You'll respect my woman," I growled.

"No need, baby," Vel said. "I don't want his respect."

He looked from me to her as Axe pressed the gun into his face a little more insistently.

"I just want to know one thing," she said.

"I'm listening," he said cautiously, and I could see him running the math on if or how he would get out of this.

"Were you there the night your club pulled the drive-by on their club?" she asked, tilting her head in our direction.

"Yeah," he said. "We all were." He grinned slowly and savagely.

Velina pushed off of him and climbed back off the bed.

"You killed my brother, Louie, that night," she said and turned her attention to Axe and me. "If it's all the same to you boys, you can go ahead and make this as slow, painful, and bloody as you'd like."

"Oh, we plan to," Axe said. "Just not here."

I took out my burner and made the call. When the line picked up, I said, "Yeah, we got a quarter slab of gator for the smokehouse."

The line went dead.

It didn't matter who had picked up, the result would be the same. A couple of the guys would come by with the van. Ol' Carver may or may not feel just what his name felt like out at the smokehouse while his bike would be left in the lot for later. With any luck, it'd be the only way to identify his body by the time we got done with our plans.

Velina stood by and said, "I'll tell you one thing, this room'll never be cleaner in its whole existence by the time I get done with it."

I nodded, but my eyes were on Carver, who was breathing heavy and was about to take a deep breath to holler. I clocked him with a set of brass knuckles I pulled out of my pocket, and he went out like a traffic light.

"I promise to make it hurt, baby," I said, and Velina smiled.

"Oh, I know y'all will. I'm counting on it, in fact," she said.

"For Louie," Axe said, and she raised her solemn green eyes to his and nodded.

"For Louie, so there are no more Louies, and for me, if you don't mind," she said.

Axe grinned. "You got it," he said.

∽

TORTURE IS A LABORIOUS BUSINESS, and Carver ended up being a tough nut to crack – but crack him, we did.

He confirmed a lot of what we already knew and gave us more than a few nuggets of wisdom that we didn't. But it was pretty fuckin' apparent by the time we finished with him that we'd wrung every-thing we were going to get out of him that we could and that we had our work cut out for us when it came to culling the Bayou Brethren herd.

Of course, we could run through every single bottom-feeding hang-around, prospect, and fuckin' member, but it wouldn't do any good.

No, we needed to cut the head off the snake, and that would prove to be much harder.

There were only a couple of guys in the upper echelon of the Bayou Brethren who knew where Lazarus hung out on the regular, and nobody knew where he laid his bald fuckin' fucked-up head.

It was frustrating, but we'd made progress.

Baby steps, I guess.

By the time Axe and I returned and got our bikes, false dawn was a glimmer on the horizon.

We posed Carver's body and torched the motel. We'd done things right. There were no broken bones. By the time the fire got done with him, there wouldn't be enough left to determine a cause of death, and it would be chalked up to smoke inhalation or burning.

It'd be a while before anyone called it in. We'd rented out practically the whole place under the table. It was on the verge of shutting down anyway, being considered a nuisance property.

Wasn't going to be a problem anymore except clearing the land and making yet another empty lot in the Ninth.

I went home.

Velina was waiting up for me, watching some shit on television that I had no interest in. Some sappy romance series or something.

I guess she needed sappy after doing what we'd done. I didn't know.

I showered and came to bed, stretching out beside her and kissing her firmly, checking with her by asking, "You doing alright?"

"Pfft," she said. "I'm fuckin' *great*. You have no idea how relieved I am that I never have to see or deal with that asshole again."

I chuckled and asked, "You quit yet?"

"If by quit you mean I walked out of my last shift with no intention of ever going back, then yeah."

I snorted and said, "I thought you liked it there."

"Yes, and no," she said with a gusty sigh. "It was alright, but I'll be much happier leaving my Louie girl persona behind and just being Velina."

"Gonna have to avoid the Quarter for a while," I said.

"That's about the only bummer out of all this," she said. "I like it there."

"Well, I thought we might head on out to Florida for a bit, soak up some sun, check on your friend, take a breather from it all."

"I really like the sound of that," she said.

"We'll get rid of your car and take Temprence hers," I said. "Make it look like Louie just moved on to another city, just like she planned all along."

"Sounds good to me. I'm not *that* attached to my car. Not sure what I'll do in the meantime, but honestly, I'm due for some kind of an upgrade."

"We'll get that shit sorted. For now, it can stay in the garage," I said. She nodded.

"So, how'd it go?" she asked, and I gave her a look.

"Good," I told her.

"Good," she said with relief and dropped the subject.

She was learning.

"I love you," she said spontaneously, cuddling up to my side and laying her head on my shoulder.

I put my arms around her and held her tight.

"I love you, too, baby," I said, then asked, "You doing alright? For sure?"

She nodded against me, and her silence told me all I needed to know. She would be okay. She would remain loyal, but for right now, in this moment, she struggled a little, which was only natural. She was still so shiny and new to all of this.

"You sleep at all?" I asked.

She said, "No, I waited for you."

Ah...

"Come on, get comfortable," I murmured, and she did, wriggling until she was close, draping her leg over mine, and closing her eyes, her eyelashes sweeping against and tickling my chest on the one side.

She had these moments when it was just her and just me, and no one else around, where she allowed herself to become almost childlike in my presence.

I liked it. It wasn't weird to me at all. It was like she needed to regress some in order to make some progress in her healing and I got that.

She spent all day, every day, putting in a herculean effort, was a badass bitch around and with everyone else, and yet with me? She would be soft and vulnerable, and that meant a fuckton to me.

"I got you, baby," I said and kissed the top of her head. She sighed out, her body losing some of the tension that rode it, right up until she was with me, and could let it all go.

I loved being her safe haven, and she had no idea what it meant to me that she was mine.

I closed my eyes, let the peace that was my woman in my arms wash over me, and looked forward to the rest of our lives.

CHAPTER THIRTY-SIX

V elina...
    We took Temperance's car out to her in Florida and stayed
for like a week. I drove, and Saint rode. I would be riding back
with him.

It was like a nine-hour drive, and that was a lot, but it was worth it
to arrive in Fort Royal and see Temperance absolutely *thriving*.

She was still stripping, but she seemed happy and was spending a
lot of time with one of the Kraken club's brothers, who looked at her
the way that I sometimes caught Saint looking at me. It made me feel
such relief.

I was glad she was going to be okay, and I hoped like hell she got
everything her heart desired.

She ended up becoming fast and pretty good friends with another
girl there named Faith. I learned quite a bit about both the Kraken and
the Voodoo Bastards, and how club life was *really* supposed to work.

I could see immediately why the Voodoo Bastards had envied the
Kraken and had wanted to adopt their business model, so-to-speak.

We spent nights on the beach around bonfires, sampling the bottles
of different liquors that the Bastards had been distilling, laughing, and
making up names for different things like *Baron's Barrel Aged Rum...*

names that went with not just the voodoo vibe but that encapsulated the feel of New Orleans herself.

Mostly, Saint and I took the time with each other, away from the heavy weight of the rivalry between the Bastards and the Brethren. We held hands and walked along the beach for hours, talking, dreaming, and making plans.

There were so many things that Saint wanted me to experience in my new home.

Greek Fest, Jazz Fest, Mardi Gras, and the history, stories, and local cultures and legends.

I was excited and ready for it all.

I had no idea what this next chapter entailed for me, but I knew one thing – I was excited and grateful that for the next, however many the fates would allow me to have, I would have them with this man, and I wouldn't be doing it all alone anymore.

We talked about a lot of things, Saint and I.

About our families, our faith, and what we wanted to keep from our pasts and what we wanted to ditch all together.

Honestly, I was okay with ditching my mother and my siblings, all together. Didn't really care if I ever spoke to them ever again.

He was surprised by that, and it took me a while to unpack it. When I did, it was to realize that they never really treated me like family was *supposed to,* at least not to my mind. It'd been so long of giving them every opportunity to just treat me right that I no longer felt the need to extend them any more opportunities.

I think that will died in me when I started talking to Louie.

I think Louie showed me the way… that the blood of the covenant was indeed thicker than the water of the womb.

"He was lucky to find that out," I said as Saint and I walked hand in hand, listening to the Gulf crash upon the shore.

"I think we're the lucky ones," Saint said. "Me especially. Not only that I got to know him for as long as I did. Not just that I got to call him 'brother' with everything that goes into that, either."

He met my eyes and raised the back of my hand to his lips, pressing a kiss to it.

"I know, for a fact, I'm the luckiest man alive that he brought you to me."

I laughed, pushed him a little, and said, "Stop!"

"Hey, I fuckin' mean it!" he cried, laughing, gripping my hand and not letting go.

"I know you mean it," I said. "It's just... awkward for me, I guess."

"Why?" he asked.

"Still not used to hearing good things about me, I guess," I said.

He pulled me into his arms and settled them around my waist, his hands smoothing along my lower back until he could palm my hips.

I wrapped my arms around his neck, and I looked at him as he looked at me.

"Well, you better get used to it and quick, because if I have to, I'm going to remind you every fuckin' day of the rest of our lives that you're beautiful, smart, funny, kind, fierce, wonderful, and whatever other things I can come up with that are equally as true."

I laughed at that, shook my head, and said, "You're gonna give me an overinflated ego."

He pulled one of my hands from around his neck and kissed my palm, sighing, and said to me, "No, I just want you to see yourself the way I see you."

I swallowed hard, eyes suddenly misting, and smacked him in the chest.

He laughed, long, boisterous, and loud, and pulled me into his chest. I clung to him in the summer breeze off of the water of the vast Gulf and held to him tightly.

Damn it, I hated when he got to me and could make me get all emotional... but I was grateful at the same time.

This man... healing the pieces of my broken heart one at a time, even though he wasn't the one to break it.

God, I loved him.

ALSO BY A.J. DOWNEY

Indigo Knights

1. Her Thin Blue Lifeline

2. His Cold Blue Command

3. A Low Blue Flame

4. His Wild Blue Rose

5. Her Pained Blue Silence

6. A Cold Blue Call

7. Her Reluctant Blue Cavalier

8. Forged Under Fire

9. Under A Blue Moon

10. Sound of Blue Thunder

Sacred Hearts MC Pacific Northwest

1. Over the High Side

2. Wind Therapy

3. Apex of the Curve

4. Low Sided

5. Eating Asphalt

6. Hammer Down

7. Only Fool Riding

The Voodoo Bastards MC

1. Bourbon & Blood

2. Whiskey Shivers

3. Moonshine Lullabies

4. Cognac Secrets

Iron Wraiths MC

1. Original Syn

2. Love & Fear

3. The Hangman's Rope

ABOUT A.J. DOWNEY

A.J. Downey is a Pacific Northwest girl living in an East Tennessee world who finds inspiration from her surroundings, through the people she meets, and likely as a byproduct of way too much caffeine. She specializes in real and relatable romance stories featuring that real-life kind of love that everyone craves.

Stalker Information:

Website
www.ajdowney.com

Sign up for her newsletter at
http://eepurl.com/dkQiIH

Facebook Group - AJ's Sacred Circle
https://www.facebook.com/groups/authorajdowney/

f facebook.com/authorajdowney
X x.com/authorajdowney
instagram.com/ajdowney
BB bookbub.com/authors/a-j-downey

www.ingramcontent.com/pod-product-compliance
Lightning Source LLC
Chambersburg PA
CBHW050740230626
47052CB00004BA/763